MAIN

# SWEET SHADOWS

ALSO BY

# Tera Lynn Childs

*Sweet Venom*

*Forgive My Fins*

*Fins Are Forever*

*Just for Fins*

# SWEET SHADOWS

## TERA LYNN CHILDS

KATHERINE TEGEN BOOKS
An Imprint of HarperCollins Publishers

Katherine Tegen Books is an imprint of HarperCollins Publishers.

Library of Congress Cataloging-in-Publication Data
Childs, Tera Lynn.
  Sweet shadows / Tera Lynn Childs. — 1st ed.
    p.  cm.
  Sequel to: Sweet venom.
  Summary: Teen triplets Gretchen, Grace, and Greer, descendants of Medusa,
continue to battle the monsters who walk the streets of San Francisco, unseen
by humans, but realize they must enter the abyss if they are to protect their
loved ones—and their world.
  ISBN 978-0-06-200183-2 (trade bdg.)
  [1. Fate and fatalism—Fiction. 2. Medusa (Greek mythology)—Fiction.
3. Mythology, Greek—Fiction. 4. Monsters—Fiction. 5. Sisters—Fiction.
6. Triplets—Fiction. 7. San Francisco (Calif.)—Fiction.] I. Title.
PZ7.C44185Svs 2012                                          2011044626
[Fic]—dc23                                                          CIP
                                                                     AC

Typography by Andrea Vandergrift
12  13  14  15  16    LP/RRDH    10  9  8  7  6  5  4  3  2  1
❖

First Edition

*For Kirsty, my first fan*

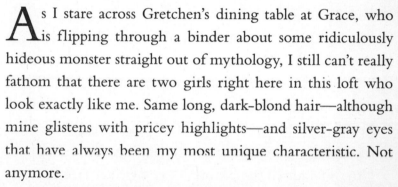

## CHAPTER 1

## GREER

As I stare across Gretchen's dining table at Grace, who is flipping through a binder about some ridiculously hideous monster straight out of mythology, I still can't really fathom that there are two girls right here in this loft who look exactly like me. Same long, dark-blond hair—although mine glistens with pricey highlights—and silver-gray eyes that have always been my most unique characteristic. Not anymore.

Same height, weight, and shape. Same size. After the fight with the giant beast that was attacking Gretchen—a manticore, she called it—not even my keen fashion sense sets me apart. My clothes were positively disgusting, and the only thing keeping me from throwing them in the nearest incinerator is the designer label. Well, that and the fact that

they're kind of a badge of honor from my second real monster fight—evidence of a success more hard-won than my string of straight A's and student government positions.

Anyway, my expensive clothes are in a trash bag by the door and I'm wearing a pair of Gretchen's gray cargos and a white tank top. One good thing about being triplets, I suppose, is that we can share clothes. Barring extreme instances like this, however, I can't imagine ever wanting to borrow anything from either of their closets. Eco-geek and military chick aren't really my style.

"Look at his feet," Grace says, sliding the open binder toward me and pointing at a drawing of a fairly normal-looking creature with backward-facing feet. It needs a good orthopedic surgeon.

"Gross," I say, because it is and because I think it's the kind of response she wants. Grace is thrilled to have found her sisters and can't wait for us to become best friends. I'm not quite as enthusiastic. I already have an established life and boyfriend and circle of friends. But knowing there's this secret side of my life is kind of exhilarating. And scary.

"You should see the panotii," she says, her face contorting into a disgusted wince. "They have ears the size of their bodies."

"Have you memorized all the binders?" I ask.

"No." Her gaze drops and I can see her cheeks flush pink. She's embarrassed by her dedication. "I've digitized most of them, though, and the funnier images stand out."

She shouldn't be ashamed to be a hard worker. She should be proud of her achievements. Instead, she seems more like the kind of girl who dismisses them. Afraid of appearing . . . *more* than others.

I'm about to tell her she should embrace her achievements, that her success should inspire others, not embarrass them. But before I can open my mouth, a violent wave of nausea assaults my stomach.

It's so strong I lurch to my feet, certain I'm about to heave all over the shiny glass table.

As soon as I'm upright, the sensation moves, spreads to the rest of my body. I'm shocked, frozen by an overwhelming sense of dread, weighted to the floor by the most horrible fear I've ever felt.

From the edge of my vision I sense Gretchen walking into the room.

"What's wrong?" Grace asks, and I can hear the worry in her voice.

"I—" I brace my hands on the table as my legs threaten to give out beneath me. "I don't know. It's just, all of a sudden, I got this really awful feeling."

My sisters exchange a look.

"What kind of feeling?" Gretchen asks.

I turn to her, needing her strength in this moment. "Like something bad is about to happen."

I've barely finished the sentence when Gretchen's phone rings. She turns and runs for it and I focus on inhaling deeply, hoping that some meditative breathing will quell this incomprehensible sensation.

*Breathe in. Breathe out. In. Out. In—*

Suddenly, Gretchen is sprinting toward us, arms wide and shouting, "Run!"

I'm still frozen, unable to process what exactly is happening, overwhelmed by the feelings assaulting me.

As Gretchen runs by, she snags my arm with one of hers. She grabs Grace with the other, pushing us toward the open door.

I feel my body take over, my feet moving to follow my sisters onto the balcony. I'm already climbing the railing when Gretchen grabs me under the arm and flings me up, over, and out.

As I fall into the water below, the debilitating feeling vanishes, and by the time I hit the freezing bay, my wits have returned. I brace myself to hit the surface.

The shock of the cold disorients me, inciting panic at being propelled under the waves, and I force myself to calm down. *Swim,* I tell myself. Thankfully Gretchen tossed me at such an angle that I haven't gone down so much as out. Within seconds I'm on the surface and paddling back toward my sisters.

I see Grace's head pop up first, just a few feet to my right. Thank goodness. Scanning the area for Gretchen, I feel my entire body flood with relief as she bursts into view.

They're okay. We're okay.

Treading water against the weight of wet clothes, I lean my head back as uncontrolled tears of shock and relief sting my eyes. That's when I see the flames. Gretchen's loft, the very space we were just standing in—joking in—is engulfed in flames and smoke.

Her home. It's just . . . gone.

"This is bad," I say.

Grace says, "Somebody tried to kill us."

"You think?" Gretchen snaps.

Grace doesn't deserve that, but I suppose this is a pretty extraordinary situation. Gretchen could use a lot of slack right now. We all could.

"All those books," Grace says, shaking her head. "Thank goodness I got most of the binders done, but all those resources . . ."

She trails off, probably mourning the lost library. Maybe that's her coping mechanism, focusing on that tangible loss instead of the reality of how close we came to dying just now.

Gretchen, on the other hand, isn't bothering to cope. Even from several feet away, in the eerie glow of the fire, I can see the fury on her face.

I glance from her to the burning shell of the loft in disbelief. What just happened? Can that have been an accident? What about that phone call?

The chill of the frigid bay finally penetrates my fear- and adrenaline-flooded body. My muscles start spasming. I can ask questions later. If we don't get out soon, we'll go

5

hypothermic. And after everything that's happened I don't exactly relish the idea of a trip to the emergency room to top it off.

"We need to get out of the water," I say, my jaw tightening against the chill. When neither of them moves, I add, "Now!"

Startled from their thoughts—Grace from mourning the loss of all those books, Gretchen from her boiling anger at our near deaths—they turn toward shore and start paddling.

With shivering limbs, I swim after them. The activity works the fear out of my system and clears my mind. I push aside all the thoughts fighting to consume me until there is only one remaining: the feeling of dread I had up in the loft. Was that a freak coincidence? Or was it a premonition? And if it was, what good is a warning like that if it petrifies me in place?

San Francisco has a reputation for winterlike temperatures even in the summertime. Never have I been as thoroughly frozen to the core as I feel right now. Standing on the pier with my borrowed clothes clinging to me, soaked with icy water, I can't stop the wave after wave of shivering chills that sweep over me.

My teeth are chattering as I say, "We need to get warm."

"We need to get out of here," Grace says, shaking just as hard as I am. "Someone will have called the fire department. And it's not like we can really explain. . . ."

She waves her hand in a circle and, as vague as the gesture is,

I understand precisely what she means. From what Gretchen has said, very little of her life is legitimately documented. She doesn't want anyone poking around, asking questions about the loft and who lives—lived—there, let alone the burning arsenal inside.

And none of us needs anyone asking about the triplets who nearly got blown up. Parents would be called, which would lead to even more questions. The kind I'm not prepared to answer yet.

"I agree," I say. "My car is right over—"

"I don't think the fire has reached the garage yet," Gretchen says.

She's looking at the building that was, until an explosion tore apart the upper level ten minutes ago, her home. Like she wants to go inside.

"You're not serious," I say. "You can't go in there."

Fine, so the flames are still in the upper level at the far end of the building. The smoke is pouring out from every opening, every crack. And where there's smoke . . .

Gretchen spears me with a serious look. "I need that car," she says. "I need what's inside that car."

Then, before I can argue the point—by telling her that it's complete lunacy to run into a burning building that just *blew up*—she sprints toward a side door that presumably leads into the garage.

She's insane. We've already almost died tonight—twice—and now she's racing back into danger.

Grace starts to go after her, but I grab her, stopping her

7

from following our sister into the inferno. One sister with a death wish is enough.

"Let me go!" she shouts, trying to twist out of my grasp. "We can't let her go in alone!"

I understand the sentiment, but I hold Grace tighter. She's not thinking clearly right now. I don't want to risk losing her too.

"Do I really have to explain why rushing into a burning building is a bad idea?"

"Greer!" Grace gives up her struggle and stands, limp, staring at the open door through which Gretchen disappeared. "What if she—?"

"She won't," I insist, with more conviction—and more faith—than I knew I had. I take a deep breath, letting my faith in Gretchen straighten my spine. "She is strong and tough and capable in more ways than we can imagine. She'll be fine."

As I say the words, I realize they're true. And I believe them.

Like Grace and me, Gretchen has had to face unimaginable changes in the last two weeks. She discovered she's a triplet—which Grace and I just discovered as well, along with the fact that we're descendants of Medusa, destined to hunt monsters and chase them out of our world. She learned that her mentor, who is also one of our immortal ancestral aunts, the Gorgon Euryale, has been taken as a prisoner the gods only know where—literally. And now, twice in one

8

night, someone has tried to kill Gretchen. She's handled all of these changes with dignity and courage. I don't believe there is anything she can't face.

Of course, a burning building isn't a mythological monster, and maybe this is one challenge she isn't trained for. A trickle of fear slides down my spine.

Just as I begin to doubt my conviction, Gretchen's black Mustang bursts through the end wall of the building in an explosion of wood and plaster, squealing backward onto the blacktop. She cuts a tight turn and shifts into forward, skidding to a stop right next to my silver Porsche.

I purse my lips to keep from grinning like a fool—Mother would be appalled at my near display of emotion. I knew she would be fine. I knew it.

Gretchen climbs out of the car, coughing.

Grace rushes forward. "Are you okay?"

She wraps Gretchen in a tight hug. I look away, trying to keep the tears of fear and relief and emotional release from spilling out.

My attention drifts to my car, catching on the set of ugly dents on my otherwise perfect hood. They're a reminder of the first near-death experience I encountered tonight—a six-armed giant who showed up at my front door—that feels so long ago now.

So much for avoiding emotional reaction.

"Yeah—" Gretchen is seized by a spasm of wheezing coughs. "I'll be fine."

"You sound fine," I say sarcastically, earning a glare from both sisters.

Gretchen walks around to her trunk, pops it open, and starts digging around inside. She pulls out a duffel bag, slams the trunk shut, and sets the bag on top.

Feeling more in control of myself, I walk up to my car and run a hand over the dents—thankfully there don't appear to be any scratches in the metallic clear-coat paint. There are so many ways the evening could have ended badly. Even if my car is a little the worse for wear, I'm relieved that we're all safe and whole. Tonight could have easily wound up a tragedy—if I hadn't managed to outrun and then outdrive that giant, if Grace hadn't autoported away from that monstrous bear in time, if she and I hadn't gotten to Gretchen's loft at just the right moment to help her fight the manticore, or if Gretchen hadn't dragged us out an instant before the explosion.

"Wait a minute," I say, my analytical mind returning to working order. Something must have compelled Gretchen to throw us out into the bay. Something more concrete than my sense of dread. I think back to those moments, trying to remember exactly what happened. My mind was clouded by the nausea, but I remember a ringing sound. "You got a phone call," I say, turning to Gretchen. "Someone warned you about the explosion, didn't they?"

I watch as her shoulders stiffen. She pauses in digging through the duffel bag just long enough for me to know she heard me. Then she simply says, "Yes," and starts pulling things out.

"Yes?" I echo. As if that's an adequate answer.

A pair of combat boots hits the trunk with a thump.

"Do you know who called?" Grace asks, shivering harder now.

"Yes."

I ask the obvious question. "Who?"

Anger rolls off Gretchen in hot waves. Yes, she knows who made the call. She's going to find out what else that person knows. And she's not going to tell us any more about it. Not acceptable.

"Did your mystery caller give any specifics about the explosion?" I ask. "Was it a bomb or a gas leak or—"

"No," Gretchen interrupts. "He only said to get out."

Her silver eyes cloud over, and I'm immediately glad I'm not on the receiving end of her shadowed looks. I have no doubt the caller will regret ever meeting her before the night is through.

Gretchen reaches back into the duffel, pulls out a dry tee, and tosses it at Grace.

Despite her obvious shyness, Grace pulls off her icy wet shirt and pulls on a dry one from Gretchen's stash. The black knit sticks to her still-damp bra, but the moisture won't show on the dark fabric. Though the wet denim of her jeans probably feels like lead dragging her down, it's probably insulating as well. She still shivers, but less violently.

"Who?" I repeat.

Gretchen glances at me, maybe surprised at my persistence. "Someone who knows more than he's let on." When I start to ask more, she says, "I'll take care of it. He's my responsibility."

There's an undercurrent of something—guilt maybe—and I let it go. We're all in shock. Right here, right now is not the time to push her for more.

"Now what?" I ask.

"Now," Gretchen says, finding another top and throwing it my direction, "you two go home and I go find the jerk. I'll get the whole story from him. For once. If I have to beat his pretty face to a pulp, I'll find out what's going on."

I quickly change into the dry tank. I don't miss her reference to his pretty face. He's not just a random acquaintance. I have a feeling there's more to their relationship than she'd ever let me and Grace know.

Gretchen finally digs a pair of dry cargos out of the bag and, without hesitation, drops her drenched ones to the ground. She steps into the dry pants—not caring that her underwear is still soaked—yanks them up, and quickly zips and buttons them with jerky, angry movements. She pulls her wet tank off, leaving just her white sports bra.

She's raring to go.

It's all well and good that she wants to go pound some information out of the pretty face who called to warn us, but that doesn't change the fact that there are big angry beasts waiting at home for me and Grace.

"What about the monsters?" I ask. "There's a six-armed giant tearing through my house. And a massive bear in the alley behind Grace's apartment."

Grace blushes. I'm not sure whether it's because she'd forgotten about the bear or because she's embarrassed to need Gretchen to help her get rid of it. Either way, Grace and I are not capable of taking on the vile creatures on our own.

Gretchen doesn't respond. Just drops her boots to the ground and steps into them. She bends over and quickly does up the laces.

"Yeah," Grace says quietly. "I don't like the idea that they're out there looking for us. Or," she adds softly, "our families."

Well, I don't need to worry about that possibility. Mother and Dad won't be home until the wee hours. But the idea of going home alone and maybe having to face that terrifying giant again—not precisely how I hoped to end the evening.

Gretchen runs a hand over her wet hair.

"Hell." She closes her eyes. "You're right. I'll deal with those first." She nods at Grace. "I'll start with the bear."

Grace gives her a relieved smile.

"Can you take her home?" Gretchen asks me. "Give me a five-minute head start and I'll have the thing back in the abyss before you get there." When I nod, she adds, "Then I'll take out your giant."

"We can help," Grace insists. "You don't have to face them alone."

As much as I don't relish the idea of ever seeing that thing again, Grace has a point. I'm not the kind of girl who lets someone else do my dirty work.

"Yes, of course," I say. "We'll go with you."

Gretchen shakes her head. "I'll be fine," she says. "Nothing I haven't faced before."

I nod, recognizing this is a matter of pride for her. And maybe an opportunity to work out some frustration.

"Where will you sleep?" I ask. "We have a comfortable sofa bed in the rec room. No one goes down there much anymore."

"You can come home with me," Grace offers. "I'll have to explain things to my parents, you know, but I'm sure it'll be fine."

"I've got a place," Gretchen says. "Ursula and I have a safe house—somewhere to go, with basic supplies and weapons, in case something like this happens."

"Are you sure?" Grace asks.

Gretchen nods. "I'll be fine."

I find myself saying "Thank you" and really meaning it. I feel a little guilty about letting Gretchen go hunting alone. I'm going to have to learn how to fight these monsters on my own eventually. I won't always have one of my sisters around to help.

But for tonight, after everything I've been through, after

everything that's changed in my world in the last few days, it's a relief to know that Gretchen is here to take care of business. I have no doubt that the creatures sent to kill us will be long gone before Grace and I get home.

Then my biggest challenge will be figuring out how to explain to my parents about the dents in my car and the damage to our front door. Frankly, that's no less terrifying than the monsters.

## CHAPTER 2

# GRACE

"Thanks for the ride," I say to Greer as she pulls up in front of my apartment building. There's no sign of Gretchen or her car, so she must have been here and moved on already.

Greer smiles—a small smile that doesn't reach her eyes—and says, "No problem. It's on my way home anyway."

I know that's a lie and that her house is in the opposite direction, but I don't call her on it. She's been through a lot—we all have—and I'm just thankful she isn't running away from our legacy. From us. I would hardly blame her after tonight.

I open the door, ready to climb out, but at the last second I lean back across the seats, the stick shift jabbing into my ribs, and wrap my arms around her. The thought of what

might have happened tonight if she had run away, if she hadn't helped me and Gretchen fight the manticore . . . it's too awful to imagine. I'm so grateful that we're together in this, the three of us.

"Thank you," I whisper against her damp hair.

I'm pretty sure it's a sign of our extreme circumstances that she hugs me back. Before she can take it back or say something to ruin the moment, I jump out of the car and slam the door behind me.

I watch, sad and happy at the same time, as she drives away. If we can survive a night like tonight with our fragile sisterhood intact, I have to believe we can survive anything as long as we stick together.

When her taillights disappear around the corner, I turn and trudge up the sidewalk to the front gate. I dig in my jeans pocket, thankful to find my keys still stashed inside. I quickly let myself in through the courtyard gate and then the main door of the building.

I don't realize how exhausted I am until I slide my key into the apartment door. It's like my mind decides that all threats are behind me now that I'm home and it's okay for my body to collapse for a while. My feet are too heavy to lift, and it's all I can do to turn the handle.

I swing the door open as quietly as possible.

I shouldn't have bothered. Every light is on and I hear my dad's voice booming from the kitchen.

"I don't care if it's only been five minutes," he shouts.

"She is not the kind of girl—"

There's a pause and my heart drops into my stomach.

I hear my mom sobbing. Oh no. Oh no-no-no-no-no. I can't believe I didn't think about them at all—at *all*—in the last few hours. I was so caught up in everything, I never once considered that they might be wondering where I went, worrying about my safety.

If they knew why, I'm sure they would understand. But I can't—won't—tell them.

Feeling like the worst daughter in history, I walk to the kitchen.

"Something has happened to my daughter," Dad continues, "and if you don't send someone to help us search, I'll—" He sees me and freezes.

I try to look as apologetic as I feel.

The look in his eyes shifts quickly from shock to relief to pure fury.

Mom gasps and rushes me, pulling me into a suffocating hug.

Dad looks like he wants to explode.

"Never mind!" he barks into the phone. Then, after hanging up on what I can only assume is the police department, he roars, "Where the hell have you been?"

"I was so worried," Mom sobs. "I sent you to take the garbage out and you never came back. That was *hours* ago. I imagined the worst."

"You had your mother scared half to death."

18

They look at me, their expressions angry and accusing and, I'm sure, relieved. But mostly angry. I never even thought about the fact that Mom would be expecting me back, would be wondering where I went.

I know I was a little preoccupied, what with almost getting killed by a giant bear and then blown up, but that's not really an excuse. I had time after the fight at Gretchen's. After my shower, while Greer and I were giggling over the binders. I had plenty of time. I could have called home to check in.

If I'm being honest, I was too caught up in spending time with my sisters.

Even though I didn't have my phone with me, since I'd only been taking out the garbage, I could have found a way. I *should* have found a way.

"I'm sorry," I say lamely. "I didn't even think—"

"You're sorry?" Dad echoes. "You should be sorry."

Mom lays a hand on his arm. "This is so unlike you, Grace. To just disappear without telling us. What's going on?"

"And look at you," Dad says, his gaze sweeping over me. "Your jeans are drenched. And your hair. Everything but that tee."

"Weren't you wearing a blue shirt when you left?" Mom asks. She shakes her head. "*What* happened?"

"I—" What can I say? That I found my sisters, that we're triplets and we're destined to hunt monsters who, apparently, want us dead? Who tried to kill us twice in one night? No,

19

that's not fair to Mom and Dad. I can't share that burden with anyone but Gretchen and Greer. It is ours alone.

It's not like it would reassure them anyway. Either they'd think I'd lost my mind or, on the off chance that they believed me, they'd be scared to death about me being in danger. If I stop to think about it for too long, *I'd* be scared to death.

No, I can't tell them any of it. I have to protect them however I can.

"I'm sorry," I repeat. "I had some things to think about and I just kind of ended up walking around."

On the scale of cover stories, I'm sure that's pretty low. But it's the best I've got. I glance down at myself, wishing I had some believable explanation for the state of my clothes and appearance.

Mom frowns, as if now she's more worried about whatever it was I needed to think about. Before meeting Gretchen— before she tossed me over her shoulder and carried me out of that nightclub—I had no secrets from my mom. Oh how I wish I could tell her everything now.

Dad shakes his head. "I can't even look at you right now."

I bite my lip to keep from crying as he turns and walks away. I know I've screwed up, but there's no way to fix this. I'm going to have to face the consequences. Another one of my new responsibilities.

"He's just worried," Mom says, trying to make me feel better, even when she probably shouldn't but should be just as angry as Dad. "Let him sleep on it and you two can talk in the morning."

I nod and let her hug me. Then she turns and follows Dad to bed.

I lean against the counter and try to process this situation. There's no win here, really. Either I tell my parents the truth and they forgive me for turning into a flake but worry that I'll be eaten by a mythological monster. Or I lie to them—I keep my secret and let them think I'm turning into a problem child, but the worst thing they imagine is falling grades and boy troubles.

As much as I want my parents to think well of me, to respect and trust me, I want to protect them more. And that means keeping them in the dark as much and for as long as possible.

Decisions like this stink. But I guess it comes with the destiny.

Pushing away from the counter, I head for the shower to wash off the bay water stink and then I'll collapse in bed. Maybe things will look better in the morning.

And maybe flying monkeys will bring me a magic broom.

Even through my closed door and theirs I can hear Mom and Dad arguing about me. It's the middle of the night and I'm so tired I just want to cry, but sleep isn't coming. The guilt over what I'm doing to my parents is eating at my stomach, so I lie there staring at the shadowed ceiling.

It's such a change for them to be arguing over me. Sure, there were lots of long nights and late discussions when we were talking about moving to San Francisco, when I got the scholarship offer from Alpha—thanks, I know now, to my immortal ancestor, the Gorgon Sthenno, in an effort to bring me and my sisters together. To reunite the Key Generation.

That was the most discord I'd ever caused in our house.

My brother, Thane, is usually the troublemaker.

I smile at that thought. If he were home, he'd find it hilarious that I'm finally at the center of the turmoil. And by hilarious I mean he might crack a small smile. He's not much for showing emotion.

It's quite a coincidence that the time he decides to disappear in his quest to "figure things out" is right when all Hades breaks loose in my world. He's only been gone since this afternoon, but it feels like weeks. So much has happened and I already miss him. I hope he comes home soon.

I'm finally starting to drift off to sleep and the world around me is going soft and fuzzy when I hear the ding-dong chime of a text message. I roll over and grab my phone off the charger. It's from Thane.

Are you okay?

I blink, trying to bring my brain back to full consciousness. Am I okay? He's the one who's run off to places unknown. I should be asking *him* that question. He doesn't know what happened tonight though. He's just checking in, letting me know he's thinking about me.

Yes. You?

I expect an immediate response, but as I sit there, staring at my phone, I realize that the ding-dong wasn't a first alert. It was a second chime to let me know about a message I hadn't read yet. I scroll through his texts and see that he's sent me five tonight, the last one almost half an hour ago. I must have been in the shower.

I'm about to fall back into bed, thinking he must have given up waiting for me and has gone to sleep, when I get a new message alert.

Good. Night.

This is cryptic, even for Thane. Does he mean that he's good? Or that it's good that I'm okay? He doesn't say a word about where he is, when he's coming back. He vanished this afternoon with nothing more than a phone call to tell me the cover story he fed Mom. That he's staying at his soccer teammate Milo's house. I have no idea where he really is or what he's doing. And all I get is Good. Night.? My irritation pushes my exhaustion to the side. I sit up and text back.

Where are you? When are you coming home?

I stare at my screen for ten minutes. Nothing. I text again.

Worried about you.

This time, I only have five minutes worth of patience. No response. Instead of texting again, I pull up my contacts and call his number.

My irritation grows as I listen to it ring. And ring. And ring-ring-ring. I tap my feet on the floor in an anxious gesture that drives Mom so crazy, I've almost managed to rid myself of it. Except in extreme circumstances.

The call goes to his voicemail, which is nothing more than the generic message that comes with the service. Now I'm starting to really worry. I hang up, ready to call again—and again and again until he finally picks up—when a message chime ding-dongs in my ear.

**Don't. I'm fine. Home soon.**

That's not really the answer I want. I want to know where he is, I want to know that he's coming home tomorrow, not just vaguely soon. I miss him. I worry about him. And—maybe most of all—I want my big brother's shoulder to lean on.

But it's better than no answer at all.

I send one more text.

**XOXO**

I set my phone back on the nightstand, knowing I won't hear from him again tonight.

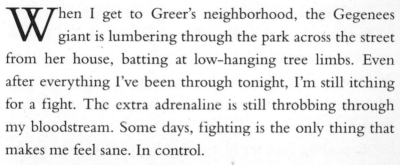

# CHAPTER 3

# GRETCHEN

When I get to Greer's neighborhood, the Gegenees giant is lumbering through the park across the street from her house, batting at low-hanging tree limbs. Even after everything I've been through tonight, I'm still itching for a fight. The extra adrenaline is still throbbing through my bloodstream. Some days, fighting is the only thing that makes me feel sane. In control.

Since that day four years ago when the oracle read my prophecy, told me I was destined for more than life as the worthless adopted daughter of abusive addict parents, I've spent my days and nights honing my skills in hand-to-hand combat. Most of my monster fights are routine. Hunt, fight, send them home. But sometimes, the fight itself is what I need. The challenge of taking down a beast gets my

brain working straight again.

Maybe that will help tonight.

The ursa hybrid behind Grace's building wasn't any trouble—it was too focused on cornering a fat rat behind the garbage bins. Never saw me coming. Talk about anticlimactic. I hope the giant proves more of a challenge.

I drive Moira up onto the sidewalk, jerking the parking brake into place as I unbuckle. The replacement cargos from my emergency kit in the trunk aren't outfitted—the pockets are empty of my usual gear. But I don't want the gear tonight. I don't need it. I only need my fists.

"Lose something?" I tease as I climb out of the car. "Kitty cat stuck up a tree?"

The Gegenees giant whirls around, its hideous face contorting into a look of shock and then rage. Good. The angrier it gets, the better the fight will be.

Then its gaze rakes over me, taking in my sports bra and cargos as I round Moira's hood. When it gets to my Doc Martens, it scowls.

"Expecting bare feet?" I ask as I approach. "Or maybe strappy stilettos?"

It looks up, its eyes widening in fear.

"Big tough guy like you?" I crack my knuckles. "Volunteered to take on one of the weaker sisters? I'm so disappointed."

It starts backing up.

"But here's a lesson to share with all your beastie buds."

I roll my shoulders. I can almost feel the first punch. "You come after one of us, you get all of us."

It backs up faster, knocking its head into one of the branches and wincing.

"Now," I say with a sick smile, "you have to deal with me."

It turns to run.

"Don't you want to play?" I call, but it keeps running. "Darn it."

I chase after it, up over the hill and down the grassy slope on the other side. When it tries to run through the playground, two of its arms get caught in the hanging rings of the jungle gym. It screams, howling into the night like a bear caught in a steel trap.

As I leap through the air, landing on its back with my legs around its waist, I sigh. "Not even putting up a fight. Where's the fun in that?"

The beast struggles more, trying to wrench its arms from the rings and dislodge me from its back. Pathetic.

My fangs drop, I lean forward over its bulging shoulder and sink a bite into a meaty forearm. I barely even have a moment to enjoy the huntress high, as the venom flows from my fangs into its bloodstream, before it vanishes beneath me.

I crash to the soft, wood chip—covered ground on my hands and knees. Why do they always have to be so easy when I'm eager for a throwdown? I need to get this angry energy out of me before I explode. Normally I would go take it out on the punching dummy at the loft, but it's ashes by now.

*Well, if the monsters want to go down easy,* I think as I stand and dust off my knees, *maybe Nick will be a challenge. And he's next on my list.*

Back in my car, I yank open the glove box and pull out the spare phone. Mine got fried when I jumped into the bay with my sisters, but hopefully the SIM card survived the dunk. I dig the card out of my old phone, dry it off on my pants, and then place it in the backup phone. I'm relieved when the phone powers up, but my recent calls list is blank.

Fine. Even if my SIM card didn't record the call, I have his number saved from when he called before.

I labeled it ANNOYING JERKWAD.

At least the annoying jerkwad called to warn us.

My brain drifts for a second, imagining what might have happened if he hadn't made that call. Only a few seconds later—I quickly shake the thought out of my mind. It's too unthinkable. He did make the call, my sisters and I are safe, and now he's going to tell me what he knows.

Whether he wants to or not.

When Nick first appeared in my life two weeks ago, I thought he was a puzzle. A guy who wouldn't take no for an answer, who wouldn't back down from me, and who was somehow immune to my hypnotic eye power. Now I know he must be something more, someone involved in this as more than just an innocent bystander.

No one else knows my phone number. No one else could

have made that call, warning me to get out of the loft. It must have been Nick.

I dial the number.

He picks up on the fourth ring.

"Hello?" He sounds sleepy.

I grit my teeth. Seriously? He went back to sleep after that?

"Where are you?" I demand.

"What?"

"Where. Are. You?"

There's silence, some shuffling, and then, "Gretchen?"

"Of course it's Gretchen," I snap. "Didn't you think I'd be calling back?"

"Calling back?" he echoes.

"Or did you think I'd be dead?"

"Dead?" His voice clears in an instant. "What's going on?"

"Tell me where you are," I demand for the last time. "Right now."

To my surprise, he actually gives me the address. I floor the accelerator, reaching for my spare gear under the passenger seat as I go. Within five minutes, I've restocked my pockets and I'm speeding into a parking spot behind the wooden apartment building on Twin Peaks. The slope is killer, but he must have a great view of the city. If I weren't about to pound his face into the dirt, I'd be jealous. It's a great spot to do a monster sniff test.

I don't notice him standing outside, waiting, until he

walks up to my window and knocks on the glass.

Without hesitation, I pull the handle and shove, sending Moira's door into Nick's hip and knocking him to the ground. I jump out, take my advantage—he's got several inches of height on me, so I'll take whatever I can get—and straddle his waist. I clamp one hand around his wrists and reach into my cargo pocket with another, pulling out a zip tie.

"What the hell are you doing?" he demands, bucking and trying to knock me off. "What happened?"

I don't say a word. I slip a zip tie around his wrists and yank, tugging it not quite tight enough to cut off circulation, but enough to secure his hands.

"Gretchen," he says, resting his blond head back against the pavement, giving up on trying to get free, "tell me what's going on."

He sounds almost reasonable, like he's not at all shocked that I've tackled him to the ground and tied him like a prize pig. I shouldn't be surprised. He knew the explosion was coming, which means he knows who—and what—I am.

Maybe I should give him a tiny bit of credit for saving our lives.

A tiny bit.

"We're going for a drive," I explain. "Either you can get in the passenger seat under your own power, or I'll put you there myself."

He studies me for a second, watching me with those

midnight-blue eyes. I can't tell what's going on in his mind—can I ever?—but he just nods and says, "I'm good."

I push back to my feet, yank him to his, and then follow him around the car. He pulls open the door and climbs in without argument. Well, that's something going right.

When I get back in the driver's seat, I can feel his eyes on me. He's waiting for me to say something, but I'm so angry I don't know what to say. All that built-up energy—the leftover fear and adrenaline—is vibrating inside me and I feel like a rubber band pulled almost to the snapping point. Maybe keeping my mouth clenched shut will make him spill more than he would otherwise.

I back out of the parking spot and wind my way down off the mountain. Silence fills the car as I navigate my way across town, down Geary, heading for a nice, safe, deserted location. Somewhere humans won't overhear us and monsters won't find us.

Ocean Beach is the perfect spot.

I zoom past Cliff House and down the hill toward the public beaches. They're closed at night and the parking lots are empty. Not even those willing to risk a citation for being on the beach after hours are out this late.

I pull Moira into a spot facing the ocean, cut the engine, and palm the keys. Just in case. I stare out over the waves, the moonlight glinting on the cresting peaks. So peaceful. So completely at odds with the fury and confusion warring inside me.

"Something happened tonight," Nick finally says, his voice gentle. Tentative. "What?"

"What?" I laugh. I can't help it. Is he seriously going to play dumb about this? "You know what."

"I don't," he insists. "Look, I'm cooperating. I got into the car. I'm not even complaining that I can't feel my fingertips anymore."

I glance down at his hands, zipped together and resting on his thighs.

I flick a glance at him. "You won't run?"

He shakes his head.

I reach down into my boot and pull out one of the backup daggers I keep there. My missing mentor, Ursula (who, I recently learned, is the immortal Gorgon Euryale—I'll never get used to calling her that), preached the wisdom of being prepared for a worst-case scenario. I've always thought that keeping the extra set of clothes in the trunk, and the gear under the seat and in my locker, was a bit of overkill. Tonight I learned why they're necessary.

With a quick flick of my wrist, hopefully fast enough to make Nick worry about getting sliced, I cut through the zip tie. As I slide the dagger back into my boot, he rubs his wrists.

I guess I underestimated how tight I tugged the tie.

He doesn't run. But he doesn't start talking, either. He's not going to fight me, but he's not going to spill his secrets unprompted. I'm going to have to take the offensive.

32

"What caused the explosion?" I ask flatly. "Was it a bomb or—"

"Explosion!" To his credit, he sounds truly shocked. "What explosion? Gretchen, what *happened*?"

"What happened?" I echo. "My home blew up! Everything I own, everything that wasn't in this car"—I pound my wrist against the steering wheel—"is gone."

"I'm so sorry," he mutters, rubbing a hand through his short wavy hair. "They must have moved up the timetable. They weren't supposed to—"

"They?" I demand, not missing his slip. "Who're *they*?"

He looks at me, his dark eyes bleak and seemingly full of pain. It's a good act. I shouldn't be surprised that he's such a good liar. He's been keeping secrets from me since the moment we met. He's something more than human, and I should have seen it sooner.

"Who are you?" I ask. "*What* are you?"

If my hypno powers worked on him, I'd have had my answers ages ago.

He shakes his head, like he can't process what's going on. I can tell he's thinking, can practically see the thoughts tearing through his mind.

Part of me—the smart part—thinks he's trying to come up with a believable lie. But the rest of me believes he's truly at a loss.

"Look," I say, "you're obviously not all bad. You called to warn me. You saved my life and my sisters' lives." I swallow hard. "I should be thanking you."

"I didn't make that call, Gretchen, I swear it." His voice is steady and—I huff—convincing. "I would have if I'd known it was coming, but I had no idea."

"Then tell me what you do know."

He takes a deep breath and drops his head back against the headrest.

Finally, after what seems like forever, especially for someone with as little patience as I've got, he says, "There is something I need to tell you."

I'm torn between the urge to make a sarcastic reply— *Really? You think?*—and shoving my fist into his nose. In the end, I just stare at him.

"I was sent to protect you," he says. "To watch over you when Euryale was taken. To guard you from those who don't want you and your sisters to be reunited."

My body reacts before my mind fully processes his words, and I give in to the urge to punch him. My knuckles hurt like hell, but the satisfaction that he'll have a bloody—and possibly broken—nose and a pair of black eyes makes the pain bearable.

Unable to sit still, I jump out of the car and walk to the seawall. I press my palms against the rough concrete along the top and stare out over the moonlit ocean.

All this time I've known that there is something wrong with Nick, something different about him. Something . . . not human. Why didn't I ask myself more questions? I should have interrogated him, pushed him for answers. If I had,

34

maybe things wouldn't be as screwed up as they are now.

Maybe I could have prevented the explosion. Maybes and what-ifs. Equally useless.

I hear the passenger door shut with a soft click and then Nick's shoes scrunching across the pavement.

"Who sent you?" I demand before he can offer more lies.

"I—" He takes the spot next to me, leaning his forearms onto the wall. "I should have told you the truth sooner. I should have told you everything. I just thought . . ."

He shakes his head and lets his words trail off.

Well, I'm not about to let him get off that easy.

"You thought *what*?" I demand. "That you could just stand by and watch while my sisters and I got killed for the bounties on our heads?"

"No, of course not." He turns to face me, and I'm disappointed to see only the tiniest trickle of blood from his nose. Either my aim is off or he's got some of that supernatural healing power my sisters and I share.

He adds, "I don't know anything about a bounty."

Anger boils through me, and I think if a scolopendra climbed out of the sea and went for Nick right now, I'd let the thing eat him. After I let its snot-covered nostril hairs rub all over him for a while. I should have let the skorpios hybrid spear him with her tail. Or let the griffin claw his face—

"You saw them." How did I not realize this earlier? My hands clench tighter. "You saw them all. The monsters I was fighting."

He nods, not even ashamed. "Yes, I saw them."

35

"I should have known you could see their true forms," I mutter. "No way you landed that punch square between the griffin's eyes by accident."

"Look, Gretchen, I wanted to tell you, but—" he begins.

"But *what*?" I interrupt. "You were having too much fun teasing me? Mocking me for thinking you might actually be interested in *me*? I am such a jerk."

"No," he insists. "That's not it at all. I was following orders." He shoves his hands into his pockets. "It's complicated."

I snort. If that isn't a code word for *I don't want to explain the truth*, then I don't know what is.

"Fine." I sneer. "What *can* you tell me?"

"Not much more than you already know," he says. "There are those who would like to see you and your sisters dead, and there are those who would like to see you succeed."

"Which side are you on?"

His eyes shift a little to the side. "I'm protecting you, aren't I?"

"I don't know—are you?" I retort. "And that wasn't an answer."

"Look, I can't give you all the answers."

"You mean you won't."

"Fine," he says with a sigh. "I won't. Too many are risking their lives—even their very immortality—to ensure the right outcome. I can't expose them any more than you would expose your sisters if you didn't have to."

I grind my teeth and try to pretend he doesn't have a point.

Just because I might believe him, though, doesn't mean I have to like it.

He grabs my shoulders and turns my body toward him. I let him do it, but I keep my face turned to the ocean.

"I *am* interested in you, Gretchen." When I still won't look at him, he presses his fingers against my jaw and gently turns my face. He is looking straight in my eyes when he says, "I'm interested in *you*."

His midnight blues burn with an intensity that almost makes me believe him. Makes me *want* to believe him. He knows just the right thing to say to mess with my mind. He always has. He leans in closer, watching me. His lips are a breath away from mine.

This time I'm not buying it.

My knee connects with his soft spot and he doubles over, gasping for air.

"Find your own way home," I snap before turning and marching back to my car.

I'm squealing out of the parking lot when it hits me that I don't have a home to go to anymore. A place to sleep, yes. Not a *home*. My vision blurs and I realize there are tears in my eyes. Tears. For the love of Medusa, I'm turning into an emotional mess.

I quickly wipe away the moisture and focus on driving. Focus on getting to the safe house. I won't find answers there, but I'll find a bed and a good night's sleep. In the morning, my head will be clearer and I'll figure out a game plan.

All I know right now is that the first item on the list will be finding and rescuing Ursula.

My first instinct is to visit the one person I know has a connection to the mythological world. When I visited her a few days ago, she helped me locate the immortal Gorgon Sthenno in the city, which helped Grace figure out that Sthenno is her school counselor. If anyone can help me figure out how to rescue Ursula, how to figure out if Nick is what he now appears to be, she's the one. The oracle.

At this time of night the streets of her neighborhood are practically deserted. I park Moira right in front of the vacant-looking storefront, facing the wrong direction so I can jump out closest to the door. I click the remote locks as I reach for the handle on the oracle's front door.

I expect the handle to turn easily, as it has the two previous times I've visited her. But the tarnished gold doesn't budge. Jerking at it a few more times, I have to accept the fact that the door is locked.

I pound on the glass, thinking that maybe she locks the door at night to keep out the unsavories. She could be inside, in the back, or maybe sleeping. I'm not sure if this is her home or simply a place where she hangs out.

There is no sound beyond the door. No light leaks out around the heavy velvet drapes. No indication of anything alive or awake within.

I give the door one final pounding, rattling the hinges

and shaking the glass in the frame.

Nothing.

I turn and stalk back to Moira, swinging into the driver's seat and turning over the engine as I click my seatbelt into place. For a second I pause, hands on the steering wheel, figuring out my next play.

Ursula is gone. Taken prisoner I don't know where, and not wanting me to come after her—or so she told Grace when she appeared to her a few days ago.

Nick is a confusion. A liar. He's something more than I thought, someone more like me than I ever imagined. But can I trust him? How do I know whether I should or not? If I can't answer that question, then I have to keep him at a distance until I can. And answers aren't available at the moment.

The oracle isn't available.

Grace is talking to Sthenno tomorrow.

I guess, for tonight, there's not much else I can do. Hopefully Sthenno will have some answers for us. Or, if she doesn't, then the oracle will. Either way, tonight's a bust.

My arms sag and I realize I'm exhausted. And no wonder. After tackling the manticore in my training room, diving out into the icy bay as the loft exploded, hunting down the two beasts that went after my sisters, and going after Nick, I feel like I've been awake for a month.

Slipping Moira into gear, I head toward the safe house Ursula and I set up. It's in the Tenderloin, maybe the dodgiest part of town—which means there are few prying eyes and even an all-out monster battle would go practically unnoticed. The police won't even patrol there.

In these early-morning hours, there isn't another soul on the street. I turn into the dark, debris-strewn alley behind the safe house. After retrieving the extra gear from under the passenger seat and the duffel bag from the trunk, I trudge up the narrow staircase to the second-floor apartment. My boots barely clear each step.

I could sleep for a year. If only I didn't have school in the morning and an appearance of normalcy to maintain.

Kneeling next to the apartment door, I use a dagger to unscrew the cover from the power outlet in the wall.

I remember the night Ursula and I installed the false outlet. We picked up the yellowed parts at a tiny hardware store in Chinatown and put a couple of cracks in the cover to give it that old, neglected look to go with the rest of the building. If any of the other tenants noticed the oddly placed outlet, they probably thought it dated to the days when the building was a cheap hotel, when someone might have actually vacuumed the hallways every few years.

The happy memory stings a little, and I pull myself back into the present. I reach inside, retrieve the hidden key, and replace the cover.

The door swings open on surprisingly silent hinges, and I find myself facing my new home. *Temporary home,* I remind myself. As soon as I get Ursula back, we'll find a new place, a better place. We'll have to rebuild the arsenal and I don't know if we can restock the library, but whatever we have to do, we'll do.

I've only been to the safe house the one time before, when we installed the hidden key safe in the hall and Ursula gave me the ten-cent tour. She pointed out the backup weapons vault behind the refrigerator. The antivenom and first aid supplies are under a loose tile in the bathroom. There are clothes for both of us in the bedroom closet, emergency cell phones under the couch cushions, and prepaid credit cards in a ziplock bag taped inside the toilet tank.

Ursula thought of everything. Everything I might need if she disappeared. Maybe she knew this was a possibility. Maybe she knew that one day I might be on my own, that she might get taken or worse. I'm glad she was so prepared, but I'd rather have her here.

The entire place looks like a pay-by-the-hour motel room. Dirty walls, ratty linens, rust and dust everywhere. Not the nicest decor, but the carefully orchestrated kind that wouldn't raise red flags if the low-rent landlord decided to pop in. On the surface it looks just like any other apartment in the building.

I can't believe this is my home now. It's such a world away from the sleek and shiny surfaces in the loft. The loft, where everything was clean and gleaming and where I had everything I needed.

The safe house reminds me too much of Phil and Barb's. It's a little too reminiscent of the place—not a *home*, never a *home*—I ran away from four years ago. There are no broken floorboards and all the furniture seems to be in working— if filthy—order, but it's got the same vibe. I can practically picture my ex-parents sitting on the couch, watching the ancient TV and drinking themselves stupid.

There are two important differences between this place and whatever rathole they're living in right now. One, I don't have to tiptoe around, terrified that I'll wake one of them up, draw attention to myself, and bring out their fury. Here, I can throw my duffel bag on the floor, toss my gear pack onto the counter, and slam the door behind me without sending adrenaline pumping into my bloodstream.

And two, if I remember correctly, is right behind the mostly empty bookshelf in the living room. I stomp through the apartment, walk up to the shelf, and grab the dusty white statue of Pan with one hand. Yanking the statue forward, I leap out of the way as the bookshelf swings down. It drops to the floor, landing with a soft thud on the well-worn carpet.

Yes, exactly as I remembered.

Spinning around, I don't bother to kick off my boots before collapsing back on the Murphy bed. A fluffy gray comforter puffs around me and, although the bedding smells a little stale, it's clean. It's comfortable. And it's just what I need.

Less than a minute later, I'm dead to the world.

# CHAPTER 4

## GREER

As I stand on my front stoop, staring at the six sets of gouges in our white-and-gold front door, I think it's reasonable to expect a little near-death-experience reaction. In my mind I see those big, meaty hands snapping my neck or tearing off body parts I'd rather keep. My heart races and I feel survivor's adrenaline coursing through my body. Is this my life now?

"Greer?"

Kyle appears in the open front door with worry etched on his handsome face. I completely blanked. When we talked on the phone a few short hours ago, I invited him over for a make-up date after my unexpected departure from dinner at Ahab's the other night. A sea dracaena climbing out of the bay is a valid excuse, I suppose, but not one I can share with Kyle.

I told him to come over and bring strawberries. Then a six-armed giant showed up at my door. Not surprising that I forgot all about my boyfriend's visit.

"Kyle," I say with a forced smile, "I totally forgot about our—"

"What the freak happened?" he shouts.

Before I can answer, he pulls me into a tight hug and squeezes me against his chest. This is an unusual display of emotion from him. I wrap my arms awkwardly around his waist and pat his back.

"I was so worried," he says next to my ear. "I got here and saw the messed-up door and then the disaster inside and—"

"Disaster?" Oh no.

"Yeah, the whole place is turned upside down," he says, leaning back. "The thieves must have gone through everything."

"Thieves?"

I open my mouth to explain. But what can I say? I can't tell Kyle it was a Gegenees giant, not a team of thieves. I can just imagine the look on his face. *Cool, calm, collected Greer has finally gone over the edge. Too much repressed emotion—it had to burst through sometime. Always knew she was destined for the psych ward.* No, the truth is unbelievable. Kyle's answer is so much easier.

Burglary is common enough in Pacific Heights. Some of the city's wealthiest residents live here, making it a prime target for high-end thefts.

44

Our security system is top-of-the-line, designed to protect all the priceless antiques and artworks my parents have collected over the years. From the Colonial china cabinet to the Picasso sketch in the library, we have a collection that would make any thief drool.

I'll be lucky if nothing *was* stolen in the time the door has remained open since I fled the giant. Maybe it's not such a lie after all.

"Really?" I reply, trying to sound shocked. "Thieves?"

"I don't know if anything's missing." He reaches up and presses his palm against my cheek. "I thought they took you. You said you were going to be home, and when I got here—"

"I'm fine," I say. I know I have to stop him when I see the emotion in his eyes. I know Kyle likes me, says he loves me, even. But I've never realized how much he actually cares.

"I wasn't here," I lie. Anything to soothe the worry from his face. "I had to make an emergency shopping run."

He smiles, a knowing kind of smile that says he knows how much I love shopping. His eyes scan me and then he frowns.

"In your bare feet?"

*Sugar.* I glance down, as if I expect shoes to magically appear. I was barefoot when I fled the giant, and didn't seek out footwear in Gretchen's loft—combat boots aren't really my style. And then there was the explosion and, well, I've been traipsing across San Francisco in my bare feet.

"Would you believe I've taken up barefoot running?" I

ask with a laugh. When he frowns harder I say, "No, I didn't think so."

"Greer, what's going on?"

"I, um—" *Oh great.* I never stammer. I need to think of a reasonable explanation quickly. "I left them in the car, silly," I tease. "My feet are killing me."

That last part isn't a lie, either. But if Kyle thought my calling him silly was out of character, he doesn't show it.

"Did you come out through the house?" he asks with a frown. "I didn't hear you."

"No, I—" Deciding to stick as close to the truth as possible, I say, "I was frightened. I saw the front door as I drove by and was afraid to go inside. I came around on the sidewalk."

He seems to accept that answer as believable.

"We need to call the cops," he says, sounding more like a future senator than ever. "They'll want to file reports, record the damage. Stuff like that. The insurance company will want documentation."

*Sugar, sugar.* I don't want the police involved. I don't want things messier than they already are. What other choice do I have, though? There is no way I can offer my parents a believable explanation for the damage. Our front door will need to be replaced, it will take our full staff days to restore the interior to rights, and there's the not insignificant matter of my dented hood.

As much as I don't relish the idea of lying to law enforcement and filing a false police report, I can't think of a better option.

"You're right," I say. "Let me go grab the house phone and I'll make the call."

By the time the police leave with enough fake details to fill a report about the supposed thieves, I'm exhausted and all I want to do is fall into a steaming hot bath with a chamomile fizzy bomb. Kyle walks up and puts his arms around me. I let my head drop onto his shoulder, glad to have someone to hold me up.

I feel a twinge of guilt about Gretchen, who took down both monsters and then went home to an empty house—an empty safe house that isn't even her home—and who doesn't have anyone to lean on.

Kyle's hands slide smoothly over my back and I close my eyes. This is just what I need. A warm, reassuring hug. Maybe a little massage. The feeling that everything will be—

His hands slip lower, cupping my bottom. He whispers in my ear, "I thought we'd never be alone."

My eyes flash open. Is he joking? I pull back to look at his face and find no trace of humor there.

He squeezes me close.

"Kyle," I warn, "I'm not really in the mood."

"Come on, babe," he complains. "I thought we were going to spend some quality time tonight."

I press my palms against his shoulders and push as I step back out of his embrace. The sudden distance between us is more than the kind that can be measured in inches.

A biting comment is right on the tip of my tongue, but I

force myself to take a calming breath first. I take inventory of my emotions. I expect to feel angry or insulted or even offended. Instead, I feel . . . disappointed.

Kyle and I have been going out for almost a year. By now, shouldn't he care more about my well-being than about getting a little action? Especially after the day I've had? Even if he doesn't know the whole truth, he knows I've been through a traumatic event. And just when I'd started believing he truly cares about me.

"I'm tired," I say dispassionately. "I need to go to bed."

And in that moment I feel my connection to Kyle fade away. All this time and effort I've put into him, and it adds up to nothing.

"I'll call you tomorrow," I tell him.

He gives me a sad, puppy-dog look and I almost want to tell him it's okay, that he can stay and we can cuddle on the couch. But I don't think he wants to cuddle, and I know I don't want anything more than that.

Then he throws me that lopsided surfer-dude smile and says, "Sure thing, babe."

Before I can even open my mouth to say good night or give him a piece of my mind for calling me babe—*again*—he's walking out the front door.

"Good night," I say with a bit of a bite.

He just waves over his shoulder and disappears into the night.

All I want to do is climb upstairs to my bathroom, run

a tub full of steaming water, and soak this night away. But when I close the damaged door and turn back into the house, I see the destruction left in the wake of the giant and I know I can't leave it such a mess. Mother would be furious.

I take a deep breath, shake off my exhaustion, and begin straightening up. I start in the foyer, righting the small nineteenth-century table that is on its side across the room and re-placing it beneath the big gilded mirror. I adjust the mirror so it's hanging square once more. There is a crack in the lower right corner and I smile at the thought of the giant having seven years of bad luck. That unluckiness probably started tonight when Gretchen found him and sent him home.

I move on to the dining room, resetting chairs and re-tying drapes. Then to the living room, where the shredded couch cushions need more than just a straightening. I'm taking a bag full of stuffing to the trash chute when I hear a car pull into the garage downstairs.

My heart thuds and my palms turn clammy. I like to think of myself as a strong young woman, prepared to face most anything with calm and poise. Anything, that is, except my mother.

I fight the instinct to run, to escape to my room and pretend it's all a bad dream. That would only make things worse.

Footsteps on the back stairs echo closer and then the door is swinging open.

Mother steps into the kitchen, looking like a queen. Her icy blond hair is swept into a crisp chignon, her deep purple business suit is still perfectly pressed after a full day of wear, with bold but tasteful jewels around her neck and wrist. No one would mistake her for anything less than she is: perfect.

"Why is the garage open?" she demands. "Are you trying to invite thieves into our home?"

"No, Mother," I say automatically. I brace myself for the lie I have to tell. "There was a break-in. I was just—"

"What did they take?" She sets her satchel on the counter and strides into the house to inspect.

Dad steps into the kitchen, worry creasing his distinguished, graying brow. "Are you okay, Greer?"

"Yes, I'm fine," I reply.

He steps close, lifts a hand, and rests it on my shoulder. For a second I think he wants to hug me. And in this moment I would let him.

But then Mother returns. "What was taken?"

"As far as I can tell," I say, hiding the quiver in my voice, "nothing."

Her eyes narrow. "What do you mean 'nothing'?"

I resist the urge to shrug. "I did a cursory inventory when the police were here, for their report, and I couldn't find anything specific missing."

She studies me, trying to gauge whether I'm telling the truth, whether she needs to interrogate me about the situation, whether I'm guilty of some minor transgression that requires punishment.

I can't take the pressure, not after tonight. For the first

time in my life, I lift my gaze and look her directly in the eye—not slightly to the left, so it appears that I'm meeting her gaze while avoiding her usual lecture on the importance of eye contact. Staring straight into her suspicious eyes, I say, slowly and carefully, "Nothing was taken. The police think it was vandals."

When Grace told me about our hypnotic powers, I thought she was being ridiculous. I also thought I would never have reason to use them, even if they were real. I have no trouble getting people to do what I want. Everyone but my mother. So I have to try.

When I see her eyes lose focus and she repeats, "Nothing taken. Vandals." I feel a giddy bubble rise up inside me.

*It worked. It really worked.*

Dad, oblivious to what has just happened, walks up to her and rests a hand against her lower back. "It sounds as if Greer has everything under control, Helen." He throws me a sympathetic smile. "We've all had long days. I'll have Natasha call the housekeepers in the morning, and the house will be back to normal when we return home tomorrow night."

"Of course." I smile, trying to appear positive when I know *I* will have to be the one to talk to Natasha because Dad will be at the office before dawn. I will take care of it, as I always do.

Mother just looks at him, her face still oddly blank, and she lets Dad lead her to the stairs up to their second-floor bedroom. As he guides her into the stairway, he looks back at me and we share a knowing smile. If he notices Mother's unusual malleability, her slightly odd behavior, he doesn't comment.

I nod good night to Dad and wait until I hear their bedroom door shut before I release the tense energy coiled up inside me.

My bath is calling me, but I have to face the rest of the cleanup first. Yes, I will make sure the housekeepers come tomorrow, but the better things look when Mother comes down in the morning, the better things will be for everyone in the household.

As I move throughout the first floor, smoothing rugs and straightening portraits of ancestors who no longer belong to me, I can't keep the tremor from my hands. Even if my hypno powers helped give me the confidence, I just told my mother and the police bald-faced lies. My boyfriend is proving to be too callous and selfish for my taste. And tonight I escaped death by six-armed giant, manticore, and explosion. My life is changing faster that I can keep up with, and for the first time in my life, I'm not 100-percent certain I can handle it.

There are little cracks forming in my controlled facade, and I'm afraid it will take more than a hot bath and a good night's sleep to repair them.

For tonight, though, they'll have to suffice.

# CHAPTER 5

# GRACE

Despite my crazy late night, I'm waiting outside Ms. West's office first thing the next morning. Actually, I left home so early, I got to school before the front doors were open. The custodian let me in when he saw me sitting on the front steps, and then the secretary let me into the office so I could wait for Ms. West on the bench outside her door.

One reason for my eagerness is that I want to talk to Ms. West and find out for certain if she's the Gorgon Sthenno. I'm pretty sure—as sure as I can be—but it pays to be cautious. Especially after last night. I have to be a little strategic.

But the other reason is that I wanted to get out of the house before Mom and Dad were up. I knew Mom said Dad and I should talk this morning about my irresponsible behavior, but I couldn't face the prospect. I couldn't sit there and listen to them explain how disappointed they are in me and how I know better and how they thought they could trust me. It breaks my heart that I can't tell them the real reason I disappeared last night. It breaks my heart that this new part of me, this shadow life with triplet sisters and a mythological legacy, might be causing a crack in the relationship I have with my parents. It kills me, but I don't have another choice. Telling them is not an option. I have to keep my shadows to myself.

"Grace?" Ms. West asks as she arrives at her door. "Is something wrong?"

She looks the same as always: tall, elegant, poised. Wearing a crisp suit in a soft shade of gray and heels that would make Greer proud. Hair in a tight, low ponytail. Simple gold jewelry. Same generically welcoming look on her face.

Even though she hasn't changed since yesterday, the way I'm looking at her has. I see the little details I missed before. The sense of strength emanating from every inch of her body. The ancient design of her earrings. And, most of all, the wisdom in her soft blue eyes. The wisdom of someone far older—by millennia—than the thirty-something image she presents.

How did I miss these signs before? Or am I just seeing them now because I want to?

I can't take the risk that I'm wrong, that I've guessed wrong. My sisters and I have too much at stake. So instead of asking, *Hey, aren't you an immortal Gorgon?* I say, "Yeah. I need to talk to you about my English class."

She smiles blandly and says, "Of course."

As she unlocks the door to her office, I mentally play through what I want to say. By the time she has settled into the chair behind her austere desk, and I'm in one of the facing chairs, I'm still trying to figure out how to begin.

The picture on the wall behind her draws my attention. The pristine white sand, the brilliant turquoise waters. There's something intensely familiar about it.

In an instant, I know what I have to say.

"That's a beautiful picture," I say, sitting on the edge of my chair. I drop my gaze to meet her eye to eye. "Is it the Aegean?"

At first she doesn't react. I sense a slight shift in her, maybe a narrowing of her eyes at the corners or an imperceptible straightening of her spine.

She blinks once. "It is."

The right side of her mouth quirks up a fraction of an inch.

"It's beautiful," I say, charging ahead now that I feel that I have the tiniest bit of reassurance. "It looks . . . timeless. Like it might have looked exactly like that for, oh"—I lift my brows—"thousands of years."

Ms. West leans back in her chair, crosses her arms over her chest, and gives me a small smile. "Not *exactly*. But it's held up quite well."

For several long moments we just watch each other across

the desk. I imagine she's trying to guess exactly how much I know, whether I've discovered my heritage, found my sisters, seen my first monster.

I'm trying to contain my excitement.

"So . . . ," she says.

I grin. "So."

She nods and asks, "What do you know?"

"I know that you're the immortal Gorgon Sthenno." I hesitate, waiting for confirmation. She nods, and when I realize I'm not getting more than that—she's as tight-lipped as Gretchen was at first—I continue. "I know that I'm a descendant of your sister, Medusa."

Her reaction is almost unnoticeable. She sucks in a little extra breath at the mention of her lost sister. There is a sadness in her eyes that clearly says not even millennia can dim the pain of her loss. I feel immediate sympathy. I've only known my sisters a short time and they're both here and healthy, but I can't imagine the pain of losing one of them. I wonder if it's the sort of pain you could ever get over.

From the sudden shine in Ms. West's eyes, I think I know the answer.

"I know that I have two sisters, triplets," I continue, trying to save us both from the painful thoughts. "And that we're the Key Generation."

"You know quite a lot," she finally says.

"Not nearly enough," I reply. "I also know that Euryale has been taken prisoner. And that last night there were coordinated, planned attacks on me and my sisters."

"Planned attacks?" she echoes. Sitting up straighter in her chair, she leans forward across the desk. "What do you mean?"

I give her the brief recap about the simultaneous attacks at our homes and then the explosion at the loft. Her jaw gets tighter with every detail.

"I've been out of contact too long, so focused on getting you here to the city that I let myself get cut off," she says. "I had no idea plans were already in motion."

"It's okay," I say, wanting to reassure her. "Gretchen, Greer, and I are fine. You couldn't have known."

"I knew things were going to change quickly now that you three are sixteen, now that the predestined clock has begun ticking," she says. "I should have known they would try to grab one or both of us."

She shakes her head, her eyes glazing over like she's getting lost in thought. Maybe thinking about her own sister, about how Euryale has been taken prisoner. I imagine she feels as responsible for protecting and taking care of Euryale as I do for protecting and taking care of Gretchen and Greer.

"They who?" I ask.

She looks at me, startled from her thoughts. "The factions," she answers. "They are trying to manipulate the path of things to come."

"Factions?"

"The two opposing sides in this brewing war," she explains.

"War?" My stomach clenches.

For once, her face softens. And that only magnifies my unease.

"The time of the Key Generation has been anticipated for longer than most can remember," she says. "It is the moment in which the mythological scales realign. For too long they have been weighted in one direction; even if that is the direction of supposed good, the scales are not meant to be unbalanced. The opportunity to maintain or reverse that imbalance makes for desperate action."

"Like trying to kill us."

"One side, yes, would see you fail," she says. "Would see the door remain forever sealed." She taps her fingernails on the desk. "The other wishes to see you open the door, only to have you overrun by monsters from the abyss who have long been plotting to take over this realm."

She scowls, looking at the ceiling as if she's trying to piece together what's going on. That makes two of us.

"The side that wants us to fail," I say. "What does that mean?"

She answers absently, "That means they want you dead before the seal can be broken. As they have killed so many of our line before you, trying to prevent your birth."

This is just getting worse and worse. I take a deep breath. Okay, I knew there were people—or monsters—trying to kill us. This isn't news. At least now I sort of know why. And I know we aren't the first.

"How many?" I ask.

She looks at me. "How many what?"

"How many of our line have they killed?" I swallow before asking the question burning in my brain. "What about our mother? Is she . . . ?"

I can't finish the question. I don't have to. The look on Ms. West's face says everything.

"Oh, Grace," she says. "Your mother has been lost to us for quite some time."

My tears shouldn't surprise me. I've just learned that the mother I'd always hoped to meet, to question, to learn more about, is gone.

"Lost," I repeat, forcing my tears away. "You mean dead."

"We honestly don't know," she says, and my heart starts beating faster. "We have had no contact with her since shortly after she gave you and your sisters up for adoption."

No contact. That means out of touch, it doesn't mean dead. Not necessarily.

She might be alive. She has to be. I have to believe that. I have to believe that when she gave us up for our protection, it also protected her. Somewhere out there, she's waiting for us. Hoping we fulfill our destiny, hoping we find her. I promise to do everything within my power to do just that.

But for now I have myself and my sisters to look out for. There are bigger things at stake. We need to figure out this situation before things get worse, before this—I shudder—war comes.

"Why?" I ask, swallowing my emotion. "Why does everyone want us dead?"

"Not everyone," she says with a sympathetic smile. Then

she answers my question. "Each side has its own motives. Those who wish to see you fail *before* the seal is broken—they believe they are acting for the greater good."

"The greater good?" I echo. "I don't see how killing us does anyone any good."

Ms. West laughs. "Good and bad, right and wrong, are not so easily defined in our world." She sighs. "Those who believe they act with righteous intent, who believe they act to protect both humankind and residents of Olympus, are all the more dangerous for their conviction."

Just because they think they're doing the right thing doesn't make them right.

"What about the other side?" I ask. "The one that wants us dead *after*?"

"That side acts with a more selfish goal," she explains, "though they believe themselves just as righteous as their opponents. They seek the freedom of monsterkind, a population that has been imprisoned and marginalized for millennia. It is a very complicated and emotion-driven dispute, on both sides."

I let all of this news sink in: the war and the factions and the players on each side who I used to believe existed only in myth. And all of them ultimately wanting me and my sisters dead. It's pretty overwhelming.

"Doesn't anyone want us to live?" I blurt. "Isn't there anyone who wants us to succeed and live long, happy lives?"

Not that I expect her to say, *Nope. Sorry. You're out of luck.*

But the last thing I expect is for Ms. West to get up, walk around her desk, and pull me up into a tight hug.

"Yes," she says against my hair. "Yes, of course we do."

"Who?" I demand, pulling back. "So far it sounds like everyone wants us dead either before or after the seal is broken."

"Euryale and I are determined to see you succeed," she says adamantly. "I believe she was trying to discover more about who is on each side when she was taken. And there are others. They work in secret and at great personal risk to pave the way for your triumph. If the gods on either side caught wind of anyone working against them, the consequences would be severe. . . ."

Her voice kind of trails off, like the sum total of everything that's happened in the last two weeks has just added up in her brain. Join the club.

At least I feel a little more reassured. My sisters and I may be caught in the middle of a brewing war, but at least we aren't working alone.

Suddenly she steps back.

"I need to go."

"What?" I gasp. "No, we need to talk."

She looks at me and gives me a true smile. "Yes, we do. All of us." She grabs her purse off the floor. "But first, I need to seek some answers. Can you meet after school?"

I nod. "Yes."

"And your sisters?" she asks. "Gretchen and Greer, those are their names?"

"Yes," I say. "I think they can be there too. I'll text them."

We agree on a place and time, a coffee shop in Union Square where the sheer volume of tourists and shoppers will give us some much-needed anonymity.

I stand and yank my backpack onto my shoulder. I give Ms. West—Sthenno—a shaky smile. She lifts her palms to my cheeks and cups my face.

"I am relieved to have the whole truth out in the open between us, Grace." She leans forward and kisses first one cheek, then the other. "Trust that we will get through this. And know that my sister Euryale and I and others are working to ensure your success."

I want to believe her, but all this talk of war and factions and people I've never even met wanting me and my sisters and the rest of my family dead is a little unnerving. My fear must show, because she drops her hands to my shoulders and gives me a reassuring squeeze.

"This is your destiny," she says. "Fate has a way of working out in the end."

As I walk out of her office, I try to think positively. I focus on her steadfast assurance that we'll survive and succeed in this upcoming battle.

But there's a little niggle of doubt at the back of my mind that says fate also has a way of playing tricks on the players. Sometimes there are unanticipated twists and turns. I just have to tell myself that Gretchen, Greer, and I will be able to hold on tight for the ride. Three times the strength. Three times the chance of success.

And, my doubts can't help adding, three times the chance of failure.

As I blend into the stream of before-school students, I try to focus on the day ahead. Answers will have to wait until our afternoon meeting.

I pull out my phone and send a quick text to Gretchen and Greer on my way to homeroom.

**Coffee with Sthenno at four at the Grindery in Union Square.**

"Texting home to mommy?" my archenemy Miranda taunts as we walk into class at the same time.

I'm so over being intimidated by her.

"Suck a lemon, Sanders," I say, repeating my friend Vail's favorite shutdown.

I fall into my seat, drop my bag on the floor, and realize that all the stress and exhaustion of the last twenty-four hours have just caught up with me. I feel like passing out.

"Lulu told me you grew a pair," Vail says from across the aisle.

I glance over to see her grinning at me, proud of me for putting Miranda in her place. The colorful tips at the ends of her otherwise black hair are now a flaming shade of red.

"Yeah," I say. "I guess I did."

The tardy bell rings and I relax back in my seat. Taking a lesson from my ordinary life, I mentally tell my doubts to take a hike. If I can stand up to Miranda, no monster stands a chance.

Ms. West—Sthenno—is right. We're going to succeed. I just have to trust in fate.

# CHAPTER 6

# GRETCHEN

I time my arrival in biology so I'm walking through the door just as the bell rings. The last thing I want to face this early in the morning is Nick, so I figure that by arriving with the bell, I can avoid that window of time when we would still be free to talk. Well, he'd be free to talk and I'd be free to ignore him.

Turns out my precision timing is wasted because the seat behind mine is empty.

"Nice of you to join us, Miss Sharpe," Mrs. Knightly warns as I stride past the front of the class. "Next time, be in your seat *before* the bell or it'll be a tardy."

Some of the sheep—I mean, other students—watch in eager anticipation, hoping I'll do something gossipworthy. I ignore them.

"Yes ma'am," I say, mostly to appease her, so I can sink into my chair and let the adrenaline in my bloodstream fade away.

Guess I was more worried than I thought.

Mrs. Knightly starts her lecture, but I can't concentrate on anything she says. Instead I'm going over everything that happened last night. I was hard on Nick, I know. But he has to know he deserved it. He kept his true identity, his reason for showing up in my life, a secret, and it nearly cost my sisters and me our lives.

I should be furious at him—I am, really—but part of me wants to believe him when he says he's watching over us, protecting us. Protecting me.

I snort at the thought—and then have to cover up the sound with a brief coughing fit when Mrs. Knightly skewers me with an angry glare. What has he done to protect me? Most of the time I was protecting him.

He must realize by now that I'm the last person on earth who needs protecting. I can take care of myself and my sisters.

Part of me *does* believe him, though. Believes that he's on our side—whatever that means. I can't help wondering where he is and if he's not here today because of the things I said last night.

My phone vibrates in my cargo pocket.

Mrs. Knightly is focused on writing something about chromosomes and reproduction on the board. Without moving my upper body, I lift my knee, reach down, unbutton the pocket holding my phone, and slide it quietly out into my palm. I pull it up into my lap and look down.

It's a text from Grace.

My heart thumps and I realize that I'd been hoping it was Nick. *Get over it*, I tell myself. If he's scared away, he's scared away. So what if he's the only boy who's ever known my secret? He isn't interested in me, anyway. He's just . . . I don't know what. Trying to get close to me? Win my trust?

Whatever. He lied to me. I shouldn't want to talk to him. I shouldn't want him to call or to be in class to pass notes over my shoulder. I shouldn't want him at all.

Shaking off these frivolous thoughts, I look down again and read Grace's message.

**Coffee with Sthenno at four at the Grindery in Union Square.**

I know the place. It's too crowded and overpriced for me, but it's kind of a landmark. I text back a quick **Okay** and am slipping my phone back into its pocket when I hear my name.

"Miss Sharpe," Mrs. Knightly says. She sounds annoyed, like she's been trying to get my attention.

"Yes?" I sit up straight, trying to look like a good, attentive student.

"What is the difference between mitosis and meiosis?"

"Um . . ." Around me, the sheep snicker. I swing a glare around the room. As if they're any better. I can see four phones hidden behind textbooks, two girls passing notes, another two with earbuds concealed beneath their hair, and one boy with his head down, pretending to read the textbook with

66

his eyes closed. None of them would be able to answer either.

"Sorry," I say, giving Mrs. Knightly my best apologetic smile. I'm not much for apologies, so I doubt even my best attempt is very successful. "I'm a little lost."

Flipping through my textbook, as if I'm looking for the answer, I hope she lets my humiliation end there. The room is silent for several long, tense moments. Then she finally says, "Please see me after class."

As she moves on, putting one of the sheep on the spot for the answer, I slump in my chair. Obviously my warnings are over. I'll be lucky to get out of this one without detention or a date with the principal.

I do my best to focus during the rest of class, forcing thoughts of Nick from my mind. I copy down everything from the board and even raise my hand once to answer a question. Mrs. Knightly ignores me, and I know I'm in big trouble.

When the bell rings, I put my notes away and walk up to her desk. She is busy writing and doesn't acknowledge my presence until the last of the sheep shuffles out of the room.

I sneak a peek at the writing and release a relieved sigh when I realize it's not about me.

She sets her pen down and finally looks up.

"Miss Sharpe," she says, her voice hard. She closes her eyes, and when she opens them again she smiles tightly. "Gretchen. I think we need to talk about what's going on."

Her eyes, the darkest I've ever seen—darker even than Nick's midnight blue—find mine. There's something almost

67

hypnotic about their cavernous dark. Which is a silly thought, really, because I'm the one with the hypnotic eyes.

I could use that power to get out of this situation in the blink of an eye, but I might as well let it play out first. Right now I'm only assuming I'm in trouble.

"We are only in the third week of school and already you have accrued several absences and tardies and you're missing three homework assignments."

"I know," I say, trying to catch her off guard by agreeing. "I've had some"—I lean forward and whisper—"*family* issues to deal with."

This is an excuse I've used many times in the last four years. Most teachers are sympathetic to complicated home lives— okay, maybe not *most* teachers, but *some*. This is the first time that the excuse is actually true. Back-to-back assassination attempts on me and my sisters and having my mentor/great-dozens-of-times-over-aunt taken prisoner definitely qualify as family issues, right?

Mrs. Knightly isn't going to let it slide that easy. "Do you want to talk about it? Perhaps I can help."

I have to bite my lip not to laugh. Yeah, right. I can just imagine the look on her face when I tell her that I'm a little out of sorts because someone blew up my loft last night, but not before a manticore tried to kill me. And that the boy I thought was just into me was actually sent by someone on one branch in the forest of family trees that make up Greek mythology to protect me because I'm a leaf on one of those branches myself, and in my spare time I hunt mythological monsters who want to kill or control the human population. Oh yeah, that would go over real well.

"Thanks," I say. "But I'll be fine."

She studies me for a minute, probably weighing whether or not she should send me to the principal anyway for good measure. I feel a connection, something drawing me toward her. Like maybe I *could* tell her all the crazy things that are going on in my life.

Then she blinks and the connection is broken. I fall back a step, as if an actual rope has been cut.

"Consider this your final warning," she says, her attention returning to the notes on her desk. She picks up her pen and starts writing. "Next time will earn you a trip to the office."

"Yes, ma'am."

Then, as quickly as possible without looking like I'm fleeing, I rush into the hall, into the between-classes crowd.

I can't afford the trouble of a trip to the principal's office. I never could—not with Ursula being a completely unofficial guardian and me having run away from my supposed parents when I was twelve—but right now it's especially crucial I stay below the administrative radar. I'm living on my own in a safe house in a dodgy part of town, without a suitable guardian in sight. It would be a trip to the principal, followed by a trip to Child Welfare or, worse, juvie.

No thanks. I have too many responsibilities, too many people relying on me to do my job, keep them safe, and bring them home. I can't afford any red flags with the authorities. I'll just have to work extra hard to keep my nose clean and uninteresting to the powers that be.

The rest of the school day goes smoothly. After the close call in first period I get my game face on and manage to impersonate a perfect student in the rest of my classes. My history teacher even comments on my attentiveness.

By the time I'm pushing through the front doors, heading to Moira's parking spot, I'm happy with my success. I just have to keep this up until all the current crazy gets settled.

"You look pretty proud of yourself," a familiar voice says. "Did somebody get a gold star?"

I spin around and see Nick leaning against the outer wall of the school, right outside the entrance. Casual as ever. As if I hadn't punched him in the nose and abandoned him at the beach in the middle of the night. Fine. Two can play the *nothing happened* game.

I ignore him and his statement and keep walking. My body may be excited to see him, if my racing heart and shaking hands are any indication, but my brain knows better.

He obviously doesn't take offense, because he falls into step beside me.

"We need to talk," he says.

I cut him a sharp glare.

"I'm serious, Gretchen." His long strides keep up easily with my fast ones. "Can we go somewhere and—"

"Can't," I interrupt. "I have an appointment."

At first I said it to give myself an out, but then I remember the coffee meeting with Sthenno. I really do have an appointment.

"I'll come with you," he insists.

I laugh. "Yeah right."

"Look." He grabs my elbow, yanking me to a stop only because I let him, and stepping around to face me. "Let me ride along. I'll say my piece and then, when you get wherever you're going, you can kick me out."

I'm skeptical. With Nick, nothing is ever that easy. The idea of kicking him out does hold some appeal, though.

"Or you can just kick me," he adds with a wicked smile, as if he has just read my thoughts. "I know how much you love that."

I glare harder.

Can I trust him? He's not exactly been forthright for the duration of our acquaintance. In fact, our whole history has been pretty much a lie. But what's the harm? It's not like he's ever tried to hurt me, and if he ever does, I can defend myself. Besides, maybe I can get some more answers out of him.

Finally I shrug.

This will be on my terms, though.

He must understand, because he falls back into step next to me as I continue toward Moira. When we get within range, I pop her trunk. I fling my backpack inside and slam it shut.

Nick hurries to the passenger door, as if he's afraid I'll change my mind and take off without him. Maybe he's right. But getting into the car doesn't guarantee him the chance to say what he has to say. If I want him out I could have him rolling across the street in less than two seconds. One, if the car is moving fast enough.

My curiosity wins out, and I wait for him to buckle in before putting Moira in gear and pulling into traffic. The seatbelt gives him at least another two seconds in the car.

I have more than half an hour before I'm supposed to meet Sthenno and my sisters at the coffee shop, so I decide to take the scenic route. In general, I try to avoid the touristy parts of town. I get drawn to them often enough on monster hunts. The sightseeing crowds make easy pickings for beastiekind. What's one missing tourist in a sea of hundreds? But there is one popular spot that I return to again and again.

Nick is silent as I make my way down Columbus and turn left onto Lombard, well below the crookedest-street-in-the-world section—talk about a tactical nightmare. I follow the road around a sharp curve and wind my way up Telegraph Hill. In the summer it's pure madness, full of visitors from across the country and around the world. But on this chilly fall day, the road is practically empty. I pull into a parking spot at the top, facing out over the bay.

I'm not sure why this is my Zen spot. Maybe it's the sweeping views of the water and the city. Maybe it's the feeling of being so far above it all. Maybe it's Pioneer Park, a pretty little green space that rarely sees visitors. For whatever reason, when I need to get away, to think about things, this is where I come.

Which in no way explains why I've brought Nick here.

"For someone who has something to say," I snap, "you're being awfully silent."

I feel him watching me. "I'm waiting until you're ready to listen."

"I never promised to listen. Only that you could come along for the ride."

He shifts in the seat—awkwardly because of the restricting seatbelt—and tries to face me. I look away. I don't want to see him, to be influenced by his pretty face, his expression, or any outward appearances of sincerity. I learned a long time ago it's easier for people to put on a false facade than to fake it in their voice.

Our view of the bay below is filtered by a light fog. Not so thick that I can't see the other side, but enough to make everything unclear. Which is exactly how I feel right now. Unclear.

"I know you're upset with me," he finally begins.

That's a ridiculously massive understatement. I snort derisively in response.

"I totally deserve that," he continues anyway. "I can't change what's already happened, but you have to know one thing."

When he doesn't explain, curiosity draws my gaze away from the hazy view of Alcatraz. His dark eyes are steady and earnest. Darn it.

"I am on your side," he says, deadly serious, like this is the most important thing he has ever said. "Whatever happens, I want to help you fulfill your destiny."

"Destiny?" I snap back. "What destiny? I didn't even know I was on a side other than the monster-hunting one."

"Things are more complicated than that," he says. "When the door was sealed, it was intended that one day—when the Key Generation came of age"—he nods at me, indicating he knows that means me and my sisters—"the seal would be broken so man and monster could once more share the world, as it was meant to be."

"Oh yeah, monsters freely roaming the streets. That's a total utopia."

"Of course it's not," he replies. "Not without regulation. Not without guardians in place."

I shake my head. I don't understand any of this. All this time my sole mission has been to send monsters home. Away. And now my destiny's supposed to be letting them out? That can't be right.

"Gretchen, I want you to know that, no matter what—" He reaches out, like he wants to rest his hand on mine, but then drops it onto the gearshift between us. "You can trust me."

It's practically a whisper, but I hear it like he used a megaphone. The effect echoes through me and I find myself *wanting* to trust him. *Wanting* to believe in him more than anyone else.

What has he done to earn my trust? He's been lying to me

since the beginning—well, if not lying, exactly, then at least keeping the truth buried. He's an unknown quantity, a new addition in my life with no proof of who he is or where he came from. And the one person whose answer I trust is being held prisoner beyond my reach.

Yet something in me wants to believe him. I can't explain it, but it's like a craving. Unfounded and unrelenting.

Maybe if he answers some questions, I'll know whether to listen to the part of me that is softening.

I'll start with an easy one. "Where are you from?" I ask.

His eyes shutter before he answers. "I was born in Greece."

I lift my brows at the incomplete answer. If he's going to ask me to trust him, then he has to trust me too. He has to tell me everything.

He sighs, as if accepting that he has to tell me the whole truth. "I was raised on Mount Olympus."

"Mount Olympus?" I sputter. "As in the home of the gods?"

He nods. Just that. No explanation or insistence or defense of his claim. Just a nod. And that is more convincing than any words.

"Are you—" I begin to ask, but I'm not sure how to phrase the question. "Who are you—? I mean, where do you—?"

"I am a descendant of Themis," he says simply. "The goddess of law and justice."

"Themis," I echo.

I suppose that shouldn't be any more surprising than the

fact that I'm a descendant of Medusa. But Medusa was only a Gorgon, a mortal guardian. Themis is a full-on goddess.

"Is that who sent you to protect me?"

"No. And I can't tell you who did," he says before I can ask. "I won't because it isn't safe. There are those on both sides of this war who can steal your thoughts, who can enter your mind and uncover your secrets. I cannot risk the lives and immortality of those who dare to help us."

*Us.* There is something both reassuring and terrifying about that word. Reassuring, because it means I'm not alone. I know I'm not *really* alone; I have my sisters and Ursula and Sthenno. But this is something different. Nick is on my side because he believes it's the right thing to do, not because we're connected by blood legacy.

Terrifying, because it means there are a lot more people counting on me than I thought.

"Fine," I say, accepting—for now—that he won't answer that particular question. I've got more. I cautiously ask the next one, hiding my concern. "What do you know about Ursula?"

The sadness in his eyes gives me the answer. "Euryale." This time he does put his hand on mine. "I know she's been taken."

"Where?"

"We don't know for sure," he says, still not bothering to explain who *we* are. "Some believe she is being held in the abyss. Others think she is in the dungeon of Olympus."

The abyss? I shudder at the thought of her in that dark,

76

dismal place. I've never seen it firsthand, but Ursula told me about it. Dark, cold, and permeated by the stench of countless monsters. I can't stop the mental image of her there. Alone. Surrounded by the monsters she's spent a very long lifetime fighting to keep contained. I can only imagine—

Nick reaches for my face and I feel his fingertips glide smoothly across the skin beneath my eye. It's damp with tears.

I pull a hard breath in through my nose and force myself to strengthen up. I need to be strong and clearheaded if I want to help Ursula. She needs me. She's been there for me from the beginning, without hesitation. I need to be here for her now.

My phone vibrates in my pocket.

It's after four. I know what it's going to say before I pull it out. Shrugging off my unexpected emotion—and Nick's warm fingers—I say, "I'm late."

"Gretchen, I—"

"Where can I drop you?"

I back out of the parking spot and steer Moira back down the hill. Nick retreats to his side of the car, and I'm glad for the distance. I need the breathing room.

"Are you meeting your sisters?" he asks.

I freeze for an instant, protective instinct taking over. I don't want him or anyone else involved in this mess to know about Grace and Greer. It's one thing for me to place my trust in him—if I've even decided I can do that—but I won't put them at risk. Not ever.

"Where can I drop you?" I repeat.

He takes the hint—for once. "Anywhere is fine."

I pull over in front of a bus stop on Stockton. I drum my fingers on the steering wheel impatiently, like I can't wait for him to get out of the car. I'm anxious to see my sisters, to reassure myself that they're okay. To meet Sthenno and find out what she has to say. And to get away from Nick.

Which in no way explains why, when he opens the door and starts to climb out, I blurt, "We can get together after."

Why did I say that?

He turns back to face me. From the corner of my eye I can see the barest hint of a smile on his face.

"Want to meet at my place?" he asks, cleverly hiding the smugness I can tell he's feeling.

I shake my head. His place. That sounds too intimate. "I'll text you when I'm done."

"Okay." He climbs the rest of the way out of the car, turns back to close the door, and then leans in the open window. "I won't let you down, Gretchen. I promise."

I don't know how to respond to that. I want to believe him, want to give him the trust he's asking for. But I'm not sure I can. I'm not sure I ever will.

I'm the girl who's meant to walk alone. Now with sisters at my back. Trusting Nick doesn't fit the game plan. Does it?

But I can't stop the longing.

So instead of replying or even acknowledging his words, I release the clutch and drive away.

# CHAPTER 7

## GREER

When I turn on my phone after school, it immediately pings with a dozen new text messages. Most of them are from Kyle, apologizing for how last night ended. I delete them without responding.

One is from the housekeepers, confirming that their work is done and the house is back to normal except for the door. I have a contractor coming this afternoon to give an estimate for replacing it. I plan on taking my car to a body shop this weekend, which will complete the restoration to pre-attack appearances.

The other three messages are from Grace.

Coffee with Sthenno at the Grindery in Union Square.

Then, when I didn't respond, she sent another.

Did you get my text? Meeting after school. Call me.

Finally, a text from just a few minutes ago.

**At the coffee shop. Coming?**

I close my eyes and count to ten. Last night, when I agreed to join up with the three mythketeers, it was with the understanding that the monster-hunting side of my life would have to balance with the responsibilities of the normal side.

Less than twenty-four hours later and already my two halves are in conflict. I have a Mock Government meeting right now and then the contractor appointment.

Last night was terrible, and I know I have responsibilities in that world. But I have to compartmentalize. I have to keep the two halves separate or I'm liable to go insane. It's a careful balance.

My phone beeps again.

**Greer?**

I sigh. I realize I don't have much of a choice. As much as I want to ignore the world of monsters and mythology, to bury my head in the sand and pretend my sisters never found me, I can't. I'm too principled for that. Mock Government pales in comparison to saving the world from mythological monsters, obviously. And I can reschedule with the contractor.

Sometimes being responsible is a challenge.

I shoot Grace a quick message.

**Just got your texts. On my way now.**

I scroll through my contacts, searching for Fog City Builders as I start toward the front entrance instead of the Mock Government classroom. I should tell Mrs. Franklin I can't make it, but there's no time.

"Are you on your way to MG?" Rory asks as she steps into my path.

Annalise says, "Cute shoes. Are they new?"

I try not to roll my eyes. This is the third time she's asked me the same question about the same shoes. I choose to ignore it.

"I have to miss the meeting," I say, finally finding the phone number I'm looking for. "I forgot about a preexisting appointment."

The looks on their faces say it all. In the years they have known me, I have never had to miss a meeting. I have never forgotten about an appointment or even scheduled a conflict by accident. I just don't.

"Are you okay?" Rory asks.

"Yeah," Annalise says. "You're not sick, are you?"

She actually takes half a step back.

I don't have time for their dramatics. I'm already late for the meeting with my sisters that I didn't even know about until moments ago. If I don't hit traffic, I can be there in ten minutes. Less if I ignore the speed limit—which I will, because I hate being late.

"I'm fine," I say, punching the number for the contractors as I walk around my friends. "I'll see you tomorrow."

I can practically feel their open-jawed stares as I disappear down the hall. Great, I spend one day as a part of a greater destiny, and already the rest of my life is suffering the consequences.

I refuse to completely sacrifice normalcy for this guardian legacy. I will just have to fight harder for balance in the future.

"My name is Greer Morgenthal," I say when a receptionist answers the phone at Fog City Builders, "and I need to reschedule my afternoon consultation."

At this time of day it's virtually impossible to find a parking spot around Union Square. Unless, of course, your father is CEO of a company on the upper floors of the Gold Rush Building. I emerge from the parking garage less than a block away from the coffee shop where I'm supposed to meet my sisters and our immortal ancestor Sthenno.

Okay, I have to admit, the idea is a little thrilling. As my irritation settled during the drive over, my curiosity grew. It's one thing to imagine I'm a descendant of a mythological being. That's a very distant and abstract kind of connection, like the one people who are descended from a *Mayflower* passenger or a Civil War general feel with their ancestors. But I'm about to meet an actual immortal, a being who can't die, who's been alive for thousands of years. Kind of makes my short life feel rather insignificant.

I can only imagine the things Sthenno must have seen—so many events both great and tragic. I wonder what she thinks of our current world, whether it measures up to or surpasses previous generations. I like to think we have a lot of great things going for us—medicine, technology, globalization—but maybe every era thinks most highly of itself.

I cross the street, careful to avoid cracks and potholes in my high-heeled peep toes.

Grace is sitting at one of the three tables set out on the sidewalk that give the cramped coffee shop some extra seating space. She waves at me, an enthusiastic smile on her face. I realize that I have a similar grin on my face and quickly school my features into a calm facade. Mother always says an external display of emotion is the sign of a weak mind. Which is probably why I've gotten so good at hiding mine over the years.

"You're the first one here," Grace cheers as I get close enough to hear her.

That's remarkable, considering I was the last one to know about the meeting. Perhaps not all that surprising though. Gretchen doesn't strike me as the most time-conscious person, and after countless millennia I suppose you could hardly expect Sthenno to take the matter of a few minutes too seriously.

"Here," Grace says, waving me into the other chair. "We can pull two more over when Gretchen and Ms. West get here."

"Ms. West?" I ask.

"My counselor," she explains. "I mean, Sthenno. She is also my school counselor."

I stare blankly at her.

"I guess that's how she could keep tabs on me." She shrugs. "And how she got me to San Francisco too."

I smile and nod. I think Grace often has thoughts that make sense in her head but come out incomplete when she tries to convey them. I understand her general meaning, however, and it's easier to agree than to ask for clarification.

Relaxing into the wrought-iron-and-wicker chair, I scan the street for signs of either Gretchen or Sthenno. Union Square is not my favorite part of town—it's dirty and crowded and always gives me an unsettled vibe. Tourists love it, though, and the shopping is first-rate.

"Oh look!" Grace shouts. "There's Gretchen." She jumps to her feet and starts waving her arms. "Gretchen! Over here!"

Her face blossoms into an even bigger smile, and I assume that Gretchen has seen us and is heading this way. I continue my relaxed survey of the street while Grace pulls over a chair for Gretchen.

I notice a woman walking up the sidewalk on the other side, about two blocks away. She is tall and poised and elegant, and although I can't seem to place her anywhere, she feels intimately familiar. I can't look away as she weaves through the crowds effortlessly, almost as if they part before her.

Gretchen drops into the chair next to me. "What are you gawking at?"

I shake my head, unable to lose the sensation that I know this woman from somewhere. I usually trust my brain over my instinct, but the feeling is so overwhelming I can't simply dismiss it.

Grace twists in her seat to get a look.

"Oh," she exclaims. "That's Ms. West. I mean Sthenno."

Our ancient immortal ancestor?

At that moment, the woman—Ms. West—Sthenno—crosses the street, and a memory flashes into my thoughts. It's been years. More than a decade. The moment plays in my mind with perfect clarity.

When I was a child, I saw a centaur in my bedroom. It was the only time before my sisterly reunion that I saw a mythological monster, and I eventually came to believe that the vision was a nightmare. A hallucination. Mother started taking me to regular hypnotherapy sessions immediately. The therapist was a middle-aged woman with dark hair that was fading into gray. Then, at one session—the very last—there was a different therapist. She was younger, blonder, and far more effective. One session with her and Mother declared me cured.

I recognize the woman stepping on the sidewalk at the end of the block because she was that final therapist.

A million confused questions flood my brain.

"I—"

Before I can say that I've met Sthenno before, a black spot appears next to her in the middle of the air. The spot grows quickly, expanding into a giant hole about the size of a double door.

"What the heck?" Grace blurts.

Gretchen bursts to her feet.

Grace and I sit there, stunned, but Gretchen takes off running. On instinct, I follow. Gretchen is still several feet away from Sthenno when a creature steps out of the hole. It almost looks human—well, it's human shaped anyway, like a gnarled old woman. She has pale green skin, stark white hair, and blood dripping down her cheeks.

"Achlys!" Gretchen shouts.

The green hag glances our way, startled, as if she didn't expect anyone to see her.

Then, without hesitation, she wraps both arms around Sthenno and throws her into the hole. Gretchen lunges, barely missing the hag, who follows Sthenno into the blackness. The hole snaps shut just as Gretchen reaches the spot.

She shouts into the empty air. "No!"

"What just happened?" I ask, skidding to a stop next to Gretchen.

Grace catches up, eyes wide. "Where did she go?"

Gretchen glares at the empty spot where the black hole was, then turns and levels a silver glare at each of us. "That was a window into the abyss," she says. "Sthenno is now their prisoner."

She looks like she wants to punch something. Anything.

I step back.

"What was that thing?" I ask. "It wasn't human."

"No," Gretchen replies, jamming her hands onto her hips. "Definitely not human. She's a dark spirit. The demon of misery. I tangled with her once." Gretchen holds up her forearm, revealing a set of four long, parallel scars. "Her nasty fingernails are tipped with an antihealing poison. Took forever for my wounds to heal."

"We have to go get her," Grace says.

My heart trips a little at the idea. Willingly walking into that . . . blackness? It's a crazy idea. But as crazy and scary as it is, we don't have many options. We need answers and Sthenno has them. We need her.

"We do," I agree. "How?"

Gretchen's eyes narrow.

"Sure," she snaps. "It's just that easy. We'll go in after her."

I can do without the sarcasm. "And why not?"

"Is that even possible?" Grace asks.

"It must be," I insist. "Right?"

"In case you haven't noticed," Gretchen says, "the portal is gone."

She waves her hands in the air, in the space that moments ago was a big black void that led into the abyss. Like we need a lesson in visual reality.

I did not get to be junior class president, alumnae tea cochair, and Women in Business liaison by allowing fears and negative thinking to dictate my actions. I am a firm believer in the adage that where there's a will, there's a way.

As annoyed as I was to get called to this emergency meeting without prior notice, now that I've seen who Sthenno is, now that I recognize her, I want to know more. It is no coincidence that she is the one who banished monsters from my life, which means that not only has she known about me for years, but she also has the ability to make the monsters disappear. At least from my mind.

If it worked once, perhaps it can again. Perhaps I can wake up one day and think this nightmare is a distant dream.

I'm not about to let her just vanish into the abyss and say, *Oops. Guess we'll catch her next time.*

"Then we should open another one," I say. "There must be a way."

Gretchen glares harder at me, and I can tell she wants to direct me to the nearest bridge so I can jump off. Then her expression changes into something more thoughtful. She's considering my suggestion. *Good.*

"Is *that* even possible?" Grace asks, echoing her last unanswered question.

"I don't—" Gretchen shakes her head. "I'm not sure. I've never wondered that. I never asked."

Her focus shifts, her eyes shadow like she's lost in thought. Lost in doubt. She's beating herself up for all those questions she never asked Euryale before the Gorgon was taken. Four years of squandered opportunities. I'm not sure how I know that's what she's thinking, but I know if I were in her shoes those thoughts would be playing through my mind.

"Did you get a chance to talk to Sthenno this morning?" I ask Grace. "Did you ask her any questions?"

"A few," Grace says, looking dismayed. "She told me there are factions, two sides in a looming war. One that wants us dead now, another that wants us dead later."

War? Factions? Dead now and dead later? Oh this nightmare just keeps getting better and better.

"That's pretty much what Nick said," Gretchen agrees.

"Nick?" Grace asks suggestively.

Gretchen cuts her a scowl. "It's not like that."

I can see the conflicted emotions playing on her face. Positive and negative. Anger and attraction. Maybe it's *not* like that, but maybe she *wants* it to be. Maybe Gretchen has a crush. I hide a smile.

"So, is no one else at all freaked out about this war?" I ask. "That apparently everyone on every side wants us dead? No one's annoyed by that?"

"Yeah," Grace says. "I'm a little freaked out. But Ms. West said there are others on our side, working to help us."

"That's good to know," Gretchen says sarcastically.

"Ms. West thinks Euryale was trying to find out who was on each side," Grace continues, "when she was taken."

Gretchen winces at the mention of her missing mentor. She's hurting, I can tell, but she's trying valiantly not to show it. "I need to question Nick again."

Partly to save her from facing her emotions right now, and partly for myself because I'm not used to dealing with this kind of pain, I steer the conversation into safe territory.

"Should we meet again after school tomorrow?" I ask. "My schedule is clear after four thirty."

"Mine too," Grace says. "Well, mine's always clear. Should

we meet at the safe house?"

"Bad idea." Gretchen shoves her hands into her back pockets, looking relieved by the change of topic. "I don't think we should meet at our homes anymore. It increases the chances of a monster or three following us there."

"They already know where we live," I argue. "Last night proves that."

"They knew where I lived, obviously," Gretchen says, "or they wouldn't have blown up the place. But I'm hoping the two beasties who showed up at your places just trailed you two home from the sushi place. We need to be hyperaware of being followed from now on."

She *hopes* they just followed us? I cross my arms over my chest. Well, I *hope* she's right.

"So where should we meet?" Grace asks. "In public?"

"That's good for talking," Gretchen replies, shaking her head. "But we need to train too."

I don't miss the subtext. Gretchen is already at the peak of her game, she's got monster butt kicking down to a science. It's Grace and I who need to train. I suppose I can't argue with that. And if one of those creatures shows up at my home again, I want to be able to do something about it.

"I know the perfect place," I say. "My school."

Since I have such extensive responsibilities at Immaculate Heart—and perhaps because my parents donated the money so the board could buy the lot next door for future expansion—I have keys to the building. Freedom and access to every room in the place. Yet another benefit of being a responsible student at a small private school.

I give both sisters the address, and they agree to come by after my student council meeting. The halls will be empty and we will have exclusive use of the gymnasium. It's not as well equipped as the training room in Gretchen's loft—and the closest thing to an arsenal is the collection of sports gear—but it will do as a temporary space.

As we walk our separate ways—Grace to the nearest bus stop, Gretchen to the public parking garage three blocks away, and me to Dad's building—I can't help feeling that the two halves of my life, my two worlds, are about to collide in an irreversible way.

## CHAPTER 8

# GRACE

Dinner at home is tense. I don't really expect it to be any other way, not with Mom and Dad still upset about my disappearance last night and Thane still . . . elsewhere. I can't remember ever feeling this awkward around my parents. Ever.

When dinner is over, I clear the table and take care of the dishes. Alone and in silence. It's like their disappointment is my punishment.

I hang the damp dish towel on the oven door handle when I'm done. I can't just let it be like this—the distance and tension are too much. I walk quietly to their bedroom and knock on the door.

"Come in," Dad says.

He's sitting at the small desk in the corner of the room—the

closest thing to an office this apartment has space for—and Mom's in the bathroom, getting ready for bed. In all my years, I've never felt like such an outsider in my own home.

Dad doesn't look up, and my heart breaks a little more.

"I'm sorry, Dad," I say with as much feeling as I can shove into three small words. "I'm really, really sorry."

His attention stays focused on the computer screen and I feel tears start to well in my eyes. He's not even going to respond.

Then I see his shoulders rise and fall in a small sigh.

"I know," he says. When he turns to look at me, his eyes are shining too. "I know you are, Gracie."

I rush over to him, practically throwing him off the chair with my hug. Then I feel Mom's arms wrap around us.

"We were so scared," she says. "Terrified that something awful might have—"

She can't finish. She doesn't have to.

As much as I want to reassure her, to tell her that nothing terrible happened, that nothing terrible *will* happen, I can't lie again. Last night was awful and dangerous and seconds away from becoming their worst nightmare. Mine too. Tonight might be just as bad. Or the next night, or the night after that. My life is suddenly more dangerous than their worst fears. I can't make a promise that everything will be fine, because I can't control the outcome.

A war that's been brewing for millennia is about to break out in San Francisco, and I'm right in the middle of it all.

If I think about it too much, the fear might overwhelm me. I need to focus on the positive, on the right now.

"I'm fine," I say. "I promise you, I'm fine."

*For now.*

"Make us one more promise," Dad says, leaning out of the hug. "Never go anywhere without your phone again."

Mom nods. "It would have saved a lot of worry."

"I promise," I say. Even though I know that if I'd had my phone last night, it would have either gotten blown up in the loft or drenched in the bay.

But I'll never leave home without it again.

I tell them I love them—and they tell me they love me right back—before retreating to my room. Speaking of my phone, it's ringing when I walk through my door.

My heart pounds when I read the screen: *Milo.*

"Hi," I say, trying to disguise how breathless I feel. "What's up?"

There's a brief pause before he says, "I thought we were."

"We—" I slap a hand over my mouth. "Omigosh, Milo, I totally forgot."

I can't believe I'm such a moron. Milo is Thane's friend, his soccer teammate at Euclid, and about the cutest boy I've ever met. He's sweet too, which is a major bonus. And he likes me.

When I was all high on confronting Miranda yesterday, I called him and asked him out. I was terrified, but I did it. And he said *yes.*

We were supposed to meet this afternoon, but after everything that happened last night and then with Sthenno at school and again at Union Square, I blanked. I totally blew my chance.

"Something, um, critical came up and—I'm so sorry."

"No worries," he says, though he sounds a little off. "I get it."

*Oh no. He thinks I blew him off on purpose. No, no, no.*

"Really," I insist. "It was something last-minute with my—" I have to stop myself from saying sisters. "A friend," I say. "She had an emergency and . . ." I stink at lying. I need to stop trying. "I swear, I really really really want to go out with you."

Great. Way to sound totally desperate, Grace. I roll my eyes at my idiocy and can picture Milo doing the same. I take a deep breath to compose myself and sink back onto my bed, ready for the rejection.

I expect him to say, *No thanks, crazy girl,* and hang up, never to be heard from again.

Instead, he says, "How about tomorrow?"

I sit back up.

"Tomorrow?" I echo. A second chance! Relief floods through me. I'm not meeting Gretchen and Greer until four thirty. "I can meet right after school. I have something later in the afternoon."

"Soccer practice," he says. "Until five."

"Shoot." I have no idea when the girls and I will be done,

so I can't make after-sister plans. "I would invite you over for dinner, but . . ."

"Thane," he finishes. "Have you heard from him?"

Not enough. "He texted me last night."

"Is he"—Milo hesitates—"okay?"

"I think so." I *hope* so. "He said he'd be home soon."

We sit in silence, listening to each other breathing for a few minutes. I'm sure Milo is wondering about his new friend's weird behavior. I'm wondering what my brother is trying to work through and whether he'll be happier when he gets back. He's a good person—he deserves a lifetime of happiness.

"So . . . ," Milo says.

I smile sadly. "So . . ."

I feel totally dumb for forgetting our date today. And I don't know when I'll be able to reschedule. I barely know what I'm doing tomorrow. Who knows what will come up the day after that? For all I know, the whole monster realm could break free and take over the city.

I wish we could make tomorrow work.

"Wait, I have an idea," I blurt. Why did it take me so long to think of this? It's the perfect solution. "How about I come to your practice? It won't be like a date or anything, but we could, you know, talk."

I can hear the smile in his voice when he repeats, "Talk. Sounds perfect."

"Great!" I flop back onto my bed, relieved. "I'll be there

as soon as school lets out. I get out earlier, so I should beat you there."

"Great," he says. "I'll see you then."

I sigh. "Good night, Milo."

"Good night, Grace."

As I set my phone on the nightstand, I feel like I could probably float all the way to my boring white ceiling.

Tomorrow, I'll get to see Milo and we'll *talk*. My parents forgive me. Now, if only Thane would come home. And my sisters and I could figure out how to rescue our kidnapped ancestors and survive the looming war. Then my world would be pretty much perfect.

## CHAPTER 9

## GRETCHEN

I text Nick to meet me at the Peace Plaza in Japantown because it's between his place and Union Square. It's also very public and very neutral. A safe place, in more ways than one. I find him waiting for me by the Peace Pagoda.

"Hey, how was your—"

"I'm starved," I say. "You like Korean?"

He blinks, like he's startled by my abrupt question. But, to his credit, he recovers quickly. "I like food, period."

I nod and then turn to head into the east building, to one of my favorite restaurants. I don't say another word until we're seated in a cozy—and discreet—booth, the waitress gone to get our drinks.

"I am going to ask you a series of questions," I say. "If you don't answer them to my liking, I'm walking away."

For a second he looks as if he wants to make a joke. His dark eyes sparkle and the hint of a smile plays at the corners of his mouth.

"Permanently," I add, just in case I'm not being clear enough. "I just saw Sthenno get kidnapped. Ursula—Euryale—is already taken. My sisters and I were nearly killed last night. And there's a war coming that we're not prepared to fight. I need answers. Either you're useful or you're not."

He makes a choking sound.

I spin my chopsticks on the table. "You won't like what happens to useless things."

He regroups and says, "Okay. I'll answer everything I can."

Everything he can? I snort. He'd better answer everything he can't too.

I've had the entire drive here to gather my thoughts, to prep my question, to decide on my first line of attack. There are so many things I need to know, and right now he's the only one who might have answers. But where to start? Since Ursula told Grace she's safe, I have to assume that she is. And that Sthenno will be too. For the time being.

The critical question then is whether my sisters and I are safe. Which makes the first question a no-brainer.

"Who wants us dead?" I ask. "My sisters and me, who's trying to kill us?"

The waitress returns with our drinks, a pair of root beers,

and Nick waits until she's gone with our food orders to respond.

"I can't know for certain," he says. Not the answer I'm looking for, and when he sees my scowl he adds, "But I can make a guess. When the gods sealed the door, the ritual included a clause stating that after a time the door would be reopened."

"By the Key Generation," I say. I take a sip of my root beer. "That's me and my sisters. I know that."

"Right," he says, giving me a look that shows he doesn't appreciate the interruption. "Well, over the years—the millennia, really—some of the gods changed their minds. They grew complacent and lazy. Deluded themselves into believing that it would be best to maintain the status quo. They decided that reopening the door, even with the Key Generation to guard it, would be a huge mistake."

"They want us dead," I say, trying to fill in the blanks, "so we can't break the seal."

He nods.

"Which gods are those?" I ask. "The ones who changed their minds."

Nick shakes his head. "We don't know for sure. Zeus is probably one of them. He's tired and checked out and doesn't want to resurrect old concerns. If that is true, then his allies are on that side as well. But that's supposition. We only know that one faction wants you taken out before you can break the seal."

Zeus. I shake my head. It's one thing to think about the

gods as a vague kind of idea. To think I'm distantly related to them, that I'm part of their family tree. But it's another thing to realize they're real and fallible and acting in ways that affect my life. To know they're aware of me and planning to kill me. It's . . . annoying. Can't they just leave me and my sisters alone to do our jobs? It's not like we asked for this destiny.

"Well, that explains the bounty," I say, thinking out loud.

"The bounty?" Nick asks. "You mentioned it last night, but you weren't exactly in the mood to answer questions."

"Yeah," I reply, swirling my glass so the ice inside starts to spin. "A few of the beasties I've hunted lately mentioned it. They get a one-way ticket to freedom if they bring one of us back."

"Another argument for Zeus then." Nick rips apart his chopsticks and uses them to dig out an ice cube from his glass. "He is probably the only god with the power to grant *eleftheria*—freedom."

"What's so great about our world anyway?" I ask. "We've got pollution and traffic and lots of stress. Why is all of monsterkind so eager to visit our sunny shores?"

Nick freezes, ice cube halfway to his mouth. "You've clearly never been in the abyss."

"No," I say, "and I'm not especially interested in visiting. Have you?"

His entire face shadows. "I have."

"Oh," I say quietly. I feel that I should apologize, but I'm not sure for what.

"It's"—he looks up at the ceiling and shudders—"horrible."

"But it's where monsters belong," I insist. "It's their home. It must be livable."

"There is a world of difference between livable and desirable." Nick drops the ice cube back into his glass. "But to answer your question, there are two main reasons that monsters want access to the human realm. First, because access to the human realm means access to humans."

"And humans mean tasty life force for beasties to feed on." I take a swig of root beer.

Nick nods. "And second, because monsters in the human realm are immortal."

"Immortal?" I cough, choking on a root beer bubble that goes down the wrong way. "I knew my venom didn't kill them, but I didn't know they were immortal."

"Only an Olympian weapon can kill a monster in this realm." Nick gives me a wry smile. "You can see why they might want to spend time here."

"I guess so," I say, still in shock.

"And there are some monsters," he adds with a twist of a smile, "that would just rather hang out in the world of trees and sunshine. Endless black can get so monotonous."

I ignore his sarcastic comment.

"So that faction, they think they're protecting the world by keeping the Key Generation from breaking the seal?"

Nick nods again, digs out another ice cube, and pops it into his mouth. While he crunches, I swirl.

I'm still mad that they're trying to kill us, but if they're doing it for what they think are the right reasons? Well, that makes it easier to understand, anyway. Not that I'm going to let them succeed.

"What about the other side?" I ask. "The ones who want us to open the door?"

Nick takes so long to finish crunching his ice that I wonder if he's buying time. With every bite, his cheek and jaw muscles tighten, showing off the chiseled lines of his face. . . . *Snap out of it!* The last thing I need to be thinking about is Nick's chiseled face.

"Oh, they want you dead too," he finally says. "But not until after the door is open. In the meantime they are amassing an army to overpower you and your allies when the gates swing wide."

Great. Win-win.

The waitress arrives with our appetizer, a variety of pajeon pancakes. As soon as she walks away, I grab my fork to spear a piece of kimchee and pop it in my mouth. I savor the burning feeling that lingers after the bite of spicy pickled cabbage is gone.

"So, we have allies?" I ask. "It's nice to know at least someone is on our side."

Grace said Sthenno insisted we weren't alone. I guess this is confirmation.

"I am," he says quietly.

So quietly I can't help but believe him. I'm usually a pretty solid lie detector, and I don't detect anything but sincerity from him right now. He's lied and kept things from me in the past, but not now. He's finally being honest.

"Anyone else?"

"A few, yes," he answers. "The Gorgons, of course."

I roll my eyes at that statement of the obvious.

"There are others. A number of minor deities," he explains. "Even some Olympians would like to see the prophecy fulfilled. Balance restored."

"What does that mean?" I ask. "Balance restored?"

"The two realms—that of man and that of monster—were not meant to be so divided," he says. I can see a true longing in his eyes, like he's lost in some distant memory. "Creatures of all kinds were meant to move in and out between the two. That is how the world began." His eyes clear, and I sense him returning to the present. "That is how the world should be. In balance."

That makes sense. Light and dark, yin and yang, man and monster. Those dichotomies are supposed to coexist, not be divided.

Still, the idea of monsters drifting in and out of our world is not exactly appealing. Monsters might be immortal in this realm, but humans aren't. And most monsters are more than happy to kill a few of us to get the extra surge of life-force energy.

"You're not convinced," Nick says, guessing my thoughts. "You think the realms should remain divided."

"Well, why not?" I ask. "Why should we let monsters free in this world to hunt and cause havoc?

"I—" He closes his mouth and shakes his head. "I can't convince you to make the right choice. You and your sisters will have to realize it for yourselves. I have enough faith in fate that you will."

I want to roll my eyes at the idea that fate will have anything to do with our decision, but his eyes are so direct and sincere that I can't make light of his conviction.

"So if we decide to break the seal, how do we do it?" I ask. "How do we reopen the door?"

Despite Nick's belief, I'm not certain that's what we should do. The world is a very different place from what it was thousands of years ago before the door was sealed. It might not be able to handle the reintegration of monsters into daily life.

My sisters and I might not be able to take up the guardianship the way our ancient ancestors did.

But I need to stay open to all possibilities. I have to understand as much about what's going on as possible. If the opposing sides are those who want the door opened and those who want it sealed permanently, I should understand what each entails. Even if the solution is none of the above.

"No idea," Nick says. "The ritual prophecy only stated that the door would be reopened. I doubt the gods wanted it to be easy. No one even knows *where* the door is anymore. It's been a very long time."

"No one? Great," I say, spearing another bite of kimchee.

"How are we supposed to find out?"

Nick shrugs, and I want to toss my root beer at him. How can he be so casual about this, when my life, my sisters' lives, maybe a whole lot of human lives, are at stake? Especially when he was so serious moments ago. The boy drives me nuts.

"Other than the gods who participated in the sealing ritual," he says, "only the Gorgons ever saw the door. Only they might know its location."

"Then how do we find the Gorgons?" I ask back. "I just saw Sthenno taken into the abyss. You said Ursula might have been taken there too. How can I get in to go after them?"

"Oh no, no, no," he says, dropping his chopsticks on the table with a clatter. "That is a bad idea. You have no idea what the abyss is like."

His face pales and he looks terrified. Before I can stop myself, I reach across the table and lay my hand over his. He looks down, startled. And then puts his other hand over mine.

I'm startled too. I'm not used to being comforting. I'm more of a smack-you-on-the-back-and-get-back-in-the-game kind of girl. It's a weird sensation, and I have to fight the urge to yank my hand away.

But as much as thoughts of the abyss obviously pain him, that doesn't change some serious facts. I can't just let this go.

"I don't have a choice," I explain. "Sthenno is in there. Ursula might be too." I shake my head. "We need them."

He doesn't meet my gaze as he says, "I know."

"I have to go after them." I tug at our entwined hands, drawing his eyes to mine. "How do I get in?"

His head swings slowly from side to side. "I don't know." He slowly withdraws his hands from mine. "But we both know someone who does."

Before I can respond, the waitress arrives with our entrees. She sets the delicious-smelling plates in front of us.

When she disappears again, I ask, "Who?"

"The same woman who told you about your legacy."

"The oracle," I say. "Wait, how did you know she—"

"Everyone knows," he answers before I can ask my question. "That's what got this whole war brewing in the first place. I'll meet you at your car tomorrow after school, and we can go talk with her."

The oracle. She's at the center of a lot of what's going on in my life. If anyone has answers—though probably cryptic ones—she does. Besides, it's the only idea we've got.

As I spear a pajeon pancake with my fork, I ask, "Will you be there?" I feel like an idiot and I think my cheeks are burning. "In school, I mean. In class."

He actually laughs. "Do you want me to be?"

I shrug, as if it doesn't matter.

"It was only a cover," he says. "An excuse to be near you without raising your suspicions."

I glance at him. "Oh, you raised my suspicions anyway."

He lifts his eyebrows in a silent question.

"Well, besides the fact that you're immune to my hypno powers," I find myself confessing. "You never could seem to take the hint that I wanted you to back off."

"Did you?" he asks.

"What?"

"Want me to back off?"

I hate that I hesitate before saying, "Of course."

"Uh-huh."

We eat silently. I have to force myself to stop stealing glances at him. This is such a strange situation. Me, eating dinner with a boy who is more than just a boy, a boy who knows my secret. He knows exactly who and what I am and he's not running for the nearest exit.

I wish I knew more about him. He's a descendant of a goddess. He says he was sent to protect me and help me and my sisters succeed. I feel like I'm missing something. Heck, I feel like I'm missing a lot of things.

He shifts on his bench, and his foot brushes mine. Startled, I look up and see a sultry smirk. He knows exactly what effect he has on me. He's teasing me. Flirting maybe.

I don't know how to flirt back, but he doesn't seem to mind. He flirts enough for both of us.

For now, he's the best link I've got to the mythological world. I don't have much choice but to accept his help. But that doesn't mean I'm not keeping my eye on him.

When our plates are clean and we head back out into the Peace Plaza, the sun is long gone. I shiver, wishing I had my leather jacket. Wishing it hadn't been destroyed in the explosion.

That's probably the thing I miss most. I spent four years breaking it in. It was soft in all the right places.

"Cold?" Nick asks.

I want to say yes, because then I think he might put his arm around my shoulder. But that's too much too fast. I'm just starting to trust him, to let him into my life.

So instead of succumbing to girly impulse, I say, "I'm fine." Then, because I can't entirely dismiss him, I ask, "You want a ride home?"

My heart does a little flip when he grins and says, "I'd love one."

As we make our way into the garage, I have a talk with myself. Just because he knows the truth, just because he seems to enjoy flirting with me—or making me blush or making me angry or whatever—doesn't mean this is a good idea. It doesn't change the fact that I know next to nothing about him. It doesn't change what I am. It doesn't change my responsibilities. I'm still a descendant of Medusa, still a monster hunter with a lifetime of guardianship ahead of me. Right now I'm not even sure how long that lifetime will be. If the various players in the game have their way, it'll be pretty short.

Even if I live a long, full life, there's no guarantee that it will be in any way normal. I reconciled myself to the lonely path a long time ago. It's only going to hurt more later if I get my hopes up now.

But as we get to my car and Nick opens the driver's door for me, I can't quash the tiny little spark that ignites in my chest. I can't help remembering that, if it weren't possible to have relationships while being a guardian, my sisters and I wouldn't even be here. Medusa made it work.

Maybe—*maybe*—I could too.

One thing is certain, though. As Nick buckles in and I put Moira in gear, I know there is something different about this boy. Something that makes me want to believe. Even when my every instinct warns that it can't be this easy. Something inside me wants to try. As I pull out into the night, I smile. Beside me I sense Nick smile too.

# CHAPTER 10

## GRACE

The bleachers overlooking Milo's soccer field are built into a hill. It's such a beautiful sunny day that part of me wants to skip the bleachers altogether, find a spot on the grassy slope, and absorb some nature.

That's one thing I miss in San Francisco. There is so much glass and concrete, I feel kind of disconnected from nature. Sure, there are trees and flowers on practically every street, and water is never hard to find, but turf is mostly reserved for the parks and the very rare backyards.

I'm early. I've got at least fifteen minutes before the team shows up for practice. Besides, how could it hurt to lie down on the grass for a little bit?

Using my backpack as a pillow, I find a spot between the base of the bleachers and the field and settle in to soak up the sun above and the earth below. With my eyes closed, I can almost believe I'm back in Orangevale, lying in our backyard.

I don't regret moving to the city. If we hadn't, I never would have met my sisters or learned about our destiny, our legacy. I wouldn't have met Milo, either. But that doesn't mean there aren't things I miss. Right now, in this moment, I feel like I have the best of both worlds.

I drift away.

Then, suddenly, I'm not on the grass anymore. I'm flying. Searching for something. For some*one*.

"Sthenno!" I try to shout, but no sound comes out. "Euryale! Where are you?"

I'm becoming desperate, soaring through fog and clouds, looking everywhere. Then I stop moving. I'm still swimming in the air, but I'm frozen in place. Panicked, I stroke harder.

Then, out of nowhere, a storm kicks up. I start rocking through the clouds like a boat caught in rough seas. Shaking, shaking, sha—

My eyes pop open.

Gasping, I blurt, "Milo?"

"Hey," he says, his lips curving into a wide smile. "You okay? Looked like you were having a rough dream."

That's an understatement.

"No, no," I say, pushing myself up, careful not to knock my head into his. I'm gasping a little, trying to catch my breath as if I've just run a race. He has no idea. "I'm fine. Just"—I gesture around at the green field—"enjoying the grass."

"Yeah," he says, smiling deeper, humoring me. "You looked like you were having a nice peaceful nightmare."

"I—" I almost don't let go of the lie. There's a part of me that wants to maintain that image of normalcy when everything in my life—dreams included, apparently—is full-on abnormal. But I've had to do enough lying and keep enough secrets and tell enough half-truths lately. The more I hide my life in the shadows, the more likely I am to get trapped there. I can't tell Milo the whole truth, obviously, but I don't have to lie about this.

I take a deep breath, force myself to relax, and ask, "Ever have one of those dreams where you're flying, but then all of a sudden you can't fly anymore?"

He holds out a hand to help pull me to my feet. "All the time."

He doesn't release my hand once I'm standing. We're only inches apart and I have to fight the urge to lean into him.

"I was worried you might not show up," he says.

After I disappeared from the nightclub when Gretchen found me, and totally spaced on our date yesterday, it's no wonder he thinks I'm unreliable. I'm not normally, but he doesn't know that.

"I'm not a flake," I insist. "Life's been more complicated than usual lately. I really, really wanted to go out with you."

"Wanted?"

"Want!" I practically shout. Then, more softly, "I *want* to go out with you."

"How about this weekend?" he suggests. "Saturday is crazy, but maybe we could catch a movie or something on Sunday."

"Sunday," I say, racking my brain for any conflicts—any prescheduled conflicts—and coming up with none. "Should be perfect."

"I'll give you a call," he says. He jerks his thumb over his shoulder, toward where the team is running warm-ups at the far end of the field. "I'd better get over there. How long can you stay?"

"Not long," I say with a sad face.

"Okay." He lifts a hand to my chin and says, "Then I'm glad I got to see you."

I grin. "Me too."

With a wink, he turns and jogs off to join the rest of his team.

I grab my backpack off the ground and move toward the gate that opens onto the street. I can watch for a few minutes before I need to leave for Greer's school.

I'm smiling as the team does drills—seeing how many times they can bounce soccer balls on their knees, feet, and heads before dropping them—when the smell hits me. It's so strong it practically knocks me to the ground. Only a strong grip on my stomach keeps me from spewing my veggie burrito lunch.

I glance out the gate just as the monster walks by. A woman—at least on the top—with the lower body of a bird. Great black-and-brown wings spread out behind her, the tips sweeping the sidewalk as she moves. At the ends of her feet, razor-sharp talons scrape on the concrete, leaving a path of scratches in her wake.

I recognize her from the monster binders. A harpy.

I must have gasped or gagged or in some way indicated my reaction to her hideous form, because she stops just outside the open gate, twists her head awkwardly to the side—like a dinosaur or something—and looks me in the eyes.

She doesn't say anything at first, and over and over in my head I tell myself to act natural. Pretend she looks entirely human. Don't let her know you—

She sweeps one of her wings wide, and I can't fight my instinct to duck.

A sick grin spreads across her black-rimmed mouth, revealing razor-sharp teeth to match her talons.

"Pretty huntress," she coos.

I back away, shaking my head and holding my hands out in front of me, as if I can ward her off with just a gesture.

Yes, I'm a huntress. Yes, it's my duty to keep the human realm clear of her kind. But I'm caught off-guard. I'm alone. And I'm all too aware of the soccer team half a field away.

"Please," I whisper, pleading for I don't know what.

When she starts advancing, I know a fight is unavoidable. I have to get to a more private location. I can't take on a harpy in front of two dozen teen boys. In front of *Milo*.

Him thinking I'm a flake is one thing, but I can't let him see this. To him it would look as though I was fighting with some random woman. That would be bad enough. The truth would be even worse. He'd never understand.

She's between me and the gate, so there's no way I can get to the street. There is a building at the far end of the field, probably for extra equipment and stuff, but that's right where the team is practicing. Besides, I don't think I'd ever make it in time.

My only chance is to move behind the near end of the bleachers. They're not open underneath, but if I move all the way to the back, I think we'll be hidden enough for the team not to notice.

After checking on the boys—who are thankfully running backward up the field, facing away from me—I dash for the bleachers. I can hear the harpy screeching and swooping behind me.

With a deep, fortifying—and shaky—breath, I turn to face her. She's closing fast.

In that instant I realize I have no idea what to do. Besides knowing that I have to bite her somewhere—I vaguely remember the drawing in the binder highlighting the spot where the wing meets the back (oh how I wish I'd had time to develop the smart phone app from the scanned data)—I don't really have a clue how to take on a bird-woman with a twelve-foot wingspan. Her talons could be poisonous,

116

her teeth are certainly dangerous, and any number of awful things might happen between the time I bite her and when she pops back into the abyss.

Panic sets in and I can't hear anything above the pounding of blood in my ears. How am I even supposed to get close enough to bite?

Too late now. She blocks the way out to the field. The end of the bleachers' wall is too high, and the exterior retaining wall is even higher. I'm completely trapped.

"Oh, shoot," I mutter.

I've maneuvered myself into a corner.

My back up against the wall—literally—I close my eyes even as my fangs drop. I have only one chance here, only one way out.

I picture myself disappearing, vanishing from this spot on the wall, and reappearing behind the harpy. I focus all my energy on autoporting myself to safety, to a tactical advantage.

I open my eyes and see the harpy still bearing down. I can feel her hot, vile breath on my cheek. She reaches out with human arms, fingers grasping.

Squeezing my eyes shut again, I let my fear take over. I can barely breathe. I feel her fingertips reaching for my neck. Then . . .

I hear a startled gasp.

My eyes flash open and I'm looking at the harpy's winged back. I give a mental shout—don't want to give away my new position—and, as she starts to turn around looking for me, I leap forward onto her back.

I know I have to act fast. One scratch of those talons or teeth and I'll be in for a world of hurt, especially since, as Gretchen says, the antivenom supply at the safe house is limited.

Grabbing a fistful of feathers with each hand, I pull myself up the bird-woman's back. She spins and backs into the wall. I hold on tight, even with the wind knocked out of me, and when she pulls away from the wall, I drag myself into position.

Hoping I remember the picture right, I stab my fangs into the wing joint. For a second I think I've got it wrong—with a mouthful of feathers to show for it—but then, a heartbeat later, the harpy evaporates.

I crash to the ground and my just-recovered breath gets knocked out again.

I'm lying there, facedown in the grass, struggling to get my breathing back to normal, when Milo appears around the corner.

"Grace!" He rushes forward, rolls me onto my back, and runs his gaze over my body. "Are you okay? We heard screaming."

*That would be the now-dispatched harpy.*

"What?" he asks.

Please don't let me have said that out loud. Especially not with half the soccer team standing there watching.

"I think that was me," I say, hoping it sounds convincing.

Milo's hands follow his gaze, checking all my limbs to make sure they're not broken or missing or something.

"I'm fine," I insist, although my voice is weak and breathy. "Really, I just . . ." I search around for some plausible—and not crazy monster-related—excuse for the screaming and my lost breath. The bleachers loom above me. "I fell," I finally say. "Off the bleachers."

"You fell?" He turns to look up at the bleachers; the nearest section is at least ten feet up. "What were you doing up there?"

"I—I didn't fall from there." I push myself to a sitting position. I wave generally at a lower section of the bleacher wall. "I rolled when I hit the ground."

"You need to go to a hospital." Milo's pale green eyes are clouded with worry. "Someone call—"

"No!" I don't need to go to the hospital. I *can't* go.

I never want to use hypno powers on Milo or anyone I care about, but right now it's my only choice.

I look him straight in the eyes and say, carefully and concisely, "I'm fine. Really." I focus all my energy on conveying my message. "I'm not hurt."

He looks at me, his expression serious, for a few more seconds. Then, finally, his expression blanks and he says, "You're not hurt."

I smile while I scream on the inside. I wish I didn't have to do this. Then I turn and tell the rest of the team they should go back to practice.

As they wander back down the field, Milo helps me to my feet again. "I'd better get back to practice. I'll call you Sunday."

"Perfect," I agree. "I'll answer your call."

He turns away to leave, but I reach out for his hand. When he turns back, his eyes full of questions—either because of the hypno trick or because I stopped him—I reach up on my tiptoes and press a soft kiss to his cheek.

"Thanks," I say.

He smiles, confused.

"For"—I shrug—"caring."

He grins, and then leans down to give me a matching kiss on the cheek.

As he turns and heads back to practice, I lift my hand to my cheek. Fight a harpy, get a kiss. A girl could get used to that deal.

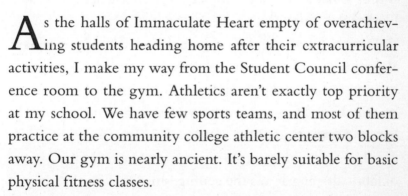

# CHAPTER 11

# GREER

As the halls of Immaculate Heart empty of overachiev-ing students heading home after their extracurricular activities, I make my way from the Student Council confer-ence room to the gym. Athletics aren't exactly top priority at my school. We have few sports teams, and most of them practice at the community college athletic center two blocks away. Our gym is nearly ancient. It's barely suitable for basic physical fitness classes.

I push open the doors and hide my revulsion at the stench of decades of gym classes. Even the semiannual industrial cleaning can't completely wipe out eau de sweat and dirty socks. I can only hope that the cleaners I've hired to prepare the space for the alumnae tea can work a miracle.

Still, if you appreciate classic architecture, the gym is a

thing of beauty. The vintage wooden parquet floors date back to the fifties. A principal in the 1980s wanted to rip it up and replace it with state-of-the-art linoleum or something, but the alumnae stood strong and finally the principal backed down. By the end of the year she was looking for another job and the gorgeous floor had been refinished and declared a historic part of the school.

Even the bleachers are vintage. Aged wood, pine I suppose, that fold back against the wall when not in use.

Since the nearest assembly is weeks away, today the bleachers are pushed out of the way, forming twin walls of worn, warm-hued pine on either side of the room.

For a moment, I allow myself to picture what it will look like for the alumnae tea a week from Saturday.

Despite my regular arguments with my cochair, Veronica—whose taste in decor is no better than her taste in starving-artist boyfriends—I know the effect will be breathtaking. Dozens of round tables with white tablecloths hanging to the floor. Place settings and centerpieces in shades of white, gold, and purple—our school colors. Giant swags of fabric draping across the ceiling, shining with the glow of thousands of fairy lights behind them.

The center attraction will be a beautiful dragon topiary, ivy and honeysuckle covering a fine wire frame, crafted by a master floral artist. That too will be filled with fairy lights, so the school mascot will appear to glow from within. I can almost smell the honeysuckle.

Almost.

"Gross," Grace says as she pushes through the door. "Do all gyms smell the same?"

I turn away from my daydream. "Probably."

She drops her backpack by the door and then rushes toward me in the middle of the room.

"Guess what!"

I stare at her for a moment, alarmed by the speed at which she is approaching. But she skids to a stop and I reply, "What?"

"I just autoported," she squeals. "On purpose!"

"Really?" That's quite impressive, since she's only recently learned she has this power. I have yet to gain the slightest control over my second sight. I think the tightening in my chest might be jealousy—a foreign sensation. "Did you autoport here?"

Her face falls. "No."

I thought that was the obvious follow-up question. It wasn't my intention to make her feel bad. Before I can explain, she continues.

"I was about to get eaten by a harpy and—"

"A harpy?" If my semester of college-level mythology serves me right—and I'm certain it does—harpies are evil creatures sent to do Zeus's dark bidding. "That must have been dangerous."

"Yeah," she says with a grin. "She had me cornered and then, *poof*, I was behind her. Got my bite in good."

"Wow, that's . . ." I'm not sure how to respond. She seems very excited, but it's also frightening. Should she be taking on such a dangerous creature alone? Gretchen does it all the time, I know, but Grace and I are different. We're . . . untrained. I suppose that only makes her victory all the more remarkable, so I say, "Great."

My encouragement seems to make her happy, because she nods and turns to look around the room. I'm surprised at how good it makes me feel to make her happy.

"I thought I was running late," she says, looking around the gym. "Where's Gretchen?"

"Not here yet."

We stand in an awkward silence.

I can hold intelligent conversations with heads of state, billionaire CEOs, and the occasional celebrity who's in town to film a movie or television show. But at the moment I can't even make small talk with my sister. What is the matter with me?

"So," Grace says, breaking—or rather, interrupting—the tension, "have you told your parents?"

"Excuse me?" I blink a few times. "Told them what? That I'm a descendant of Medusa?"

"No. That you, you know . . ." She lifts her eyebrows. "That you know you're adopted."

I jerk back.

"Of course not."

The idea of having that conversation with my parents is

not a pleasant one. Dad would feel sorry for me, sorry that I found out. Mother would tell me to grow up and deal with it, to be grateful for the opportunities they have given me. It certainly wouldn't improve our relationships.

"Why not?" she asks. "I mean, they have to know you'd find out eventually. I've known since forever. My mom and dad never tried to pretend—"

"My parents," I interrupt, giving the easiest explanation, "are too busy."

"Too busy? To talk to their own daughter?"

She sounds aghast, and I suppose to an outside observer our relationship might be a bit unusual. But she has no idea the kind of pressure they're under. They have not only our livelihoods and lifestyle to support, but also the jobs and livelihoods of thousands upon thousands of employees. Their positions are not as simple as bringing home a hefty paycheck. They feel enormous pressure because so many people are relying upon them to make their companies succeed.

Do I wish we could spend more time together? That I could talk with them about homework and boyfriends and the pressures I feel at school? Of course. But I understand.

In some ways, they face the same kind of pressure I feel to take up my duty as a descendant of Medusa. Countless people are relying on me and I cannot let them down.

For some reason, I feel the urge to explain the situation to Grace.

"They're just—" My phone beeps, saving me from trying

to justify my parents' busy lives to Grace. I pull it out of my purse and see a message from Gretchen.

**Going to be late. Start without me.**

I show the message to Grace, who frowns. "Start without her? What does that mean?"

"I suspect she wants us to start training," I say.

Grace gives me a surprisingly sarcastic look. "But *how*?" she asks. "I've only had a few sessions with her. I barely got through defensive techniques. I know hardly anything about offensive tactics."

"Is that all the training entails?" I ask. "Defensive and offensive combat techniques?"

"Well, pretty much." She makes a face. "At least as far as I know."

I shrug. "Then we've nothing to worry about. I have eight years of tae kwon do training. I'm a fourth-level black belt."

"A black belt?" Grace's eyes widen and she looks like she wants to fall over in shock. "Are you kidding me? You acted so, so . . . *helpless* when we were fighting those monsters."

"Not helpless," I explain. "Out of my element. I can split a two-inch-thick block of wood with the palm of my hand, but I have obviously never trained in manticore-fighting tactics."

She stares at me as if I've told her the Loch Ness monster is alive and well and living in San Francisco Bay. Come to think of it, that wouldn't be such a shock, considering the sea dracaena Grace and I saw climb out of the water the other night.

"You're a black belt?" she repeats. "For real?"

"Of course."

"But you seem so . . ." She waves her hand up and down at me. "Fragile."

I purse my lips. "I prefer *elegant.*"

"Fine, *elegant,*" she throws back with an eye roll. "You look like a stiff wind could take you down. Like you'd shatter into a million pieces if a monster got too close. And those shoes . . ."

I glance down at my heels. They are the height of fashion and, after years of wearing nothing less, I'm as comfortable in them as Grace probably is in tennis shoes.

"You shouldn't judge a girl by her exterior," I say, although I know I am occasionally—often—guilty of doing the same. Even when it comes to my sisters. "Besides, tae kwon do is a barefoot endeavor. My shoes come off easily enough."

"Show me something," she says, as if she still doesn't believe me.

"A demonstration?"

She nods. All right, that's a challenge I'm happy to accept.

I step out of my shoes and set them next to my purse. I move to face Grace, a few feet in front of her, and stand in ready position.

"Block me," I say.

"What—?"

Before she can finish, I execute a swift jab with my right hand, landing it softly against her neck. Regrouping into ready position, I explain, "Stop me."

Grace spreads her feet—clearly Gretchen has taught her the benefit of a solid stance—and makes her hands into fists. This time, when I come at her with my left, she swings a forearm up to block my strike.

"Nice," I say.

She shakes her head. "I can't believe you're giving me tae kwon do lessons. I thought for sure I had you beat when it came to combat."

"Had me beat?" I swing my right foot around in a round-house, pleased when she casually blocks it with her left arm. "This is not a competition, Grace."

"I know that." She blocks a series of punches and kicks without really concentrating. Either Gretchen taught her well or her instincts are strong. I suspect the answer is a bit of both. "I just . . . I thought I was ahead of the curve."

"I'm sure you are in something," I assure her. "Just not this."

She shouldn't feel bad about her training level. In fact, for someone so inexperienced, her moves are quite advanced. This explains how she defeated the harpy.

I go at her harder, testing her defensive reactions. She deflects most of them, but as I increase my speed and start delivering more advanced moves, she starts to lose control. Backing away rather than fail under my onslaught, she waves her hands up in surrender.

"See," she complains. "I can't even defend myself properly."

"You defended yourself excellently," I say, settling back into ready position. "Far better than I expected from you, with such limited training. Besides, there are times when retreat is the better defense."

"Oh." Her posture softens. "I guess you're right."

I know we are both picturing the other night, when the monsters sought us out at our homes. Probably the one place we each let our guard down. Fighting wasn't an option. Grace fled by autoporting to Gretchen's loft. I fled by speeding through red lights and ignoring one-way street signs.

My heart raced harder in those moments, in my sprint from the front door to the garage, in the desperate chase from my home to the loft, than it ever had in my life. Training in martial arts is one thing, but an actual fight-for-your-life battle is another. If I am being brutally honest with myself, I was terrified. At night I'm haunted by nightmares where the giant grabs me before I can run, where the bear claws through Grace's throat before she can autoport away, and where we don't get there in time to save Gretchen from the manticore. Every time I fall asleep, I wake up in a cold sweat.

I've been telling myself the fear was exhilarating, that I've never felt so very alive, and so very proud of my abilities. I try to reassure myself that I reacted quickly and decisively and those reactions saved my life. As Grace's saved hers. But my hands still shake and the nightmares still come.

Fear is not a familiar emotion. In my normal life, I insist that fear is for the weak willed. I am not afraid to tackle any social situation, academic project, or other challenge that comes my way.

In this new, unfamiliar world, I find myself fighting to hide my fear, to keep up the cool, calm, collected facade I've perfected over the years. Because the thing that scares me most of all is the thought that I won't be able to hold it all together.

I refuse to allow that to happen. Stiffening my spine, I push the fear aside and focus on the moment. On the training. On Grace. If she can face these fears, so can I.

"We've proven that I have human-fighting technique," I say, "and that you have had excellent defense training." I take a deep breath and say, "Now I'd like you to give me some real training in monster hunting."

"Me?" She looks around, startled.

I nod. "You're the only one here. Teach me everything Gretchen has taught you so far."

She hesitates, probably worried about being inadequate to the task. Clearly Gretchen is a solid tutor; otherwise Grace never would have been able to defend against my attack. I'm sure she has some monster-fighting skills as well.

"Okay," she says, like she's bracing herself. "I can do this."

I smile. "Of course you can."

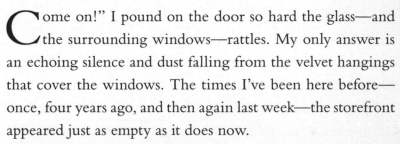

# CHAPTER 12

## GRETCHEN

"Come on!" I pound on the door so hard the glass—and the surrounding windows—rattles. My only answer is an echoing silence and dust falling from the velvet hangings that cover the windows. The times I've been here before— once, four years ago, and then again last week—the storefront appeared just as empty as it does now.

Yet both times the door was unlocked. Both times I walked right inside and she was waiting for me. The oracle.

Last night I assumed she had gone home. That she is still gone and the door still locked this afternoon is not acceptable.

"*Aaargh!*" I pound my right hand harder on the glass, not caring if I shatter the ancient thing, not caring if I spill some magical healing blood that flows through the veins of my right arm. Just so long as I can get inside.

"Way to be discreet," Nick says, wrapping a hand around my wrist and pulling my arm away from the door. "You want the whole neighborhood to take an interest?"

I glare at him. And then at the few pairs of curious eyes that are watching me assault the door. Whatever. One look in my eyes with a little subliminal suggestion, and they'll forget they ever saw me. They'll forget their own names for a while.

"I can take care of them."

Nick steps into my line of sight, blocking my view of the interested spectators.

"That's not necessary," he says, his voice low and adamant.

I yank my wrist out of his grasp. "What would you know about it?"

"I've been around the mythological block a time or two," he says, as if I've forgotten. "I know all about what happens when you mess with someone's mind."

His dark eyes get a faraway look, and I have a feeling he's lost in some kind of shadowed memory. Or maybe a dream. I don't have the time—or patience—to care right now.

"I'm just frustrated," I admit. I turn and give the bottom of the door a solid kick. "Where could she be? Why isn't she here?"

Nick snaps out of his memory. "I don't know," he says. "Oracles are meant to be tied to a location, to a mystical spot where their powers are strongest. If she has moved on—"

"Then something must have happened," I finish. She

132

might have been attacked or frightened away. Or, if current trends continue, taken prisoner. Anyone who helps me and my sisters seems to disappear. "We need to get inside."

Nick nods.

I pull my long-sleeved tee down at one wrist, securing it tight against my arm. I wish I still had my leather jacket. "Shield me," I say as I turn and lift my elbow. One swift jab to the glass and we'll be inside before I can say *Bring it, beastie.*

"Whoa, hold on there, eager beaver." Nick stops my momentum and tugs me away from the door. "Violence isn't always the answer."

He reaches into his back pocket and pulls out something small and shiny. I can't tell exactly what it is, but he steps up to the door and grabs the handle. "You," he says with a smirk, "shield me."

I scowl and then turn to face the sidewalk, keeping him at my back and hiding his actions from the view of the passersby. I hear the faint scrape of metal on metal. A few seconds later, a quiet whine announces his success. I turn around just in time to see the door swing open.

He flashes me a cocky grin. "After you."

I stomp past him, a little irritated by his arrogance—and by the fact that he has gotten us inside without destruction of property. And that he's right. It would be much easier to explain an "unlocked" door than shattered glass to a squad of cops.

Inside, the space is as dark and dusty as ever. There is no

furniture in the front room, which does its best interpretation of a deserted building.

But I know better.

Pulling out my car keys, I flick on my keychain flashlight and shine the brilliant blue beam around the room. At first, I don't notice anything unusual. A thick layer of gray-brown dust covers the floor, the curtain rods, and the defunct chandelier hanging at the center of the room. I can see the faint outline of my bootprints from my last visit.

Clearly, this place is not on a regular cleaning schedule.

As my light sweeps over the room, Nick says, "Wait. Look."

I shine my light where he's pointing, at a disturbance in the dust. In the doorway to the back room there is a sweep of fainter dust, like something slid or was dragged through. The resettled layer of dust there is almost as thick as the dust covering my old bootprints. Whatever happened there must have been shortly after my last visit.

Leaving Nick in the dark, I run into the back room. My heart plummets. It's a disaster. There are candles strewn across the floor. The small, scarred table is on its side in the corner, where it probably rolled after being tipped over. One of the wooden chairs lies in a pile of splintered wood, as if it was smashed over something.

"Whoa," Nick exclaims as he looks in from the doorway.

"I don't—" I shake my head and scan the room. "There isn't any blood. She's probably—"

"I'm sure she's fine," he says, stepping into the room and to my side. "Oracles generally are. She probably saw it coming and was gone before this even happened."

"What about the drag marks?" I demand, pointing at the tracks in the dust. "It sure looks like she was here when they showed up."

"Not necessarily." He turns to study the marks. "I can name a dozen creatures that might leave those marks with heavy tails or dragging limbs."

I take a deep breath and hope that he's right, that the oracle left before the creatures showed up. True, I barely know the woman. I've only spoken with her on two occasions, and neither time was exactly a social visit. But she guided me toward my destiny, helped me see the major turning point in my life when I went from worthless daughter to powerful descendant. I can never repay that gift.

"We need to find her," I say.

"Gretchen," Nick says, sounding disgustingly hesitant. "She could be . . . anywhere."

"Then we'll search anywhere. Everywhere." I picture the matching layers of dust in my bootprints and the drag mark in the other room. "Whatever happened to her might be because of me. Because I visited her here."

"You don't know that."

I stalk over to the table and pull it upright. "I owe her my help."

Nick doesn't say a word, but he moves to help me pull the

table into the middle of the room.

"Besides," I say, bending down to pick up some candles, "we need her. She's the only one left who can help us find the Gorgons."

To his credit, Nick just nods. He must sense how important this is to me—or how important her help is to us. While I gather candles from the floor, he returns the chairs to the table.

I'm setting the candles on the shelves when he picks up the broken chair.

"Hey, Gretch," he says, sounding odd, "look at this."

Shoving my armful of candles onto a nearby shelf, I hurry to his side. He holds out the seat of the chair, facedown.

I take the seat and study the bottom. There in the middle, held in place by pieces of masking tape that look decades old, is a square of yellowed paper that looks older still. I peel the paper off and set the seat on the table. As I unfold the square, the aged paper crackles like it might break in pieces.

"What does it say?" Nick asks.

The paper is covered in strange symbols. Just like the sign on the door written in ancient Greek.

I hold the paper toward him. "Can you read Greek?"

"Not a word."

"Great," I mutter.

I'll have to find a translator. The note might have nothing to do with my situation. It looks as if it's been there since before I was even born. But just in case, I fold the paper and stuff it into my back pocket. Maybe there's another clue—one in a language I can understand—somewhere in the room.

"Search the rest of this room." I walk toward a door leading into another room. "I'm going to check back here."

The other room turns out to be a hall that leads to a back door and a back alley. There's a door off to the right that opens onto a tiny bathroom. A brand-new bar of soap sits next to the faucet on the pedestal sink. There is a dark red hand towel on a small bar next to it and an antique-looking mirror, cloudy and oxidized, hanging above.

Nothing out of the ordinary for a bathroom.

As I turn to head into the hall, I flip off the light and a strange glint on the mirror catches my eye. I turn back and, leaving the light off, I shine my flashlight across the surface of the mirror. In the sideways light, an otherwise invisible message appears.

## FIND THE LOST.

"Seriously?" The woman does not know how to leave a comprehensible clue. As if she could say anything more vague. There are so many lost things right now: the Gorgons, the oracle, my sanity.

But the clue does give me hope that there is something more for me to find here in the bathroom.

I turn the light back on and check around the base of the sink and in and around the toilet tank. Nothing. I stand on the toilet seat and use one of my daggers to unscrew the vent cover in the ceiling. All I find there is a century's worth of dust and grime.

I wipe my hand off on my cargos and replace the vent cover.

As I hop down, I study the room critically. Analytically. Something's not right, doesn't fit, and I can't quite put my finger on it. . . .

I scan the tiny space, my eyes drawn again and again to the bar of soap. Why?

"It's new." I think it through out loud. "It's new and clean and completely out of place in this filthy room."

It must be another clue.

There isn't a handy pipe wrench hanging around, so I drop to my knees in front of the sink, grab the U-shaped pipe underneath with both hands, and twist hard in opposite directions. The pieces give. When the connectors are unthreaded, I pull the pipe out and examine it. Black gunk. So thick I can't see how water gets through.

I suppress my gag reflex and hold the pipe out over the sink. Banging it against the porcelain, I try to dislodge some of the crud. The sludge is lodged in place, and as I bang the pipe as hard as I can, the sound of metal on porcelain echoes out into the hall.

"What are you doing in here?" Nick asks, appearing in the doorway.

"I don't know," I reply honestly. "There's something funny about this—"

As I answer, a metallic sound clinks in the sink. Our wide eyes meet before I jump to my feet.

There, in the sink basin, solid against the sea of black muck I managed to knock out of the pipe, is a gunk-covered object—a big lump with what looks like a chain attached.

Quickly replacing the pipe, and hand tightening the connectors back in place, I grab the object by the chain and turn on the water. I hold it under the icy stream, watching as the blackness slowly swirls down the drain. When it's clean enough to see clearly, I hold it up.

"It's a necklace," I say, disappointed.

I'm not sure what I expected. A sign, maybe, or a clue. Or a key. Not . . . jewelry.

"That's not a necklace," Nick says, stepping into the tiny space and lifting my arm so he can study the object at eye level. "It's a pendant of Apollo."

"What's that?"

To me, it looks like a boring old necklace. A little tacky, with bright gold links, some leafy gold filigrees, and a giant golden gem in the center. Amber, maybe, or topaz. It's not very well cut, either. It looks more like a shiny blob than a rare gemstone.

"Apollo, the god of prophecy," Nick explains, "gives one to each of his oracles. It creates a mystical connection with the god himself, allowing them to receive information from him and allowing him to keep track of his priestesses." Nick's sad, dark eyes look into mine. "It is also the source of their power."

139

"That means—" No, I can't say it.

And I don't have to. Nick finishes for me.

"The oracle is without prophecy."

My fist tightens around the gold chain. This can't be good. If things were so dire that the oracle had to discard her pendant, discard her powers, then she must have been truly frightened.

"You know," Nick says, interrupting my thoughts, "there is another possibility."

"What?"

"She might have shed her powers intentionally."

"Why would she do that?"

He shrugs. "Maybe to prevent herself from helping you further."

"No," I answer without hesitation. The woman who first told me about my destiny, who helped me find Sthenno and who promised that I *could* save Ursula . . . that woman is not my enemy. "I don't believe that."

"Then maybe she ditched the pendant so she couldn't be tracked," he suggests. "It's as accurate as a GPS signal for anyone with access to Apollo's powers."

That sounds more believable.

"I think she threw this in here so I would find it," I say. "She fled before the attack, but she left this for me to protect. I need to return it to her."

I expect Nick to argue. Heck, he's argued about practically everything since we met.

140

But he nods and says, "Okay. Then let's find her."

I stuff the necklace—the pendant of Apollo—into one of my cargo pockets and make sure the flap is secured.

"First," I say, pushing Nick out of the bathroom and shutting off the light behind me, "we need to go talk to my sisters."

He glances back over his shoulder, not hiding his shock. I don't answer. It's not like I'm going to say, *Yeah, totally, it's time for you to meet the other triplets since I, like, trust you now.* Instead, I just shove him forward.

It can't be a coincidence that he was with me when I found the pendant, that he could explain to me what it is and what it means. The oracle must have known he would be there. It must have been fated to happen.

Which means, like it or not—and I'm not about to admit which side of *that* fence I'm on—Nick's fate and mine are intertwined. Looks like I don't have much choice but to bring him into the fold. Besides, keeping him close means keeping a close eye on him. Just because I'm letting him in doesn't mean I trust him completely.

When Nick and I walk into the gym at Greer's school, my sisters freeze. Well, almost. Greer is in the middle of executing a complicated flip-kick, and she has to finish the rotation before she lands on the ground and stares.

*When did she learn how to do that?*

"Gretchen," Grace greets me, with awkward warning in

her voice. "Hi. Um, I thought we were, you know—"

"Who's the guy?" Greer doesn't mince words.

"This is Nick," I explain. "He's here to help us."

Grace's eyes get wider. "Is he, um . . ."

"I'm a descendant of Themis," he offers, stepping forward and holding out his hand. As Grace carefully takes it and shakes it, he says, "The goddess of law and justice. I was sent to protect Gretchen. To protect all of you."

I don't bother adding my opinion on him protecting me.

Greer looks skeptical, arms crossed over her chest and mouth pursed tight. I don't blame her—if one of them brought a random dude to a sisterly gathering, I'd be pretty ticked off—but we don't have time for that now.

"Don't worry," I say. "If he betrays us, I'll skin him alive."

Grace drops his hand and Greer looks slightly less irritated.

"Nick has an idea of where the Gorgons are likely being held prisoner," I say. "Either in the abyss itself or in the dungeons of Mount Olympus."

"Mount Olympus?" Grace repeats. "That's . . . real?"

I'm about to throw her a look that says *Hello—where do you think your powers come from?* but Greer beats me to it.

Not missing a beat, Grace asks, "Which one do we check first?"

Nick and I answer simultaneously. "The abyss."

"Mount Olympus is a dangerous and volatile place," he

explains. "If any of us were caught trespassing there . . ."

He leaves the consequences hanging, but I think we all know what he means. Cross one of the gods on their own turf and my threats toward Nick will seem like playground teasing in comparison.

"Plus, we saw Sthenno get taken into the abyss," Grace says. "There's a good chance that's where she's being kept."

"That," I say, "and we don't know how to get to Olympus."

"We don't know how to get to the abyss either," Greer says, cutting to the chase as usual.

"Yes, that's the tricky part," Nick says. "As far as I know, on this side the portals between the realms are random, showing up at irregular times and in unpredictable places."

"The one Sthenno was pulled into just *appeared*," Grace offers.

"So—what?" Greer shifts her weight onto one hip. "We walk around, waiting for a portal to open? That could take forever."

"There is one person who might help us," I say.

"The oracle?" Grace suggests. "The one who helped us figure out that Ms. West is Sthenno?"

I nod. "We just came from her place. Everything's been tossed around and she's nowhere to be found."

"Oh no," Grace gasps.

"Has she been taken too?" Greer asks.

"I'm not sure," I say honestly. "She might have fled under her own power. She had time to leave a note and to ditch this in the bathroom sink."

I pull the pendant out of my pocket. The light streaming in the high windows along one wall of the gym catches the gold stone and beams of amber light spread out in every direction.

"Wow!" Grace steps closer, studying the dangling pendant. "It's beautiful."

Greer gets a very strange, distant look on her face—kind of like the look humans get when I use my hypno powers on them. She walks toward me, her eyes glazed, her steps awkward.

"Can I see it?" she asks.

As she's reaching out, I'm about to hand it to her when Nick knocks her arm out of the way.

"No," he says quietly. "Put it away, Gretchen."

"What—?"

Greer lunges for me. Nick blocks her, holding her back as he yells at me to hide the pendant. I stuff it back into my pocket. As soon as it's out of sight, Greer relaxes like she's come back to her senses.

She shakes her head. "What just happened?"

"You're the sister with Medusa's power, aren't you?" Nick asks. "You have the second sight?"

Frowning in confusion, she nods. "Yes, but what does that—"

"The pendant of Apollo," he explains, "is a very powerful conduit of prophecy. If you came into contact with it, it would magnify your abilities exponentially."

We all give him matching looks that say, *So?*

"Combined with her natural ability, it would make her a beacon of Apollo's power here on Earth. If she is not mentally prepared, trained to control her powers and more, then it could overload her brain. She could fall into a coma."

"All right, then," Greer says. "Maybe you should keep that away from me for now."

"You think?" I ask, reaching down to secure the flap on the pocket where the pendant will stay from now on.

"What about the note?" Grace asks. "What did it say?"

"We have no idea. It's in ancient Greek." I glance at my sisters. "Either of you happen to be fluent?"

They both shake their heads.

"Ms. West—Sthenno," Grace says, "suggested I take another language as an elective, but I thought Spanish was enough. I could have chosen Modern Greek maybe. Or I could have started the Rosetta Stone course as soon as I learned about my legacy."

She looks upset, like she might cry. As much as I have no patience for tears, I can't fight the urge to comfort her. She's my sister, and it stabs at my heart to see her hurting.

"You couldn't have known," I say, giving her a reassuring pat on the back. "And you wouldn't be fluent yet anyway."

"I know." She sniffs. "It's just that everything is going so wrong so quickly, I wish I could—I don't know, I feel so helpless."

145

"You weren't feeling helpless when you took on that harpy," Greer says.

"What?" I can't have heard her right. "A harpy?"

"Yeah." Grace wipes at her tears. "On my way over here I ran into one."

"You fought her?" I ask, shocked.

She nods.

"And won?"

"She even used her autoporting power," Greer adds, a clear look of pride on her face. Maybe the Ice Queen has a heart after all. "Almost at will."

"Wow, Grace," I say, "that's great."

"Yeah, well, that doesn't help us now," she says. "We still need to find out how to get our ancestors back. Do you think the oracle left town?"

"I don't know," I admit. "Maybe she—"

"No," Greer interrupts. "She is still in the city. Still in San Francisco."

"How can you know that?" Grace asks.

Greer shakes her head. "I just know."

"That's likely true," Nick says. "An oracle wouldn't stray far from her home, from the vortex of her power."

"Okay then," I say, "if she's still in the city, we need to find her."

"It's a big city," Grace says.

"And if the oracle doesn't want to be found," Nick adds, "she won't be."

"If she didn't want to be found," I reply, confident that the oracle wouldn't just abandon me—us, "she wouldn't have left the pendant and the note."

"Where do we start?" Grace asks.

There are two logical places to begin. Either she's sticking close to home, to a territory she knows well, like the neighborhood around her storefront. Or she's getting as far from her usual haunts as possible, trying to avoid whoever—or whatever—is looking for her.

"I think we need to split up," I suggest. "Go out in pairs. We'll cover more of the city faster."

"Good idea," Nick says.

"Grace, you can go with Greer," I say. "She probably knows the city better than any of us."

Besides, I want to keep Nick close to me. Not because I want him close—fine, that might be a tiny bit of my motivation—but because I don't trust him enough yet to send one of my sisters out with him to scour the city for a missing oracle and whatever mythological players are hunting her.

"We'll divide the city into sectors," I continue. "It will probably take a few days to search everywhere, but hopefully we'll find her before then."

"Where should we search first?" Grace grabs her backpack off the floor and slips her arms through the straps.

I admire how she is always ready to go, always ready to leap into any situation, no matter the danger or uncertainty.

She fully embraces our destiny and whatever challenges come with the package. Greer, on the other hand, is a little more reticent.

"Do you really think this is worth the time?" She doesn't make a move for her purse. "Won't the oracle show up if she wants us to find her? Won't she know we're looking for her?"

I ignore her questions. I'm not going to sit around waiting when I can be out looking. Passive isn't in my personality.

"You two can use Greer's car and start by driving the perimeter." That will place them far from the oracle's neighborhood, and hopefully far from whatever might be hunting her. Besides—I glance down at the impossibly high heels Greer is stepping back into—she won't be much good on foot anyway. Nick is in sneakers and I'm in Doc Martens. We'll make better time on foot than she ever would.

She must sense my displeasure, because she starts tapping her foot on the parquet floor. "I'll have you know I could run a marathon in stilettos."

"Nick and I will start in the oracle's neighborhood," I say, ignoring her again. "We'll radiate out from there. You two can radiate in."

Greer shifts. "I have hours of homework to do. I can't be out all night."

My jaw clenches and I have to force my hands not to fist. So much for thinking she cares about anything but herself.

"You signed up for this," I snap. "You knew what you were getting into when you agreed to join us.

"Yes," she snaps back, "with the caveat that it wouldn't interfere with my normal life."

"Well, I'm sorry if all Hades is breaking loose and disrupting your plans." I step toward her and shrug off Nick's hand when he tries to hold me back. "You might not have lost anyone you care about yet. Grace and I have. Grace and I know that the sacrifice is worth it."

For an instant I think I see a crack in her facade, a tremor at the tips of her perfectly manicured hands. I blink and it's gone. I must have imagined it.

Her gaze is steady and almost a little vacant, like she's retreated.

I frown.

"Actually, I need to be home before dark too," Grace says. "My parents are pretty mad about my disappearing for hours the other night. They've given me a curfew."

I sigh. "Fine, search until dusk." I'm irritated, but I guess I also understand. Being a huntress is my entire life. Family is nonexistent and school is more of a necessary evil than a priority. For my sisters, things are different. If I want them to keep as much normalcy in their lives as they can, then I can't exactly begrudge them trying to do that.

"We can meet to compare notes and restrategize tomorrow after school," I say. "Here again?"

Both girls nod, and I'm shocked that Greer doesn't insist that we have to meet later, that she has some club meeting or tea party or study date that we have to work around. Every little step of progress counts.

"And in the meantime," I say, "text if you find anything."

"How will we know if we've found her?" Grace asks. "I mean, neither of us has ever seen her."

Darn it. I hadn't thought of that. I look at Nick, but he just shrugs. "I've never seen her in person either."

I give my sisters a brief description of the oracle, of her dark robes, wrinkled face, and hunkered body. Hopefully enough to make her stand out against a crowd. And they agree to text a photo if they think they've found her.

Minutes later, we emerge from the gym. Grace and Greer head for Greer's Porsche to make a circuit of the city along its outer edges. Nick and I take Moira back to the storefront. By the time night falls, we've found nothing. Exhausted, I drive Nick back to his apartment and then head for the safe house. I hope my sisters have had better luck.

# CHAPTER 13

## GRACE

You're driving too fast!" I squeal as Greer speeds through the same intersection for the third time. "We're not going to find the oracle if you get arrested for reckless driving."

Greer throws me a warning look. "It's called offensive driving."

"It's something offensive," I mutter under my breath, and when she asks what I said, I reply, "Nothing. Haven't we been down this street before?"

"Yes," she growls. "But I had to cut back through here to get across Mission."

This is our third straight afternoon of searching, and as the sun dips down into the west, it looks like Friday is going to be just as fruitless as Wednesday and Thursday were. It's no surprise that Greer is getting testy. Driving back and forth along the streets of San Francisco isn't exactly all fun and games. It's also panhandlers and homeless people and kids playing soccer in the street. I've stopped counting how many times her car has been hit by something. Soccer ball, dragon kite, and an overeager taxi.

Right now Greer's hands are gripping the steering wheel so hard, her knuckles are snow white.

"Maybe we should take a break," I suggest. "Stop for a coffee or something."

Instead of answering, Greer jags the car hard to the left, U-turns in the middle of the street, and speeds back the way we came. Before I can ask her what she's doing, the Porsche is pulling into a tiny parking spot and Greer is climbing out of the car.

I guess that's a yes.

I follow her down the sidewalk and into a store with a bright pink-and-orange sign that reads JUST GELATO.

"Better than coffee," she mumbles as she walks up to the counter. "A double scoop of hazelnut and espresso, please."

The girl behind the counter nods and starts scooping two big balls of gelato from the freezer display. I've never had gelato, but it looks kind of like ice cream. And I do love ice cream.

"I'm buying," Greer says. "What do you want?"

I study the case for a minute, trying to decide if I want something sweet and yummy, like strawberry or cotton candy, or rich and sophisticated, like Greer's choice. In the end I can't resist the allure of cotton candy *anything*.

The gelato girl hands me my cup, and while Greer pays, I take a seat at a table in the front window. It's a tiny table, small and round with delicate black scrolls for legs. There's barely enough room for two. It reminds me of something from a European café. Well, what I *imagine* a European café would look like. I bet Greer has firsthand experience.

When she sits down across from me, though, I don't ask her about Europe or cafés or even gelatos. She's a little—a lot—intimidating. Especially with that stormy scowl in place. Even though she's my sister, I still feel like she's far above my reach. I can't think of anything to say that won't make me look stupid, so I remain silent.

"This is precisely what I needed," she exclaims as she swallows her first bite of gelato. "Sugar, cream, and caffeine. Perfect."

I smile and take another bite of my cotton candy. No caffeine, of course, but it's beyond amazingly good. I could eat an entire tub.

As we sit there, silently eating our frozen treats, my mind wanders. I wonder what it would be like to be Greer, to be raised with so many extra advantages. I've never wanted for anything—nothing truly necessary, anyway—but the kind of money she comes from boggles my mind.

There is a cost, I'm sure. From what I've gathered, she doesn't have a very close relationship with her parents. Or much of a relationship at all. As much as she acts as if the topic is off-limits, I'm curious.

"What are your parents like?"

She looks startled for a moment, pausing to lick her spoon before answering. "They're . . ." She sounds like she's trying to choose her words carefully. "Very successful."

"I know that. But what are they like as people? As parents."

She shrugs and I think she's about to shut down. To pull the shutters and keep me out of her personal life. We might be sisters, but that doesn't mean we're family.

Then, to my surprise, she says, "Absent."

She takes a big bite of gelato. I don't try to force the conversation by saying or asking anything more. I leave her the option of continuing.

"I mean, don't get me wrong," she says, as if I'm passing judgment. "They're great people. Truly great. Smart, dedicated, and they give back a lot."

"But . . . ," I prod.

She takes a deep breath and sighs. "Sometimes I wish they were a little less driven and a little more . . . around."

"It must have been hard," I say, "growing up with parents who were rarely home."

"I shouldn't complain," she says with a small smile. "I've had every advantage. The best nannies, the best schools, the best everything. I could have been far worse off."

We fall silent and I think we're both imagining Gretchen's childhood. She doesn't talk about her adoptive parents. Ever.

But from the few hints she's let slip, I gather they are pretty rotten excuses for human beings. Abusive addicts. I gaze out the window. It breaks my heart to think of her growing up in that environment. I may not have had all the economic advantages that Greer has, but I have parents who love me, who care for and provide for me. Gretchen definitely got the short end of the stick.

"Does it frighten you?"

I look up, startled by Greer's question. "What?"

"Our destiny," she says. "This guardianship we're supposed to take up. Does it ever scare you?"

I laugh. I can't help it. "Of course it does."

She looks at me, studying me. Her elegantly waxed eyebrows pinch into a scowl.

"Any time I let myself stop to think about it for too long," I say, "I'm terrified."

She shakes her head. "You don't show it."

"Maybe I'm like you in that way," I say with a smile. But I don't think she wants a flip answer. "Every time I start to get scared, I think about our ancestors. About Medusa and how she gave her life for this destiny. About all the generations of ancestors after her who worked and sacrificed to keep our line alive."

"And that helps?" she asks with disbelief.

"A little," I say. "When I think of everything that's been done to make sure the three of us would be right here, right now . . . Well, it makes the thought of walking away unthinkable."

Greer nods, as if my answer helps, and goes back to her gelato.

I think we just bonded. To keep from beaming at her—that might undo our progress—I turn and study the world outside.

Across the street, I notice a familiar-looking boy standing outside a Mexican restaurant. He's of average height with brown hair that's golden at the ends, like he spends a lot of time in the sun.

"Oh, hey, isn't that your—" I catch myself when I see who he's standing with, and how they're standing together. A girl. *Close* together.

But it's too late. Greer turns and looks.

Maybe I'm wrong, maybe it's not the boy I saw her with at Fisherman's Wharf. Maybe it's not her—

She slams her bowl down on the table. "That scumbag."

Nope, not wrong.

She's out the door before her spoon, bounced free from the bowl, slaps to the floor. I start to follow after her, to be her support. But then the thought of her boyfriend seeing me, her identical triplet, stops me short. That could only make the situation worse. I watch, helpless through the glass, as she crosses the street to confront him.

# CHAPTER 14

# GREER

Kyle has his back to the street corner, so he isn't aware of my approach. The girl he's wrapping his arms around, however, has a full-on view.

She must sense my fury, because she says something quietly to Kyle and pulls out of his embrace. I'm already not having the best day ever. If she's smart, she'll back far, far away.

As I close the distance between us, Kyle turns around. I catch just the hint of shock before he recovers. His mouth spreads into a vast surfer-dude grin and he says, "Babe!"

My palm connects with his cheek before the drawled-out word is done. He lifts a hand to his stinging cheek.

"Babe, I can explain."

"Don't. Call. Me. Babe." How many times in the last year

have I asked—ordered, begged—him not to call me that? Countless. But has he listened or learned or even *cared* that it bothers me? No.

"Look, Greer," he says, dropping the surfer-dude affect, "this isn't what it—"

"Looks like?" I interrupt. "Then what exactly is it? Is she some long-lost cousin? Or a helpless girl you met on the street who can't stand without help?"

"Greer—"

"Or *maybe* this is *exactly* what it looks like." I spear the girl, who is cowering behind Kyle like a frightened kitten, with a fierce glare. My voice honey sweet, I ask her, "Is this a date?"

Her eyes widen, like she's been hoping to be left out of this confrontation. No such luck. She nudges Kyle from behind.

"Listen, Greer," he says, trying to sound calm and reasonable. "Why don't we go somewhere and talk about this?"

"Is this a date?" I repeat, trying to sound more reasonable myself.

My entire life as I know it might be spiraling out of control, but I can still keep my emotions in check. I can control *them*, if nothing else.

Kyle glances over his shoulder as if he's hoping the girl has disappeared—nope, his hoochie chick is still there—and then back at me with sad eyes. As if I might sympathize. He doesn't have to say anything. I know the answer—and not because of my special mental powers, either. A girl just knows.

"I cannot believe I wasted my time on you," I say. "I'm so much more than you deserve."

A look crosses his face, a combination of shame and anger. I've wounded his pride and now he wants to win it back. Not by apologizing, I'm sure. There is something hateful on his tongue and I don't need to stick around to listen. I'm not sure I could handle it at the moment.

I spin on my heels and storm away, ruining my perfect exit by stumbling over a crack in the sidewalk. Kyle calls after me and I have to fight the urge to lift my hand and show him a crude gesture. But no, I won't let him make me stoop to his low-class level. I stalk to the end of the block and around the corner with my head held high. My dignity intact.

But the moment I'm out of sight, my facade shatters. I duck into the nearest alcove and lean my back against the brick wall, not caring what the rough surface will do to my silk top. I cover my face with my hands and it all just comes out.

The emotion surprises me. I thought I had kept my feelings for Kyle superficial. I knew I liked him, but I never really let it go deeper than that. Ours was more of a business relationship—popular girl with bright future plus popular boy with (potentially) equally bright future. A perfect match.

Or so I thought.

Clearly my attachment ran deeper than I let myself believe.

I never thought Kyle could make me cry.

When I feel a pair of hands on my shoulders, I jerk back, afraid it's Kyle coming after me and seeing me in this state. My head knocks against the brick.

"Ow," I exclaim.

The sympathetic look on Grace's face only makes me sob harder.

"He's a jerk," she says.

Her arms wrap around me and I let her hug me tight. I don't usually break down—as in *never*—but it's like all the stresses and new pressures of the past couple of weeks have built up and Kyle's betrayal is just the final straw. Everything burst, and now it's leaking out onto Grace's tee.

For some reason, her support calms me. I let myself be comforted in a way I never have before. My parents don't hug. Kyle's hugs always seemed to have ulterior motives. Grace only wants me to feel better, only wants to ease my pain. And it works.

"I'm sorry," I say, sniffing. "I'm not usually such a mess."

"There's nothing to be sorry about," she insists. "Some boys are a waste of breath and bone."

"It's not just Kyle," I whisper against her shoulder. Though that is more of it than I'd like to admit. "It's everything. It's school and my parents and our destiny. I'm trying so hard to be the perfect daughter, the perfect girlfriend, the perfect monster huntress. I'm not sure I can do it all."

Grace leans back and lifts my chin up. With her silver eyes

staring straight into mine, she says, "No one is asking you to be perfect."

I wish that were true. I wish I didn't know my parents and teachers expect just that. I wish I didn't expect perfection myself. But it does make me feel a little better to hear Grace say it.

I think about what she said earlier, about living up to the sacrifice our ancestors made for us. That makes me feel better too. More focused, more driven.

"Thank you," I say, recovering some semblance of control over my emotions. I wipe the tears from beneath my eyes. "I feel all right now."

"Good." She gives me an enthusiastic grin. "Now what do you say we text Gretchen and schedule a rendezvous? We're having no luck. There must be another way to find a missing oracle than to grid search the entire city."

"Sounds good," I say.

As Grace and I walk to my car, I straighten my spine. I have a lot of expectations to live up to, most of all my own. My mother may not be perfect, but she has taught me to hold my head high.

## CHAPTER 15

## GRETCHEN

W e've searched half the city, Gretchen," Nick says as we walk back toward my car. "You're going to have to face the fact that either the oracle is gone or—"

"She doesn't want to be found," I finish. "I can't believe she'd vanish willingly and leave me without a source for answers. She must know the Gorgons have been taken. She's our only chance. My only connection to the mythological world."

Nick grins at me over Moira's roof. "Not your *only* connection."

I scowl at him. "You know what I mean."

"I know," he says as we climb into the car. "I wish I could help more with this. Maybe it's part of her plan. Maybe she wants you to figure the next step out on your own."

"Then maybe she should have left better clues."

I shift Moira into gear and head toward the bakery where Grace suggested we meet. It's far enough from their homes that I feel comfortable getting together.

There is a double danger each time we meet. Not only might the monsters track us home again, but the girls' friends and families might see us. That's not a worry for me. The guy in the passenger seat is the closest thing to a friend I've got, and I'm not even sure I'd call him that. He's been nothing but helpful since that night I forced him into my car. Maybe it's time to cut him some slack. But for Grace and Greer, being spotted together by their nearest and dearest is a real danger. Their lives could be turned upside down—well, *more* upside down—if people found out the truth.

Nick points out a parking spot about two blocks from the bakery. In this neighborhood I'll be lucky to find another spot, period. I take it.

As we start up the hill toward the bakery, side by side, I'm amazed at how comfortable I am with Nick. In just a few short days, he's gone from a boy who confused and irritated me to one I thought had betrayed me and my sisters in the worst way to one whom I trust with the most precious of my secrets. With my sister's lives—and mine.

"What?" he asks.

"I didn't say anything."

"You don't have to say anything," he says. "You've got a look."

I laugh. "A look?"

"Yeah." He stops, and I stop to face him.

"What kind of look?"

"I don't know," he says, his grin growing. "But I think it might be . . . a smile."

I smack him on the shoulder. Hard.

"I can't be sure," he continues, "because I'm not sure I've ever seen one on your face before, but it definitely looks like— Hey!"

I start smacking him with greater frequency, my good mood growing with every hit. He's laughing, I'm laughing. I feel completely . . . free. When he grabs each of my wrists in a fist, my laughter slowly dies. The look in his dark eyes says he feels the same comfortable connection as I do.

His gaze drops to my mouth and I suck in a breath.

"Gretchen . . ."

His head starts moving closer with aching slowness. My eyes drift shut. I can feel his breath on my lips, hot and damp.

As his mouth approaches mine, I feel a jolt of magic arc between our lips, like the spark of static electricity when you reach for a metal doorknob in winter. I shiver as the sensation skitters down my spine.

Then our lips meet, barely a touch. Lighter than a butterfly on a flower. But I feel it . . . *everywhere*.

Then Nick is pulling back and my eyes open. He has the same dazed look on his face that I feel. I clamp my lips together, marveling at the feeling. His smile takes over his face.

"Gretchen!" Grace's voice echoes around me. "Here we are!"

I look up the sidewalk to where Grace and Greer are standing outside the bakery. Grace is waving like wild, trying to get my attention.

I sigh. "We'd better go."

Nick doesn't release my wrists. "This isn't finished."

No, it's not. I shake my head, and he lets me go. I turn away from his serious expression and start up the street.

"Oh no," Nick says.

I turn back. A black spot has appeared in the street a few feet from where I'm standing. Right next to Nick.

Not now. Can't the beastie realm hold off for a little while? Taking down a monster isn't exactly convenient at the moment, but it's still part of the job description.

I face the portal, ready for whatever steps through. The creature that appears in the middle of the street is the stuff of bogeymen legends. A geryon—a hideous thing with three giant bodies joined at the shoulders, three ugly heads, and three sets of beady eyes. It's backed by two pairs of diseased-looking wings with feathers falling off, leaving raw, gaping wounds. Technically, the thing is my cousin. A descendant of Medusa's other offspring, the giant Chrysaor. But the gene pool definitely got corrupted along the way.

The geryon looks at me and grunts. I don't think it can even speak.

Nick moves to my side, like he wants to protect me. He

of all people should know I can take care of this myself. He'll only get in the way.

I'm about to tell him that when the creature shifts its attention. Its three gazes focus on my companion. Looking directly at Nick, one of its faces contorts into a look of pure fury.

Everything happens in an instant.

The creature steps forward, shoves me to the side with one pair of beefy paws, and wraps its four other arms around Nick's body. One tightens around his neck.

"No!" I shout.

With faster reflexes than I gave it credit for, the creature drags Nick back over to the portal. I run forward, reaching for Nick or the creature or both. But it's too late. I'm not fast enough.

With one backward step, the creature disappears into the void. Nick disappears with him.

"No!" I shout again.

I turn and see my sisters running down the street toward me. They saw what just happened and are coming to help. But they're too far away.

I have only seconds to make my decision. Let Nick go, and with him our only connection to the mythological world. Or . . .

I face my sisters, still half a block away. I make sure they're watching as I reach down and pull the oracle's note and the pendant of Apollo out of my cargo pocket and drop them on the ground. I only hope they can figure out how to use them.

Then, with the clock ticking, I turn back to the portal.

"Gretchen, no!" Grace shouts.

There's no time. Already the edges of the portal are shrinking.

Without another thought I dive headfirst into the black.

## CHAPTER 16

## GREER

Grace and I rush down the hill, even though we can both clearly see that Gretchen, Nick, and the portal are all gone. When we reach the empty space, we stand there in shock. Our sister, the girl who is ultimately responsible for bringing us together, for introducing us to this world . . . is gone.

It stings. The thought that she has abandoned us, when we're already so very alone in this, leaves me at a loss. But then I picture the look on her face—both when Grace and I caught her getting so close to Nick and in the instant before she dived in after him—and I understand.

"Why?" Grace cries. "Why would she do that?"

"To go after Nick, obviously," I say. "Did you see the way they were looking at each other?"

"You think they—" Grace blinks. "Oh. Well, then."

Still, feelings or not, I can't imagine diving into that world, putting my life at risk, willingly. Not for a boy, not for anyone. Who knows what she'll find—what she's finding—on the other side?

"What are we going to do?" Grace asks. "We have to do something. We have to . . . I don't know what."

*Yeah, I don't know what either.*

Kneeling down, I reach for the objects Gretchen left on the ground. Before I can wrap my fingers around them, Grace drops down and snatches them up.

"No you don't," she says, quickly stuffing the oracle's note and pendant into her pocket. "That thing is too dangerous for you."

I roll my eyes. "I wasn't going for the pendant," I insist, although I'm not entirely certain I wouldn't have. The object has a strange pull on me, and I might have grabbed it without thinking. "I was checking to see if there was anything else here."

Grace scowls at me, like she knows I'm lying.

I turn away, studying the space where Gretchen disappeared. Moments ago, it was a mystical portal to another realm. Now it looks just like any other piece of air in the city. No magical sparkles or lingering shadows.

"Greer," Grace says, sounding a little lost, "what are we going to do? We can't just let her go. Who knows what might happen to her in there? What if she can't get back out? We have to do something."

"And how do you expect us to get her back?" I ask. When

did I become the one with the answers, anyway? I'm newer to this world than even Grace. "Last time I checked, we have no idea how to find a portal, no idea how to open one, and no idea how to find out how to do either of those things."

"I know that," she says, with more hostility in her voice than I expect. "But she is our sister. We don't just let her vanish into the abyss. We can't. I can't."

I sigh. She's scared and she's right. But that doesn't change the circumstances.

"I don't know what to do," I answer honestly. "We're facing the same situation as Sthenno being taken—"

"Only this is Gretchen," she exclaims. "This is so much more important!"

"I know," I say, laying a reassuring hand on her shoulder. "But the problem is the same. And if the problem is the same, then the solution is the same."

"What solution?" she asks. Then, apparently getting my meaning, "You mean what we've already been doing. Searching for the oracle."

"We have no one left to ask for help." I shrug, adjusting my purse on my shoulder. I tick the names off on my fingers. "Euryale, gone. Sthenno, gone. Gretchen and Nick, gone. The oracle is our only hope. Can you think of another idea?"

Grace is silent for several long moments. "No, no yet," she says. "But I'll keep thinking. I'll dig deeper into my online hunt for resources. Maybe there's a library somewhere in the world with something that can help."

"Maybe there is." I can tell that feeling useful and productive makes Grace feel better. "Why don't we go home for tonight, like we were already planning to do? We can get a good night's sleep, you can start your research, and we'll resume in the morning."

She looks up at the sky. "But there are still a couple of hours of daylight left," she says. "Maybe we should keep looking."

"We'll only exhaust ourselves," I insist. "We won't do any good if we're too drained to concentrate. A fresh perspective will make a big difference."

Her silver eyes scan the street, like she'll find an answer there. Or maybe someone who can help. But the people of San Francisco are ignorant of that world, and it's our job to keep it that way. I have to believe the best thing we can do is continue our search in the morning, refreshed.

"I guess you're right," she finally says. "I'll get started on my research. Maybe I can design a program to explore all the special archives in the world libraries. It can search online while we search for the oracle."

"That sounds like an excellent plan." A fresh start, a fresh chance to solve this puzzle. "Can I give you a ride home? Last chance before my car goes into the shop tomorrow."

"No thanks," she says. "I'm not far. I feel like walking."

"Okay, then I'll see you in the morning."

She starts down the sidewalk, heading toward her neighborhood. I have to go in the opposite direction to get to my car, but I stand there and watch her walk away.

"Hey, Grace," I call out before she gets too far. She turns around, a question on her face. "Be careful."

She gives me a small smile. "You too."

I smile back and we both turn and head our separate ways. I'm more worried than I let Grace see. Not specifically about Gretchen—if anyone can take care of herself in the monster abyss, it's her—but about us. About our chances.

I wasn't wrong when I said there was no one left to answer our questions. With the Gorgons and now Nick and Gretchen out of this realm and the oracle on the run, we have no one to turn to. We're completely on our own, with no resources and only limited experience with the world of mythology.

My optimism was mostly a show for Grace. We're two girls with minimal powers, alone in the city. I don't hold out a lot of hope for our success.

But that doesn't mean I won't try.

"Of course I want to find her," I say, pressing the phone to my ear. Does Grace think I'm completely unfeeling? Gretchen is my sister too. But that doesn't change my responsibilities. Normal life continues, even if the world of myth is spiraling out of control. "I can't possibly get out of the alumnae tea planning meeting Monday afternoon, however."

I dropped the Porsche off at the body shop this morning to get her dents removed, so I decided to walk home from my evening workout at the gym. Gives me a little extra exercise.

172

The climb up the hill alone would give me rock-star quads if I did it every night.

"That's ridiculous," she says. "It's a *meeting*, Greer. What about your priorities? Our sister is in the abyss. She could be dead already."

No. She can't be dead. That's not an option. I have to believe that I would *know* if she were gone.

As if I haven't already processed that fear, over and over, in the twenty-four hours since we watched, helpless, as Gretchen dived into the monster realm. Hours that feel like years. Hours in which we've spent every spare daylight moment searching for her, for the oracle, or for any clue of how to get her back. Not that we found *anything*. Every person we know who is connected to the mythological world is missing. We don't even know where to turn, but we keep looking. I can cancel every other appointment on my schedule for the next few days, but this one is unmissable.

We're hunting blind, and I'm going to do this one thing that keeps my semblance of normalcy intact. If anything, taking a break will give me a clearer mind.

"It will only take a couple of hours," I promise. "Besides, I'm committing all of tomorrow to our fruitless searching again."

Sunday is usually my home spa day.

"Greer—"

Her voice cracks and I can guess what she's thinking. We'd only just found Gretchen, and each other. We'd only been reunited a short while. What if we can't get her back?

"We will find her," I say with more certainty than I necessarily feel. This is one time when I wish my magical power of knowing things would produce more tangible results. I could use some second sight at this point. I feel optimistic, but I'm not sure if that's because of my untapped ability or because I've been raised to believe in the power of positive thinking.

"But what if—"

"Grace," I say, cutting her off before she can voice her fears. My fears. "We will find her."

She sniffles for a minute and I can tell she's pulling herself together.

"I know," she says, her voice stronger than before. "I wish I could do more."

"You're doing everything you can," I assure her. "We both are."

"Are we?"

"Of course we are."

"I feel like we're missing something," she says. "Like the answer is right in front of us and we keep looking the other way."

I've had the same feeling. Not a fully realized thought, perhaps, but a sensation that the answer is near. "Me too. We just have to open our minds to the solution," I say, hating how New Age-y I sound. "The answer will reveal itself."

"I hope you're right," she says. "We're still meeting at the bus stop first thing tomorrow morning?"

"The very first."

"Okay." She sighs. "I'm going to do some more research. See if I can track down anything that can help."

If anyone can find clues to help us, it's Grace. The girl is a bona fide computer genius and has done her fair share of hacking. But I don't think there is anything out there for her to find. The mythological world has kept itself well off the grid.

"Let me know what you find," I tell her.

"Definitely."

I slide my phone back into my purse and quicken my steps.

I cross Franklin and turn left so I can walk past the Haas-Lilienthal House. A beautiful, towering gray Victorian that dates back to 1886, the architectural wonder is open a couple of days a week as a museum. I enjoy walking by. It makes me feel like I'm part of a bygone era, like I've stepped back into the nineteenth century.

At night, though, the house is positively spooky.

I'm walking past the driveway, glancing up at the cramped third-floor window where I always expect to see a ghost staring down at me, when I get the feeling. At first it's just a tickle at the back of my neck, like someone with hot breath is blowing on my sensitive skin. It quickly spreads down my spine in a burning river of fear.

A small part of me wants to turn around, to see if this sensation of being watched, being followed, is legitimate. The rest of me screams to run.

Adrenaline pumps into my veins. It's the same feeling as when the giant knocked on my front door. Only this time I force myself to stay.

I pause for a moment, like I want to take in the full facade of the house, eerily illuminated by the glow of streetlamps and light pollution. A small plastic smile in place, I focus my attention on my peripheral vision. From the corner of my eye I sense an out-of-place shadow.

Maintaining my blank face, I turn and continue up the sidewalk at my leisurely pace. I feel the shadow follow, keeping a safe distance.

I start making mental plans. I reach into my purse, casually looking for my compact. When I pull it out, I flip it open and raise it to eye level, pretending to check the state of my lipstick.

What I see in the reflection almost takes my breath away.

The creature following me is hideous. No larger than me, it is obviously part man and part sea . . . something. Great clumps of black seaweed hang off its torso like some comic-book villain who took a dip in a radioactive aquarium.

It's standing beneath a streetlamp, and the downlight distorts its features into something out of a horror movie. My heart pounds faster.

Now that I've seen my opponent, I drop my compact back in my purse and speed up my steps. I turn the corner at the intersection and break into a run, hoping to give myself a little distance between me and my pursuer. I'm not running away this time, though, I'm getting into position.

I have only seconds to decide on the best concealed location. There are raised stoops and clusters of garbage cans to the right, cars and trees and a mailbox to the left.

I decide on the big, boxy SUV with tires massive enough to hide a small hybrid hatchback. I'm just crouching behind the front bumper when I sense the creature shuffling around the corner. I slow my breathing and try to reach out with my mind, to see where the creature is and what it's planning. I have to learn how to harness my power eventually, and now seems like as good a time as any.

I sense . . . nothing. *Sugar.*

I peer out around the tire and see the creature looking around, its soggy shoulders slumped. It looks disappointed.

It thinks it's lost me. Clearly it's too stupid to realize I might be hiding. Which might be a good reaction if I were trying to get away, but I have a duty to send it home. I'm ready to fight.

Against all my instincts and better judgment, I step out of my hiding place and say, "Looking for something?"

I can tell I've startled it. *Good.*

It tilts its head to the side, confused by my actions I suppose, and grunts. Lurching forward, it holds its arms out straight like Frankenstein's monster. Wow, this is going to be easier than I thought.

I stash my gym bag in front of the tire. I'm braced, ready

to deliver a strong kick to send it flying, followed by a hand chop to bring it to the ground. Then I get the weirdest sensation. It's like slivers of ice all down my back.

The creature freezes, staring blankly at a spot just over my right shoulder. I know I probably shouldn't—turning away from the vile creature in front of me is perhaps not the smartest idea ever—but I can't ignore the icicles on my spine.

Walking down the sidewalk, about half a block away, is a woman. A very ordinary, nothing-monsterlike-about-her woman. She's maybe middle-aged, forty-something, with her black hair swirled into a loose bun. Despite her diminutive size, she's covering the sidewalk between us quickly.

The creature grunts. I turn back, not sure why the woman's presence gave me such shivers, and find the thing lurching away.

Now I'm not sure what to do. Go after the creature, in front of the woman, and risk having to answer questions about a fight and a disappearing opponent? Or maintain the appearance of normalcy and let it get away?

With a sigh, I lower my hands and watch as the monster waddles down the street. Err on the side of normalcy, I always say.

"You're not going to let it get away, are you?" the woman asks.

What did she say? No, I must have misunderstood.

"Don't play coy with me, Greer Morgenthal," she says. "I know exactly who and what you are."

"I— What?"

"You're a huntress." The woman points at the retreating creature. "Hunt."

I regain my ability to speak.

"Who are you?"

"Who do you think I am?"

Honestly, I have no clue. But I make the only guess I can. "Are you one of the Gorgons? Are you Euryale?"

The woman's laughter turns my stomach. It's dark and nasty and curls around my neck like tentacles. I back away.

"No," she barks, her voice echoing over me, "I am not a Gorgon."

A crash sounds behind me and I turn away from the woman. The escaping creature ran headfirst into a group of trashcans and is now trying to climb over and out of the piles of garbage.

"Oh for the love of darkness," the woman says.

I watch, transfixed, as she storms past me, walks up to the creature, grabs it by the neck, and hauls it to its feet. Hurrying after her—because I feel that I have to do *something*—I'm not sure if I should stop her or help her.

The woman speaks to the monster in a language I don't understand.

*"Tolmáte apsi foún tis parangelíes mou?"*

Her tone, though, tells me everything I need to know. She is not happy with this sad creature. At all.

The seaweed beast lets out a nauseating scream.

I don't know why, but instinct tells me to protect the creature from the woman.

"Stop it," I cry. "You're scaring him."

The woman twists to face me, to glare at me, and snarls. "Scaring him? Of course I'm—" She stops in midsentence, turns her head slightly, and smiles. "Ah. You have the dead queen's power."

I shake my head, not understanding her confusing statement.

"The queen Medusa, with her second sight," she says. "You are the seer."

"Who are you?" I repeat. "How do you know this?"

She smiles, still holding the creature by the throat. "I know more than you can possibly imagine. I know more than anyone else in this game."

"This isn't a game," I assert, stepping forward. I don't know where I find the sudden courage, but I refuse to let her bully me. "There are lives at stake. Now tell me who you are."

In an instant, she flings the creature toward me, and while I'm reeling backward—trying to keep from collapsing under its weight—there is a bright flash of light. When I regain my footing, keeping the creature at arm's length, I start to give her a piece of my mind.

"That was—"

The woman is gone. Whoever she is—*what*ever she is— she has disappeared.

"What in the world was that?"

180

The creature grunts.

I glare at it, like this is all its fault. I'm not sure that it isn't, but I have a feeling the woman was here for me. She wanted to see me, to test me maybe.

Seriously, after everything that's been going on, I'm at the end of my rope.

Without another word, I turn and sink my fangs into the creature. When it's gone back to the abyss, I retrieve my discarded gym bag and continue on my way home. What else could go sideways in my world? I only hope that's it for tonight.

## CHAPTER SEVENTEEN

## GRETCHEN

The worst thing about the abyss is the dark. The smell is a close second, what with it being the home of all monsterkind, but the suffocating darkness is worse. It's like a massive, endless cavern carved from black rock. What little light there is gets sucked into the nearest surface. If not for the eerie green glow of the lights—for lack of a better word—hanging from above, the entire place would be in pitch darkness.

This is exactly how I would picture Hades, only I imagine the underworld with more fire and sulfur.

The rocky surfaces are shiny—smooth like glass—and they look wet to the touch. They're bone dry.

Everything here is dry except for the black river that cuts through the center of the cavern. I haven't gotten desperate

enough to drink from it. Yet. But if I don't find Nick and get out of here soon, I'll have no choice. My mouth already feels like sandpaper.

When I first came through the portal, I had an expectation of what I'd find on the other side. The several seconds I spent flying through the swirling tunnel gave me the chance to form a mental picture—and to ask myself why I'd just done such a stupid thing, but it was a pointless question by then. I pictured myself flying out into a sea of monsters, a crowd of creatures already shredding Nick to tiny little pieces and eager to do the same to me. Eager to get a part of me so they could claim their bounty and earn their freedom.

I didn't expect to be dumped into an empty corner of a vast space, with not another creature in sight. I landed, yanked my daggers from my boots, and braced myself for the onslaught that never came.

I have no idea how long I've been here—hours, days, longer?—because there is no sun to mark the passage of time. My phone got fried on the way through and I can't get it to power up. I've never worn a watch in my life, but now I wish I did.

At first I stayed in my empty corner, certain that hordes of angry, bounty-hunting monsters would be descending on me at any moment. When they didn't come, I realized how stupid I was being. I came through the portal to rescue Nick. Sitting around on my butt waiting to be attacked was not going to accomplish anything.

Finally, I decided I couldn't sit still waiting. I walked forward to the river, looked up- and downstream, and tried to make an educated guess. The whole bleak mess looked the same in both directions. I chose downstream, figuring that, if this river behaved like those in the real world, it would grow larger and more full of life the farther it went.

I've been walking downstream ever since.

The flashlight on my keychain isn't the most powerful light source in the world, but it does the job to keep me from tripping over a rock and tumbling headfirst into the river. The light is dimming, though, and I'm not sure how much longer it will—

Even as I have that thought, the flashlight dims even more, burns bright for a second, and then goes out completely.

"Great."

I close my eyes, trying to adjust to the near black so I'll be able to see as well as possible in the faint green glow. When I open them, I can barely make out the ground beneath my feet. I start walking, slower than before, making my way downstream. Questioning myself with every step.

"What were you thinking?" I ask myself aloud. "Diving into the freaking monster abyss after a boy you barely know."

I stumble over an extrarough patch and barely catch myself before I pitch face-first to the ground. I kick at the rock, like that will make a difference.

"And why?" I ask myself. "Because he's cute? Because he likes you?"

*Because he kissed me?* I can't even ask that question out loud, despite the bleak solitude around me. The memory is too strong.

I lift my hand to my mouth, brushing my fingertips over my lips. I swear I can still feel the kiss.

But no, that's not why I dived in after him. I need him. I need his help to get Ursula and Sthenno back. I need his help to figure out the world of mythology. Without Ursula, I'm lost, and he's a lifeline.

At the same time, I realize I've left my sisters alone and unprotected. I have to believe they can take care of themselves, of each other. At least until I can get back to their sides.

Walking along the rough path, lost in thought, I sense the presence more than see it. A slightly different shadow in the black-on-black world.

Instinct takes over and I drop into a crouch. There is nothing to duck behind for cover—not that that would help, because I can't get a solid location on the whatever that just showed up. The first creature I've encountered since my arrival.

A shadow passes between me and the green light at my two o'clock. I spin, about to make a leap, when a pair of hands clamps over my shoulder. Another pair wraps around my waist.

"Mmmm, human," the thing behind me says.

The other beastie steps closer, into my direct line of sight.

"Out of place down here."

I struggle against the twin pairs of arms that are securing me against the chest of the monster I can't see. My fangs drop and I reach back, trying to grab at one of the arms holding me in place.

"No," the beast in front of me shouts as I pull a big, hairy forearm to within biting distance and sink my fangs into the tough flesh.

I don't expect the creature to vanish right away—there're pretty low odds that this forearm is the pulse point on this particular beastie—but I expect it to go eventually. What I don't expect is for the four arms holding me to suddenly slacken.

I stumble forward at my sudden freedom, into the arms of the other monster, whose green-glinting eyes aren't focused on me. It's watching its bitten friend.

I turn, expecting to see the thing angry that I've sent—

But wait, how can I send it home when it's already there?

The creature crumples to the ground. I can see now that it's a laestrygon, normally an unrelenting, man-eating giant that is as hard to fight as it is to hunt.

The laestrygon looks piteous. Clutching at one arm, at the spot where my fangs hit home, it's writhing in pain, groaning and growling and howling into the echoing abyss.

"What's going on?"

The other monster, still behind me, roars, "You've killed him."

"What?"

Killed him? No, that can't be. My venom doesn't kill monsters, it just sends them home. But he is home. And maybe that restriction only applies in the human realm, where monsters are virtually immortal. Here, in the home of the beasts, there is nowhere else to send them. Here, they die.

Just like the glow of my dying flashlight moments before, the shouts of the writhing creature on the ground gradually fade. Moans turn into whimpers, growls into labored breathing. Then, with a final sigh, everything stops.

Everything.

It's like a stab to my chest.

I've hunted monsters for four years without hesitation. I've taken them down hard and fast and with more than a little joy at watching them vanish back into the realm where they belong.

But this? This is different.

This is final.

"I—" I turn to look at the other creature, feeling helpless for the first time in a long, long time. For the first time since the last time I let Phil lay a hand on me. It's not a feeling I enjoy. "I didn't know."

The other creature, a minotaur, looks at me, eyes wide, and whispers, "Huntress."

It turns and runs into the black.

"Wait!" I call after it.

That thing is the only living creature—besides its now

deceased friend—that I've seen since landing in the abyss. I should have grabbed it, questioned it about this place, about the layout of the realm, about where I might find prisoners or food or light or a way out.

The thing might as well have poofed back to my world for whatever chance I have of finding it now. I can barely see my hand in front of my face, let alone a creature running away, deeper and deeper into shadow, at full speed.

I mutter a curse and start walking again, the same direction I've been heading. Away from the dead laestrygon.

My feet are dragging more than before. Part of it is the shock of having actually killed a monster. I have no pity for them, obviously. They are bloodthirsty, evil creatures for the most part. But in the space of a bite I've become a killer. Not just a huntress, a warden who herds her wild beasties back into their pen. A killer.

Before this, my biggest worry was accidentally killing a human if some of the deadly blood from the left side of my body got spilled in their presence. That's why I wear the Kevlar wrist cuffs. I couldn't have planned for this.

I feel like I've crossed an invisible line. Like a world that was black-and-white has turned into a million shades of gray. It's not a good feeling.

For the first time in my life, I wish someone were here to comfort me, to reassure me. No, not just someone. I wish my sisters were here. Greer would tell me to suck it up and Grace would give me a hug. Even though I would probably shrug off their efforts, it would make me feel better.

The other reason for my sluggish steps, I know, is dehydration. My mind may not know what time it is, or how much time has passed since I jumped into this realm, but my body is giving me signs. Dry mouth, heavy limbs, the beginnings of a killer headache. I've been at least thirty-six hours without water, maybe closer to forty-eight. If I don't get some moisture into my system soon, it's going to start shutting down.

The black water is hardly inviting. I have no idea if it's sanitary, let alone drinkable. I don't even know if it *is* water. Who knows what might be living in there?

I'm going to have to risk it at some point. Soon it will be either certain death by dehydration or risk other ailments by drinking the questionable water.

For now, I keep walking.

Eventually, the river changes course. The main flow of the water turns left, continuing on into the black cavern. To the right, an eddy of water forms a pool. A small lake with a narrow natural bridge just below the surface, separating it from the fast-moving river.

This looks like as good a place as any to try a drink. At least I won't risk getting carried away by the current.

I make my way around the lake, searching for a secluded spot. About a quarter of the way along the shore, the lake spreads out over a rocky shelf, forming a wide, thin sheet of water.

I move up to the corner, where the lake becomes shallow,

and drop to my knees. With my body drying out, the cushioning effect of my skin and muscle is depleted. The impact of my kneecaps on rock rattles my entire body. My entire skeleton.

As much as I don't want to try this water, I know I'm out of options. Out of time.

On my hands and knees, I lean forward, reach down to scoop a handful of lake, and lift it to my mouth. I hesitate only an instant before parting my lips and drinking in the liquid.

Cool and crisp, the water tastes clean. That doesn't mean there aren't bacteria or viruses floating around in there, but at least it tastes like pure water.

As it flows over my tongue, down my throat, into my belly, it feels like icy rivulets. Lightning flashes of cool, refreshing, life-giving water. My stomach grumbles in protest, reminding me that it would like some food too. That will have to wait. I can survive for days, weeks even, without food.

For the love of Medusa, I don't think water has ever tasted this good in my life. I scoop up handful after handful, guzzling it down like my energy drinks back home.

I've never felt so far from home. So far from everything I care about. Even knowing that some of the people I care about—Ursula, Sthenno, and, yes, Nick—are possibly here, in this realm with me, I feel a million miles away from them.

My sisters feel even farther away.

When I've drunk my fill and my stomach feels like it's

going to explode, like I might float away, I sit back on my heels. Hands on my knees, I close my eyes for a minute, reveling in the feeling of moisture on my tongue.

I can't sit here for long. I need to get back on my feet, back on the path that might lead me to Nick. To answers about the missing Gorgons. And then—hopefully—home.

But for now, for right now, I could sit here and listen to the gently lapping water forever. I'm tired, beyond exhausted. I haven't slept since I got here, and I'm sure my body and my brain would appreciate a quick nap. I can't afford to wait, though.

Finally, after I feel that some of the water bloating my stomach has been absorbed into my body, I slowly open my eyes. I'm ready to push back to my feet, to head back to the river, make my way over the bridge, and keep walking.

Across the lake, about a third of the way around the shore from my location, is a light. I'm pretty certain I would have noticed a light when I first got here. Which means I'm also pretty certain it's a late addition. Which means something—or some*one*—must have brought it there.

I jump to my feet, relieved to have my quick-healing reflexes back in working order, and take off toward the light. The glow is strong enough that I can see the ground in front of me more clearly. I can move faster than before. There's one big rock outcropping between me and the light, and when I approach it, I realize I'll either have to swim around it on the lake side or do some serious rock climbing to get over it.

I weigh my options. If I go into the lake, all my clothes—and what gear I do have—will get soaked. If I go with the rocks, I might not be able to find foot- and handholds to get me over. I'm without proper climbing gear and my boots aren't exactly the most agile of footwear. I survey the rock face and find it almost perfectly smooth. From ground level I can't even see how high the rock wall goes. It might go all the way to the ceiling for all I know.

"No way can I make it over," I mutter.

Which means the lake is my only option.

If I have to get wet, I want to lessen the consequences as much as possible. I quickly strip down to my essentials and tie my boots up in the bundle of my clothes. Hopefully I can hold them out of the water, keeping them safe and dry.

With a tight grip on my things, I make my way to the water's edge and slowly start to wade in. I knew the water was cold, but I had no idea how freezing it would feel to walk into it. Maybe it's colder in this deeper end of the lake, or maybe my toes are just more sensitive than my hands. Either way, the shivers start before I'm even knee-deep.

As the water rises, I set the bundle on my head and try to stick close to the rock outcropping. The lakebed—all solid rock, of course—drops off quickly, and soon I can barely reach the bottom with my tiptoes. Jutting my chin up to keep my head and my bundle above water, I start to dog-paddle as I reach the end of the rock outcropping.

I pass the barrier and start swimming for the shore on the

other side. I feel the first scrape of my toes on the rising bottom when something wraps around my ankle. I scream, but my shout turns into a gurgle as I get dragged under. Before I disappear beneath the surface, I heave my bundle as far toward the shore as I can, hoping to at least keep my clothes dry. With both arms free, I can concentrate on extricating my ankle from the iron grip of something that feels too much like a hand.

I dive under, reaching for my ankle. I wish I'd kept one of my daggers out instead of tying them both up with everything else in my bundle. I try to claw at whatever is pulling me, but the downward momentum and my natural buoyancy keep the hand just out of reach.

I feel the water pressure change as I'm dragged deeper and deeper. The lungful of air in my chest is running out of oxygen. Primal instinct starts forcing air out, trying to compel me to take another breath. The survival core of my brain doesn't realize that there is no air out there, only water.

The last whoosh of air escapes. I'm out of time. And to think, moments ago I was worried about going days without water. Lack of oxygen will do the same trick in minutes.

Then, suddenly, I'm being yanked to the surface. The hand around my ankle holds on tight, but the creature it's connected to gets pulled up with me. As we approach the surface, the hand releases, and I fly out of the water and out onto the rocky shore.

I suck in great gasping gulps of air, struggling to get

oxygen back into my panicking bloodstream. My stomach heaves, rejecting the black water that it welcomed a short while ago.

I'm on my hands and knees, gasping and gagging, when a woman's voice says, "What kind of fool goes wading into the Lake of the Dead?"

I look up and try to focus my blurry vision on the speaker, but my attention is drawn to a beautiful black horse standing a few feet away. It takes me a moment to realize that the reason I can tell the horse is black is that the single horn in the middle of its forehead is glowing like a ship's lantern in the fog.

"No way," I whisper, fighting off another coughing fit. "You're a unicorn."

The unicorn tilts its head to the side and gives me what can only be a bemused look. That's the last thing I see before I black out.

# CHAPTER 18

## GRACE

When Milo calls and asks if I want to go grab lunch somewhere, I almost put him off. Since Gretchen dived into the abyss just two days ago, I've been half crazed. I stayed up most of the last two nights working on my library archives search program—I call it the LASP—and then meeting Greer at first light to search the streets.

I'm exhausted and desperate, and those don't seem like good things to throw into the mix between me and Milo.

"I'd love to go to lunch, Milo," I say, "but—"

Before I can tell him I have to cancel our plans, Greer snatches the phone from my hand, clears her throat, and says, "I'm halfway across town. Can we meet in, say, twenty minutes?"

She sounded just like me.

I reach for my phone, but she jerks it out of reach.

"Greer!" I shout-whisper.

"Uh-huh," she says, twisting to avoid my efforts at phone retrieval. "Okay, I'll find it. Sounds perfect."

She hangs up, hands my phone back, and says, "You're welcome."

"I'm welcome?" *Is she insane?* "I can't go on a date. I have to keep looking for the oracle."

"We're covering the same ground," she says. "I'll keep searching while you have lunch with Milo. Consider this my penance for attending my tea committee meeting tomorrow afternoon."

"I—I can't."

"You need to." She looks me over. "How much sleep did you get last night?"

"I don't know." I shrug. "A few hours."

"More like a couple of hours," she guesses. "You look like the walking dead."

"Great, all the more reason to go on a date."

Greer walks over to the nearest car and sets her purse on the hood. She pulls out a small silk pouch. "That," she says, "I can take care of."

"This is a stupid idea," I argue. "I'll never be able to have a coherent conversation. I *shouldn't* be able to. Greer, I need to keep searching."

She holds my face between her palms and looks me straight in the eye. "Listen to me, Grace Whitfield. You are not a machine. You cannot operate on no sleep and, I imagine, no food."

I feel my cheeks burn at the truth of her accusation. I was too rushed to grab even a granola bar for breakfast.

"If you run yourself into the dirt, you will be no good to Gretchen." She releases me and grabs a silver tube out of the silk pouch. "Go on this date. Enjoy yourself. Flirt with the cute boy." She pulls the top off the tube and twists the bottom, pushing a stick of skin-colored makeup out of the end. "When you're done, you will be reenergized and we will meet back up and resume our searching."

I sigh. Maybe it's okay, maybe this is a good thing.

I relax and let Greer work her magic. Ten minutes later she pronounces my face ready for Milo. She unbuttons her lilac-colored cardigan, shrugs her way out of the sleeves, and hands it to me.

"Wear this over your . . ." She makes a face at my navy-blue SAVE THE OCEANS tee. "That thing."

"You're sure?" I ask her. "You don't think this is selfish?"

"Of course it is," she says. "But selfish isn't necessarily a bad thing. It only means you take care of yourself, and you have to do that to be able to take care of others. Now, let's get you to Crepetude."

As I follow her to the bus stop, I wonder if I'm letting Gretchen down. Maybe Greer is right. Maybe I need this break to clear my mind, to get a fresh perspective. This could be just the thing to help me figure out what to do.

I only hope I'm not rationalizing so I can hang out with Milo.

Sitting across the table from Milo an hour later, pushing my half-eaten peanut-butter-and-jelly crepe around on the plate, the guilt hits me hard. I should be out hunting for Gretchen. Not that anything useful has come from our hunting, but it feels wrong to be on a date when I could be—should be—trying.

"Earth to Grace," Milo says, a cautious smile on his adorable face. "You know they don't give refunds for the part you don't eat, so you might as well finish."

I manage a weak smile. "I'm sorry," I say. "I'm not very good company today."

"You're worried about something," he says, pushing his empty plate aside and leaning forward over the table. "Want to talk about it?"

Oh how I wish I could. I think I would feel so much better if I could just blurt out, *I'm a monster-hunting descendant of Medusa and my sister has gone missing in the abyss!* My relief would last only half a second, though. Milo would think I'm insane, that I deserve to be dropped off at the nearest nuthouse, never to be seen—or dated—again.

It's funny how, just a couple of weeks ago, I thought I *was* going nuts. Some days I wish I was.

"No," I say, forcing a smile. "I just have a lot on my mind."

I pick up my fork and lift a bite of crepe to my mouth.

"Are you worried about Thane?" he asks. "He's been gone almost a week."

There's that too.

I haven't had much time to worry about Thane, what with my immortal ancestor getting kidnapped and my sister disappearing into another realm, but I know he can take care of himself. Gretchen can too, but Thane's not fighting monsters in the abyss. He's somewhere he can still text Mom every day so she doesn't get suspicious. He'll come back to me whole, and hopefully happy. I'm not even sure how Gretchen will make it back at all.

"Yeah, I am," I say, because that's something easy to talk about. "I miss him."

I could really use my big brother right now, even if I can't tell him what's really going on. I could use his strong shoulder to lean on.

"Have you heard from him?"

"He's texted mc a couple of times." I flip open the crepe with my fork and swirl it through the peanut-butter-and-jelly filling. "He texts Mom every night. She's starting to get almost worried, but I'm doing what I can to keep her from suspecting anything."

Milo picks up his paper placemat and folds it in half. "You don't have any idea where he went? Is it somewhere in the city?"

"I honestly don't know." I watch as he folds and refolds

the paper. "He might have gone back to our old hometown for all I know."

The folds start to take shape, and I can tell Milo is making some kind of origami object.

"It's nice that you worry about Thane," he says. "Growing up, my sisters would have loved for me to disappear for a few days. They'd have divvied up my bathroom time like jackals."

I can't help a laugh. Maybe it's a pressure release, but I'm picturing three girls—with dark curls like Milo's—fighting over his precious time in the bathroom, and it just cracks me up. Milo starts laughing too, like it's contagious. I'm grateful for the light moment.

"One time," he says between laughs, "Maura snuck into my room and changed my alarm so she could have an extra fifteen minutes before school."

"They sound ruthless," I say. "Thane hardly uses the bathroom enough to count. He showers and brushes his teeth. Ten minutes max." I glance down self-consciously at my jeans and tee and borrowed cardigan, acutely aware that my hair is in a ponytail and that if Greer hadn't intervened, my face would be totally bare. "Besides, you can probably tell I'm not much of a primper."

He shrugs, focusing on his origami folds. "You don't need primping."

My cheeks burn and I feel the compliment all over.

I mumble a quiet "Thanks" and we fall into a gentle

silence, listening to the sounds of paper folding and the other diners chatting. His fingers move fast and light, folding here, tucking there. Then, with a quick pull, the mess of folds pops up into the shape of a unicorn.

"Wow!" I say, truly in awe of his skill. "That's amazing."

He pushes the unicorn across the table toward me. "It's no big deal."

"Where did you learn to do that?" I ask. I pick up the unicorn and study it, turning it around and over to see where the paper folds go.

"I was in a Japanese immersion kindergarten."

"You speak Japanese?"

"Uh, no," he says with a laugh. "The origami stuck. The language didn't."

"Well still," I say, setting the unicorn on the table between us. "It's pretty awesome."

"Then I should probably ask you out again," he says, giving me a quirky grin, "while you're so impressed."

I blush again.

"How about tomorrow after my soccer practice?" he suggests. "We could go for pizza."

Tomorrow feels a long way away. Who knows what will have gone crazy—crazier—in my life by then.

But if I've realized anything in the last hour, it's that Greer was right. This break was just what I needed to rejuvenate my energy. I feel refreshed and ready to hit the streets to find an oracle again.

Besides, Greer will be in her tea meeting until at least early afternoon. I might as well get a little more refresh time with Milo.

"Tomorrow sounds perfect," I say. "It's a date."

Sitting on the bleachers above Milo's soccer field, I hope the bright afternoon sunshine can burn away my despair. Three full days since Gretchen dived into the abyss, three days of searching the city with Greer, three nights of running my archives search and scouring the internet for anything—*anything*—that might help. And what do I have to show for my efforts?

Absolutely nothing.

To say I'm frustrated would be an overwhelming understatement.

So rather than scream like a crazy person in front of the Euclid High soccer team, I close my eyes and point my nose toward the sun. When a shadow blocks my light a few minutes later, I have a momentary panic attack that it might be another harpy.

Until Milo says, "Hey there."

I open my eyes and smile. "Hi."

"Ready to eat?" he asks. "I'm starved."

"Me too."

I grab my backpack and fall in step beside him as we head for the pizza place around the corner from the soccer field. I smile as I realize we're both wearing Chuck Taylors.

I knew we were a good match.

"What did you do this weekend?" he asks. "Other than have the most amazing crepe lunch ever."

I laugh. "Oh, I kept myself busy." Scouring the city for a mythological fortune-teller. The frustration is about to burst from me, so I decide to let it out in a manageable amount. "I'm working on this really impossible project. It's taking up all my time and I feel like I'm not making any progress."

Whew. It feels good to share even a little bit of what's going on.

"That's tough," he says. "What class is it for?"

Ooops. I didn't think that far ahead. I try to think of a subject that he's probably not taking. "Oh, um, computer science."

He whistles. "Can't help you with that one."

"Darn," I say. "And I was so hoping you were up on your JavaScript coding skills."

"I may not know about computer stuff," he says, kicking a pebble up the sidewalk as we walk. "But I am brilliant at motivation. Want some?"

"Definitely."

I smile as he stops and turns me to face him. His mint-green eyes look steadily into my silver ones. He's taking this very seriously.

"If you really want something," he says, "you go after it. Even if you think it's impossible. Even if it scares you. Even if you think it might kill you. You go after it."

I know a thing or two about scary. Especially the kind that might actually kill me. In fact, scary has been a big part of my life lately. If it's not one of the factions in the brewing war plotting my death, it's a monster pouring out of the abyss or disappearing into—

"Omigosh!"

Milo jerks back, startled.

I have an idea how to find out how to get Gretchen back.

"I'm sorry." I can't keep the huge grin off my face. "I have to go."

"Are you okay?"

"I'm great," I say. "You helped me figure out the next step of my project," I explain, hoping he doesn't ask any specific questions. "And now that I know what to do, I want to go attack it right away."

Attack being the key word.

He nods. "I understand."

He sounds resigned.

I can't leave like this. I don't want him thinking I'm ditching him, or that I don't want to be here. I do want to spend time with him, so badly. But I want to rescue my sister from the monster abyss more. And now I have an idea of how I can do that.

I'm so excited by my idea, it's like happy-filled bubbles are popping in my chest, and I act without thinking. I step forward, lean up, and plant a quick kiss on his adorable mouth.

As I pull back, my cheeks flaming with embarrassment, I see Milo's eyes widen.

"I promise," I say with as much conviction as possible. "I want to spend time with you. I want to go out every night and eat weird food I've never even heard of and make fun of bad movies and just . . . be together."

"Me too," he says quietly.

"But right now," I say, backing slowly away from him, "I have to go."

This time, when he says, "I understand," I think he really does.

With one last, beaming grin, I turn and run to the nearest bus stop. I want to call Greer immediately and tell her my plan, but she is in her tea meeting right now. Her phone will be off, so there's no point in calling. I'll be waiting when she gets out.

# CHAPTER 19

# GREER

"Greer. . . . Greer? . . . Greer!"

"What?" I glare at the source of the shouting, my alumnae tea cochair nemesis, Veronica. I am seriously over the sound of her voice.

"There is a motion to have the sugar cubes formed in the shape of a fleur-de-lis." Veronica gives me an annoyed look. "We need your vote."

"Oh," I say. "I vote yes. Fine."

She marks down the vote and starts counting them up.

I know I'm distracted. I've barely paid attention to anything that has happened during this meeting. For all I know, Veronica has resurrected her horrid ice sculpture idea and there will now be a frozen dragon at Saturday's event.

This is so unlike me. I can usually shake off anything,

focus on the task at hand, and get things done. When I put my foot down with Grace about having to be present at this meeting, I fully expected to leave my other worries at the door. I'm failing miserably.

My mind keeps drifting, trying to find a solution to the current problem. And that is not whether to have the string quartet begin with the school anthem or Ravel's *Bolero*, as the ladies around me are debating. For once, the minute details of planning an elaborate event seem trivial to me. I have more pressing, more important life-or-death matters to worry about.

I feel that the answer I'm looking for is somewhere close by. That if I just reach out—with my mind, with my fingertips, with *something*—I'll grab it. I close my eyes and try to focus my thoughts entirely on the problem. Using meditation techniques my personal trainer taught me, I visualize the problem—Gretchen in the abyss—and then a solution appearing in a sealed envelope. Mentally, I reach out and take the envelope. I break the seal, lift the flap, and pull out the paper inside. It says—

"Greer!" Veronica screeches, her whiny voice shattering my visualization into a million tiny pieces.

Enough. As much as I want to tell them to leave me alone with my thoughts, for the time being I need to focus. I need to get through this meeting, get everything on track for Saturday's big day, and then I can work on the Gretchen problem. I put the mythology half of my life into a mental box and lock it tight. I will reopen it when the meeting is over.

"Sorry," I say, still tossing a glare at Veronica for good measure. "What's the vote?"

An hour later, I declare the meeting over and I can't get out of the conference room fast enough. I've had enough color choices and garnish preferences and last-minute seating arrangement quandaries to last me a lifetime. I stuff everything into my satchel and rush out, trying to get away before anyone can stop to ask me questions—about the tea, fashion, homework, whatever.

As soon as I step into the street, I sense Grace. It's like the mythology box in my brain bursts open. I don't know how I know she's here, but I'm getting used to just knowing some things. Head whipping around, I spot her standing across the street.

"Greer!" she calls out, waving from a spot next to a streetlamp.

I look over my shoulder, relieved to see no one behind me. Yet. I wave her out of sight as I hurry across the street.

"Are you crazy?" I demand, irritation flaring. How would I explain to the tea committee about my previously unknown twin sister showing up at my school? "What if someone saw you? What if—"

"I know what to do," she interrupts. "I mean, I think I do. I have an idea how to get some answers."

"You what?"

Across the street, the front doors swing open and the rest of the committee emerges from the building. I duck down, pulling Grace with me.

"Stay low," I instruct. "Meet me at my car around the corner. Go."

I give her a gentle shove. She stays low, below the roofline of the cars lining the street. I stand and pretend to check my lipstick, giving her time to get around the corner before following.

When we're both safely in my car, I say, "You didn't have to come here. I was going to call you."

"I know," she says, sounding contrite. "But I couldn't wait."

"Okay." I nod. "Tell me about your big idea." She fidgets with the hem of her tee, not taking her eyes off her lap. "Grace," I say as I turn onto my street. "What do we have to do?"

"We need to capture a monster."

I pace the carpet in the basement rec room. Grace has spent the last twenty minutes trying to convince me this is a good idea, but I'm not so sure. Monsters are, for the most part, dangerous and deadly creatures. Especially for a pair of newbie huntresses whose dead bodies could win a couple of bounty-hunting beasts their freedom. We're a temptation for even the not-so-dangerous ones.

The idea is certifiably insane.

The problem is, it's our *only* idea.

"This is crazy," I say for the twentieth time.

"I know." She sits on her hands on the couch. "What other choice do we have?"

I drop onto the couch next to her. I run through the scenarios in my mind, trying to come up with any other plan. Nothing. This is the first viable idea we've had since Gretchen left. Grace is right, I know she's right. I just don't *want* her to be right.

The image of Gretchen, leaping into the portal, into the abyss, to save her friend, flashes through my mind. She had no thought beyond protecting her own, even at the cost of her safety. She is courageous and loyal. She would have done the same for me or Grace without hesitation. What kind of sister—what kind of *guardian*—would I be if I didn't show just as much courage when it comes to rescuing her? I might be scared—terrified—but she's my blood.

"All right," I finally say. "We can do this."

"I think I know where to find one," she says. "Gretchen told me about a kind of hotspot. An abandoned warehouse pier where she found tons of monsters over the years."

I nod. For a moment I think about suggesting something safer, like the giant spider who is the custodian at my school. But that would mean bringing the two parts of my life together, and I want to avoid that at all cost. For as long as possible.

Besides, I like Harold. I don't want to torture him for information.

"Sounds good," I say, even though it sounds terrifying. "We can bring it back here."

No one ever comes down here anymore, not since I stopped having slumber parties. Mother and Dad won't be home until late and the housekeepers only clean this room once a month. I won't have to explain why there's a monster—who looks like a man—tied up in my basement. I only hope this hunt brings us the answers we need.

An hour later, Grace and I crouch on a stack of crates outside the warehouse, peering in a filthy window.

"Holy goalie," Grace gasps.

I shake my head. "What in the world is going on in there?"

The scene before us, in the dark abandoned warehouse, is like something out of a postapocalyptic movie. The space is crowded with stacks of boxes and pallets, tarp-covered piles, and dusty forklifts. In the center of the floor there is a clearing, a square about fifty feet on each side, where there is a gathering.

Two dozen monsters of all different kinds, but all of them evil looking, stand guard around the clearing, circling the space to form an impenetrable barrier. Keeping the humans from escaping.

My heart stutters.

In the middle of the clearing, standing in very military-looking formation, perfect lines in perfect rows, are dozens of humans. Maybe more than a hundred.

They are dressed in ordinary street clothes and many of them look pretty out of shape, so they clearly aren't real military personnel. They stand, unmoving, like someone has turned off their power switches.

The creepiest part is their faces. They are completely and utterly blank, as if someone—or something—or a lot of somethings—has hypnotized them. Not only are the lights off, but nobody's home either.

Grace gasps again.

I follow the direction of her gaze, to the front of the human formation, where one of the monster guards is approaching a tall, middle-aged man who is wearing a business suit. The monster lifts the man's wrist and chomps down.

I smack a hand over my mouth.

"What is he doing?" I whisper.

"I'm not sure," Grace replies, "but Gretchen said the monsters drain human life force."

"Drain them?"

"Something about feeding on human energy gives the monsters extra power in our realm." She stares blankly through the window. "I think . . . it looks like they've *hypnotized* them."

"Curiosity killed the cat," a mocking male voice says behind us. "Killed the cat."

I turn, slowly, afraid of what I'll find.

There is a two-headed monster standing on the crate just below us. He must have snuck up on us while our attention was on the humans inside. He grins, a pair of sickening smiles, like he's just found the biggest prize ever.

One head says, "Killed the huntress too."

Grace elbows me in the ribs. I cast her a sideways glance and see her gesturing with her eyebrows. She's kind of jerking her head at the double monster below us.

She mouths, *This one.*

*Really?* I mouth back.

She nods.

I take a deep breath and sigh. Guess we've found our potential informant. And I suppose it's my job to distract the thing. I take another deep breath, reminding myself of my duty.

"I must have hit my head, because I'm seeing double," I say with a big fake smile on my face. "Double ugly, that is."

One of the beast's faces scowls in confusion while the other contorts in anger.

"Actually," I say, moving slightly to my left and stepping toward the edge of our crate, "I think you might have two of the ugliest faces I've ever seen."

The creature lunges for me. I leap down to the next crate over—grateful that I changed into flats for the hunt—trying to keep my balance and keep out of the monster's reach. The monster follows after me, turning his back on Grace.

While his attention is focused on me, Grace steps up to his back, reaches out wide with both hands, and then—*crack!* In a swift movement, she knocks the two heads together. Hard.

I dodge to the side as the creature crumples to the ground, tumbling down the pile of crates until he lands on the wooden pier with a thud.

"Perfect!" Grace squeals.

I stare down at the unconscious creature. "How are we going to get him home?"

Grace makes a face. Clearly she hasn't thought that far ahead either.

"Come on," I say, bounding down from crate to crate. "We'll figure it out."

While Grace stands guard over our quarry, I fetch my car—dent free and fresh from the body shop this morning—from its parking spot two blocks away. I lower the convertible roof. That's the only way the thing will ever fit in my tiny backseat.

I execute a quick turn and then I'm backing down the pier toward Grace. I stop in front of the still-unconscious creature.

"I tried to drag him into the open," Grace says as I climb out of my car. "He's too heavy."

"We can do it," I insist.

We each lean down and grab a shoulder. Together we manage to inch him over to my car. As we struggle to shove him up into my backseat, I say, "Sure could use Gretchen's superstrength right about now."

"Tell me about it," Grace says, panting.

A minute later we have the monster strapped into the

backseat and I'm speeding home, desperate to get him there and secured before the thing—things?—wakes up.

After I back my car into the garage, we drag the unconscious two-headed creature through the door to the rec room. We manage to hoist him up onto a bar stool. Neither of us is very skilled with knots, so we do our best to secure his arms behind him and his ankles to the legs of the stool. When we feel sure that he's not going anywhere, we step back. I take a seat on the coffee table while Grace paces. We wait.

The first sign of life is a soft groan. Grace slammed the heads together pretty hard, so they probably hurt like hell now.

Slowly, with awkward flutters, both pairs of eyes open. The beast glances around the room and, finally seeing us, affixes us with twin glares. If the creature's eyes could burn, Grace and I would be deep-fried right now.

"You'll pay for this, little huntresses," he snarls. "When I'm free, I'm coming for you first."

I'm prepared for this. "I'd be a little ticked too, if a pair of girls took me down."

One head growls.

"We're happy to let you go," Grace says, walking over to her backpack. She reaches in and pulls out the square of paper Gretchen left before diving into the portal. The oracle's note. "Just translate this for us first."

Both heads glance at the paper, at the lines of symbols that I can't read.

"What will you give me for this?" he asks.

"I told you he couldn't read," I say to Grace, taking the note from her.

"Guess we'll just have to send him home without his supper."

We both face the prisoner and drop our fangs simultaneously.

The creature's eyes widen—all four of them.

"I can read," the head on the left says. "Hold it up where I can see."

I step close enough for him to read the note but keep enough distance to avoid gnashing teeth or something equally dangerous. I hadn't expected our little game to work so quickly. I don't trust his easy acquiescence.

Slowly, he reads.

*"In the space beneath the sky, between harbor and haunted*
   *ground,*
*Where graces and muses weep at gentle water's shore,*
*Be three within three, join life with death in thee,*
*To find the lost and take up destiny."*

As the creature speaks, Grace types the confusing words into her phone. I let the strange phrases dance through my brain. They seem important—critical even—but not the answer to our current problem. It's a riddle, obviously, but to what? Leading to where? Not into the abyss to rescue Gretchen, that much is clear.

216

"Do you know what that means?" I ask the creature. "What is it referring to?"

"How should I know?" one head snarls.

"I read the thing," the other says. "Now let me go."

"Sorry," I say sarcastically, "can't do that yet."

"We have a few more questions," Grace says, putting her phone away and stepping to my side.

"Answer those," I say.

"To our liking," she adds.

"And then we might let you go."

The heads grumble, but the thing knows we have him secured. I glance at the knots just to make sure, before I keep on with the taunting.

"We need to know how to get into the abyss," Grace says.

"Why?" both heads say.

"No one *wants* to go into the abyss," one head adds.

The other echoes, "No one."

The whole creature shudders.

There is such disgust in his voices that I almost feel sorry for him, for being sentenced to life in what I'm sure is a horrible place. Then I remember that he's an evil, human-eating monster, and I don't feel quite so sympathetic.

"Well, we do," Grace says. "How do we get there?"

I dare to step a little closer. "How do we find a portal?"

"You don't *find* a portal," one head says.

"Monsters don't look for portals," the other head says. "We only go back if one of you sends us."

Well, I suppose that makes sense. From what I've seen, the creatures that come from the abyss aren't terribly eager to go back. That's why my sisters and I have to hunt them down and fill them with venom.

"Then tell us how you get here," Grace says. "Maybe if we understand that, we can figure out the reverse."

Both heads clamp their mouths tight.

I give Grace a sympathetic look. "Guess he wants to go home after all," I say.

"Yeah," Grace says. "Too bad we'll have to make it painful."

"Do you remember where the pulse point is on this one?"

Grace circles the monster. "I think so. Right"—she points at the thing's knee—"here."

"Then if we bite here"—I point at the opposite wrist—"it should take the longest for the venom to work."

Grace nods. "It will cause the most pain."

One head remains tight-lipped, but the eyes on the other widen in fear. As I reach for the wrist, he blurts, "There's a door."

"Shut it," the other head says.

"You shut it." The talkative head focuses on me. "In the abyss, there is a door."

"A door," Grace echoes. "As in *the* door?"

"Yes," the eager head nods. "The door between the realms is sealed on this side but not the other. There have always been cracks in the seal. When we step through the door in the abyss, it leads to an ever-moving portal. We never know where we'll come through in the city."

That makes sense. That's why portals keep showing up in different places, why we never know where a monster is going to come from.

For the first time, I see the benefit of unsealing this side of the door. At least then we would have only one location to guard.

"So you have no idea how to locate a portal?" I ask. "How to predict where one will show up?"

"No idea," the helpful head says.

The other one parrots, "No idea. Now be good girls and let us go."

"Oh, I think we all know that's not going to happen," I say.

What I don't realize is that, while the one head has been spilling his guts, the other has been quietly plotting. In an instant, the thing has both arms loose and is wrapping them around Grace's waist.

She screams.

I react. In a heartbeat, I'm sinking my fangs into the crea-ture's thigh.

It howls in pain but doesn't vanish immediately, and for three long seconds—which feel like three long years—I have to listen to Grace cry out as the creature tightens his grip on her.

Then, with one final screech, he's gone.

Grace crashes to the floor.

"Are you all right?" I ask, kneeling at her side.

"Yeah, I—" She turns and rests her back against the end of the loveseat. "Man, that thing had a grip."

I wipe at my mouth—the taste of whatever that was is not five-star dining—and move to sit next to her. Great. I sent away our best chances at getting answers. "I'm sorry."

"What?" she asks. "Why?"

"I just reacted." I'd seen the thing grab Grace and protective instinct took over. "I should have knocked it out again. Now we can't ask it any more questions."

"It wasn't being that helpful anyway," Grace says.

"At least it translated the note." I can't get the taste out of my mouth. "You want something to drink?"

She nods and I push myself to my feet. I run upstairs and grab a pair of San Pellegrino Limonatas, and when I get back Grace is dropping onto the couch.

"Now what?" Grace asks, wincing. She ignores her pain and pulls out her phone. She studies the translation she transcribed as the monster spoke. "It doesn't make any sense."

"I know." I sink onto the couch next to her and hand her one of the cans.

She shakes her head. "I thought for sure . . ."

"It was a good idea," I concede, popping the top on my can. "A great idea. I thought the oracle's note would help too. I think it's really important."

I down the entire beverage, relieved when my palate clears of the beastie flavor.

"Just not for this," she says, sounding defeated. "Guess we're back to square one."

I don't answer. I don't have to.

With a sigh, Grace leans to the side and rests her head on my shoulder. I reach down and pat her knee. Then, because I feel suddenly relaxed and comfortable, I let my head rest against hers.

But my mind is still on the problem. On the hope that somewhere just out of reach is the clue we need to get Gretchen home. As much as I love Grace, it's not the same with only two of us. The Key Generation is meant to be three. We have to get Gretchen back, by whatever means necessary.

# CHAPTER 20

# GRETCHEN

I think she's waking up."

"Is she still breathing?"

"What if she bites me?"

"Bited me once."

"I've never seen a huntress before. Maybe she'll—"

"Shut up!" a final, resounding voice barks. Then, quieter, "Look, give her some space. We have to see what she has to say."

I pry open one eye just as one of the earlier voices snickers and says, "Don't you mean *hear*?"

There's a soft growl and I spot the source, a golden woman who looks like she might be made out of the precious metal. Her body, clothing, even her hair is gold, cascading down her back in a solid, unmoving wave. When she turns to look

at me, the motions are robotic. Stiff.

"Hello, huntress." She smiles. "Welcome to Abyssos."

I frown. Abyssos? My voice scratches as I whisper, "Where?"

"That is the native term for this realm," she explains. "The original Greek."

"Oh," I say, my cloudy mind not quite understanding. "Okay."

"I imagine you call it the abyss."

That I understand.

Everything comes back to me in a flash. Nick, the portal, a dead monster, and almost drowning in the black lake.

"Who are you?" I ask, pushing into a sitting position. My head throbs and I pinch the bridge of my nose. "*What* are you?"

I've never seen anything like her before. All the creatures that come into the human realm are full-on creatures. Part human, part monster, part whatever. There hasn't been a robot lady—or a robot anything—since I've been hunting. There aren't any listed in the case files, either. I would remember that.

"I am a golden maiden," she says patiently. "Crafted by Hephaestus to serve at his will."

I force my headache under control and open my eyes to look at her. "But you're not . . ."

"A monster?" She laughs, making a light, tinkling sound similar to the clinking of a knife against a glass goblet. "No,

I am not. Neither are my friends, here, in the negative sense of the word. We are, however, nonhuman creatures."

She swings her golden arm wide, drawing my attention to the rest of the group gathered around me. There are a number of beings—some nearly human looking, some barely recognizable—including the unicorn I saw after I came out of the lake.

"The water," I say as my memory returns. "Something grabbed me. Something else—"

"A merdaemon," the golden maiden says. "The dark, deadly version of a mermaid. They control the waters here. They keep everything else out, guarding it for their wicked kin."

"Merdaemons," I repeat. Now those *are* in the case files. I've never had to hunt one because they can't come out of the water. But Ursula warned me that if seal carcasses ever started washing up on the beach or if surfers started disappearing, I'd have to break out the scuba gear and go deep-sea hunting.

"It had me," I say. "But something pulled me out, made it release me."

"That would be Achilla."

I follow the direction of her gaze, to a . . . person standing on the far side of the circle. I can't say whether it's a man or a woman because it appears to be half of each. The left side female, the right male.

"I am a machlyes," it says, dipping its head.

"Whatever you are," I say, giving Achilla a sincere look, "I am grateful for the help."

It looks embarrassed by the thanks and takes a step back, out of the light. The light, I notice, that is emanating from the unicorn's horn. Its bright blue glow beats back the darkness that pervades this place.

None of this makes any sense. I've never seen a unicorn before, just as I've never seen a golden maiden. Or a machlyes, for that matter. None of them are in the records. How is that possible?

I scan the rest of the circle, the seven or eight creatures gathered, and I don't recognize one of them.

"What's the matter?" the unicorn asks. "Never seen a monocerata before?"

"A what?"

The unicorn lowers its head and the light in its horn flashes off and back on. When the light goes out, everything around me plunges into inky dark. I'm not ashamed to admit my relief when the light comes back on.

"Oh, a unicorn," I say, feeling stupid but relieved. "No. I haven't."

The unicorn nickers the way I've seen horses do in movies but doesn't comment further.

"What exactly is going on here?" I ask. "I've been hunting for four years, and I've never seen any of your kinds before."

"You see me," a small voice says. Stepping out from behind the golden maiden, a small monkey—a cercopes— waves at me.

"Sillus?" I ask.

The beastie who was camped out under the Bay Bridge overpass. I feel a surge of awkwardness having to face a creature I sent back to this horrid place. He doesn't seem angry though.

"It is not surprising that you do not know us," the golden maiden says. "Our kinds are not usually allowed through the door."

"What do you mean?"

A roar, the likes of which I've never heard, rumbles from somewhere deeper in the cavern. It echoes off the rock surfaces, amplifying until I can literally feel it shaking my bones. Worse than any earthquake I've ever experienced.

"Come," the golden maiden says, stepping toward me and bending down to hand me my forgotten bundle of clothes and boots. "Let us get to a safer place. Then we will answer all your questions."

I take the bundle and quickly untie it, embarrassed to realize I've been sitting here in my underwear the whole time. I yank my pants up to my knees, then bounce to my feet to pull them all the way up. Within seconds I have my tank over my head and my boots on my feet and roughly laced, and am shrugging into my long-sleeved shirt.

"And perhaps," the golden maiden says before turning and walking away, "you can answer our questions as well."

I start after her, buttoning my shirt as I go, but the unicorn blocks my path.

"You must be tired after your ordeal," he says. "You want a ride?"

I study him. This feels like a test, like I'm supposed to prove myself. Only I'm not sure if I'm supposed to refuse and prove my independence, or accept and prove my willingness to trust. Since trust is not exactly my strong suit, I hope it's the other.

"Thanks," I say. "But I'll be fine."

He nods, not giving away anything by his reaction. I fall into step with him and the others as they make their way toward a tall crack in the rock wall beyond the lake. Sillus walks at my side, his little furry feet moving double-time to keep up. The golden maiden leads the way into the crack, and the others follow. When the unicorn is the only other one left, he nudges me toward the opening.

I face the crack, trying to remind myself that I'm not claustrophobic. Walking into a narrow, uncertain space should not leave me petrified, frozen to the spot.

"Don't make me use the horn," the unicorn says.

I twist around to look over my shoulder. Although I can't tell by looking at his horse's mouth—there's no obvious smirk—I think he might be teasing me. With no other real choice to make, I turn and step into the crack. It's dark inside, darker even than in the cavern of the abyss. But as soon as the unicorn steps in behind me, the entire place glows with a beautiful blue light. I can see now that the crack does not go infinitely up to the top of the cavern. It ends just a few feet above my head—making it a really good thing that I'm not afraid of confined spaces.

"Keep moving, huntress," the unicorn says.

"Yes, come," Sillus says. "Move faster."

As much as I don't like being told what to do, I'm squished against a narrow opening in a rock, with a unicorn behind me and a cercopes and a bunch of other creatures straight out of mythology in front of me. Arguing doesn't really seem like the best choice.

Soon the light from the unicorn's horn isn't the only thing illuminating the crack. There's an exit up ahead—thank goodness, because I'm starting to believe I was lying to myself about not being claustrophobic—and it's glowing with a soft yellow light.

When I step out into the open, I see an oasis from the dark. The yellow light glows from a massive bonfire at the center of the cave, casting a flickering light up onto the ceiling and out across the space. The ground here is softer, squishier. Like sand. There are some sad-looking plants, maybe something related to a cactus or a desert tree. A few makeshift shelters are clustered along the edge, made by leaning pieces of the trees up against a ledge in the rock wall.

There must be hundreds of creatures in this cave.

"What's this?" a gruff voice asks as I walk out of the crack.

Two sets of hands clamp around my arms as a pair of guards who look like they're carved from a polished version of the same stone that forms the cave walls hold me in place.

Neither creature—obsidian statues come to life—has eyes. But both have long spears and bulging muscles, and if they don't want to let me go, I won't be going anywhere.

Thankfully, the golden maiden intervenes. "She is under our protection. She is a huntress."

They immediately release me.

"Come," the golden maiden says, "let us go to the fire and talk."

I follow her across the sandy floor. As we get closer, I notice two unusual things about this fire. First, there is no smoke gathering below the ceiling above—there is no smoke, period. Second, even when I stand just a few feet from the licking flames, there is no heat.

"It is powered by magic," she explains to me as she takes a seat on a stone bench before the fire. "To shine light against the dark."

I sit, and Sillus sits next to me.

I stare into the dancing flames, marveling at the play of colors, at the swirling blues and greens and oranges and every color in the rainbow. It's like someone took sunlight, broke it up into its rainbow parts, and then contained it all in this fire.

It's beautiful. Far too beautiful to be part of the monster abyss.

"You have questions," she says. "I will try to answer them. But first, can you tell me how you came to be in Abyssos?"

Drawing my attention away from the beautiful fire, I look

at her. I have to figure out how to word this properly. I don't want to put Nick in any added danger. If anyone thought I cared about him more than I do, he could be at even greater risk.

"A friend of mine, he was taken. A monster stepped into my world and dragged him back into yours." I suppress a shudder at the memory of seeing Nick grabbed. "I followed after him."

"To rescue him?"

"Yes." I nod. "And for other reasons too."

She doesn't prod me for answers, waiting for me to continue.

"My mentor, Ur—" I begin, then correct myself. "The Gorgon Euryale, she was taken as well."

"Yes," the golden maiden says, "along with her sister, Sthenno."

"You know this?" Hope rises in my chest. "Then you know where they are? Where I can find them?"

"I know where the Gorgons are," she replies. "But you cannot find them. They have been taken to Olympus. To the dungeon of the gods."

She practically spits the last word. I get the feeling she is none too fond of the gods.

"You have a problem with Olympus?" I ask.

"I have no love for the gods, no," she says. "When they sealed the great door, after the guardian Medusa was slain, they had to decide who would be contained within Abyssos and who would be free to roam Olympus and Panogia, the human realm."

Until recently, I would have thought this was an easy answer. Monsters in the abyss, everyone else not. But after meeting Sillus, a harmless cercopes monkey, hearing about the friendly janitor spider at Greer's school, and now seeing these creatures here . . . Well, I'm starting to think the dividing line isn't as well defined as I used to believe.

"They decided that any creature not of wholly human appearance or godly descent would be condemned to this life." She sweeps her hand wide, shaking her head. "Even those of us with good hearts and kind intentions. Who wish only to coexist with humans and gods alike."

"You could earn your freedom," I say, testing the true goodness of her heart. "By turning me in, collecting the bounty. You could be out of here tomorrow."

"That is not true freedom." Her golden face falls. "Not when my brothers and sisters remain imprisoned."

"Can't you get out?" I ask. "Like the other creatures, can't you come through the portal?"

"There is a hierarchy here, and those with the greatest strength and darkest power are in control. We are lucky to find enough food and water to live. We could never win favor enough to be granted a release."

"Only sneaky one," Sillus says, sounding proud of himself. "Sillus get through."

We sit in silence for a minute. I can't believe it, but I

actually feel sorry for these creatures. I wish I could help them.

"We have heard," the golden maiden says, "that the Key Generation has been born. That those in power on both sides are preparing for a war over the gate." When I don't respond right away, she asks, "Is this true? Have you two identical sisters?"

I hesitate only a moment before answering. My every instinct tells me these creatures are trustworthy, and I have to trust my instincts. They're all I have in here. "Yes."

"Then you—" She turns and looks me in the eyes, her shiny gold orbs focused on me. "You are our only hope. For you and your sisters to break the seal, to resume the guardianship that is the destiny of your line. That is the only way for us and our kind to be free."

I can't really process all of this right now. The idea that so many are counting on our success—not just the ignorant humans who know nothing of the monsters that threaten their safety every day, not just my sisters and their families and our ancestral aunts, but countless creatures in here who only want a chance at a life in the light. It's a little overwhelming.

In the end, the best I can say is "I know."

She smiles, and I get the feeling she knows exactly what I'm thinking. As she pats me on the knee, her metal hand strangely cold, she says, "But you wish to know about your friend, no?"

"Yes." I nod, trying to bring my focus back to the task at

hand. "He was brought in maybe a couple of days ago, I'm not really sure, since there's no sun in here."

"Time does not pass the same in this realm anyway," she replies with a smile. "I did hear tale of a Panogian boy brought into our world. He would have been taken to the Den. I cannot promise that he is still—"

"How do I get there?" I ask, pushing to my feet. I've delayed too long already.

"You cannot go alone," she says. "It is too dangerous. Even for one with your . . . weapons."

"Weapons?" I echo. "I don't have anything special. Just a pair of daggers."

"Those are not the weapons of which I speak." She taps a finger against her mouth, metal clinking on metal.

I trace my tongue over my teeth. My fangs—which are suddenly a deadly weapon—are safely retracted at the moment. Guilt over what those fangs are capable of, over what they *have* done, washes over me.

"I had no idea," I insist. I still can't believe I actually murdered a monster. "I never meant to kill—"

"*Tsk, tsk.* It is as it is meant to be."

"Is it?"

I know what she is saying. If my venom weren't meant to kill monsters here in the abyss, it wouldn't. That doesn't make the realization any easier to accept.

She stands, the glow of the fire shining off her side in rainbow streaks. "We shall escort you as close as the line.

From there, your fate will be in your own hands."

She leaves me alone with my thoughts.

As she walks away toward a group of curious creatures—both curious looking and looking curiously at me—I ball my hands into fists in preparation for whatever I have to do. My fate—and Nick's—in my hands. Just how I like it.

## CHAPTER 21

## GREER

The solution comes to me in Contemporary Civilization. My final class of the week and we're talking about Boccaccio's *Decameron*—not exactly the most thrilling book ever written, but I usually enjoy a lively discussion about what makes a perfect form of government.

Today, however, I'm distracted. I'm doodling—something I never do—and the pattern of hypnotic swirls that appears on my sheet of notebook paper kind of draws me in. Calls to me. As I stare, the rest of the room gradually fades away, and the swirls start spinning. Around and around, until I think I might get nauseous from the motion.

Then, suddenly, the swirling stops. My vision blurs for a moment and, in a flash of light, an image appears. Crystal clear, like the object is right here in front of me where, moments ago, there were only doodles on paper.

The pendant.

Hanging before my eyes, turning gently in a counter-clockwise direction, is the oracle's pendant. The pendant of Apollo.

The one Nick said I shouldn't touch.

But everything about this image in front of me begs me to touch the pendant. It's like a craving. I need to touch the pendant more than I need chocolate, deep tissue massage, and another pair of Louboutins. That's *need*.

Maybe Nick was wrong. Maybe I'm *supposed* to touch it. Or, even if I'm not, maybe it's the clue the oracle left. The note is a false clue, or a clue to something else.

The pendant is the key.

When I reach for it, the image dissolves like fog in the afternoon sun.

My teacher is standing over me, concern creasing his brow.

"Miss Morgenthal," he says, "are you unwell?"

"What?" I feel a little disoriented, like an alien ship has dropped me off in the classroom. Then I remember where I am, where I'm supposed to be. "Oh, sorry." But right now I need to be somewhere else. I press a hand to my head. "I think I have a migraine coming on."

He nods—he's always been very caring and understanding (or maybe respectful of the family name)—and says, "Why don't you go ahead and go? We're only five minutes from the bell. You can beat the rush."

I nod gratefully.

I quickly gather up my things and try to maintain a pained look as I rush out of the classroom. As soon as I hit the hallway, I break into a run. I know my heels echo down the long corridor, but I don't care. I need to get to Grace immediately.

She has the pendant. She has the key to getting Gretchen back. She's had it all along—we just didn't know it yet. Now that we do, I feel a sense of urgency. We need to get Gretchen now. Today. Before something awful happens to her.

"Miss Greer?"

I'm almost out the front door when I hear my name being called. I turn and see Harold—the spider-monster custodian—walking toward me. I take a deep breath, focusing my vision on the wall behind him so I don't have to watch his eight legs tap-tap-tap across the floor.

"Yes, Harold?" I say with a cheery smile.

He shakes his furry head.

I force myself to stand still until he's inches away. He leans in as close as his wide stance will let him and says, "It's okay, Miss Greer. I know you can see me. I know who you are."

This is ridiculous. "I don't know what you're—"

"Others say you work to help us," he says. "You and your sisters will break the seal. Guard the door."

I imagine a loud *snap* as mythology meets real life.

"Harold, I—" Oh, really. What's the point? "Yes," I reluctantly admit. "We are."

His smile—at least I think it's a smile—is . . . joyous.

237

For a moment I think he wants to hug me, but either he realizes he's got spider legs or he notices how I stiffen and lean away, because he pulls back.

"Dangers are rising," he says. "The armies are building, training. You must take care."

This is perhaps the most surreal conversation I've ever had. "Um, thank you." I think.

"If you need help"—he leans close again, his voice urgent—"ever, anytime, you tell me. I will get word out and help will come."

I can't believe I'm about to say this to a giant spider talking and mopping, but I find myself replying, "I appreciate that, Harold."

Then, as if this isn't odd enough, I lift one hand and pat him on his furry black body.

As I'm climbing into my car a few minutes later, I'm still shaking my head. Clearly, the two halves of my life are colliding. And I'm not sure how to stop the inevitable.

# CHAPTER 22

# GRACE

The apartment is way too empty when I get home. Dad is at work, as usual lately. Mom has left a note saying she's going to the home improvement store and will be home around dinnertime. Thane is still gone.

I miss Gretchen. She is such a presence, being around her is like being in a full house.

I head to my room and plop into my desk chair.

With the Gorgons gone, Gretchen and her friend Nick—who apparently knows something about what's going on—in the abyss, and Greer and me completely clueless since the oracle's note was a bust, I feel helpless. How am I supposed to figure out how to get Gretchen back? Or break the seal on the door? Or take up the guardianship that is my destiny, that was prophesied when the door was sealed?

Is there any way for me to figure this out? I don't even know where to start.

Well, I'm not giving up. I need to approach this the way I do any other problem. Research, analyze, evaluate.

Reaching into the bottom drawer of my desk, I pull out the one piece of reference material I have. The book about the Gorgons.

I've read it cover to cover a dozen times since the loft blew up. There is a lot of information about Medusa, about her sisters, about the generations to come after them. Some things, I can tell, have been covered only vaguely, for the protection of the line. For my protection and that of my sisters.

I wish for the billionth time that I'd had the chance to start digitizing the books in Gretchen's library before it blew up. Sure, I got to most of the monster binders, and I'm sure that information will be helpful at some point. Especially when I have time to put the info into an app. But right now, I wish I had more than this lone book. More than a single source of information.

Gretchen has been gone a week and we're no closer to getting her back. I'm desperate for any possible clues.

I flip it open to a familiar page, where it talks about the Key Generation.

*Into every generation since have been born three children, three daughters to carry on the guardian legacy.*

*When the time to break the seal draws near, a time*

*predestined by the fates upon the moment of closure, the Key Generation will arrive. It will be a generation born in the same moment of the same womb.*

*The Key Generation is safe from neither the forces of supposed good nor those of confirmed evil. The children must be protected at any cost, by any measure, separated to prevent their discovery by those who wish to render the scales unbalanced.*

*Only when the Key Generation has reached maturity will the three be able to join together to break the seal, thus restoring the natural order. There are those on both sides of this war who would prevent this occurrence by any means available.*


I reread the passage several times, trying to brainstorm new ideas from old information.

Three girls. Every generation. Same womb. Separated at birth.

Same womb. Same mother.

*Mother.*

"Dummy," I blurt. "Why didn't I think of this earlier?"

Our biological mother. She must know something. She *must.* She knew enough to give us up, to separate us. She might know more. If she's even still alive or still around. Ms. West said they haven't been in contact for ages, but I might be able to find a digital trail. Even if she's not findable, there are three girls in every generation. There might be aunts and cousins out there too. Maybe they know something. Maybe they can help.

At this point, I'm willing to try anything.

Flipping open my laptop, I power it up and get ready to do some master hacking. I've gotten into the adoption records before to find Greer. Surely I can get in again, and into other databases.

Breaking through the firewall is easy. I've been there before. But once I'm inside and looking at our adoption records, things become trickier. Birth mother records are under heavier protection. Her name doesn't appear in any of our files, and when I try to search for our three names, I only come up with things I've already found.

"Come on." I tap my fingers lightly on the keys, thinking. "Be smarter than the system. Be logical."

Okay, so if there's no connection between our records and hers, maybe I'll have to search just for her. I create a search using what information I do know. I'm looking for a female, a mother of triplets, who participated in an adoption sixteen years ago. I also make a guess at her age, thinking she could have been anywhere between twenty and thirty-five when she had us.

I click *submit* and wait while the computer thinks.

Maybe this is pointless. She might have had her record wiped clean, or those who want me and my sisters to fail might have done it for her. To prevent us from ever finding her.

I get up and start pacing.

For sixteen years—or at least as many of them as I can

remember—I've known I was adopted. I've known Mom and Dad were my parents in every way that mattered. And I've never felt that desperate urge to find my birth mother. Until now.

It's not just the mythological thing either. Thinking about her, imagining her and what her life has been like since she gave us up, has made me curious. I want her help, yes, but I want to know her too.

*Beep-beep.*

I stop and turn to stare at the computer screen. Even from several feet away I can see that there is a result.

Racing back to my desk, I bang my knee against the wood as I fly back into my chair. There, on the screen, in digital black on white, is a single entry.

Cassandra Gregory

I bite my lip to contain my excitement. With a shaking hand, I reach for the mouse. When I click on the name, it takes me to a scanned profile record. The data is limited. Her age and address at the time of adoption. She was twenty-four and lived somewhere in the Mission district.

I scroll down, past dozens of empty fields. No phone number, no father's name, no next of kin, no physical description. At the bottom there is a notes field. Two comments are scribbled in that field in two different handwritings. They look like they were written years apart.

Requests daughters be given following names:
Greer, Grace, and Gretchen.

Contacted agency, requested access to adoption records. Request denied, per California Family Code § 9203.


After the second note is a date—four years ago—and a phone number. A phone number! It might not be much to go on, but people have been found using less. It's a place to start, anyway.

I've just sent the profile to my printer when I hear the front-door lock click open.

My heart pounds. Dad will be at work until late. Mom said she wouldn't be home for a few more hours. Who could it be? My imagination comes up with all sorts of possibilities, none of them good. All of them monster filled.

Since the hall outside my room leads straight to the front door, I can't sneak out and get in a better position. Instead, I press my back up against the wall next to my open door, listening for sounds of the intruder.

At first, I don't hear anything. I wonder if I imagined the sound. I was pretty focused on my search. Maybe I—

*Squeak.*

A floorboard in the hall, just outside my bedroom, creaks under the weight of a footstep. My heart punches against my chest.

*I can do this. I'm trained. I can face whatever monster has come to get me.*

I squeeze my eyes for a second, take a deep breath, and then leap out into the hallway as the intruder walks by.

*"Aaaarrrrggh!"* I scream as I land on his back, tackling him to the ground.

Using one of Gretchen's moves, I shove his face into the carpet, grab one arm, and twist it behind to his back to get leverage.

"What do you want?" I demand.

"Grace?" a deep—familiar—muffled voice asks.

I jerk back. "Thane?"

"Yes." He heaves a heavy breath. "Let me up."

"Omigosh." I release his arm and jump to my feet, quickly rushing to help him. "I didn't know it was you."

He shakes his arm and gives me a wry look.

For a moment, I just take him in. He's been gone only a week and a half, but it feels like a lifetime. He looks older. The skin around his left eye is yellow, like a healing bruise. His lower lip is split and—I glance down at his hands—so are his knuckles.

"Thane, what happened?" I reach out to take one of his hands, but he pulls away. "Were you in a fight?"

He rolls his shoulder and doesn't say anything.

When he starts to walk past me, like he's going to his room or the bathroom as if nothing's happened, I grab his elbow.

"Leave it, Grace," he says, shrugging out of my grip.

Well, doormat Grace might have let him get away with that, but she's long gone. I reach for him with both hands, wrapping them around his arm and yanking him back to face me.

He winces in pain and I almost let him go.

"You said you were going to be gone for two or three days," I say. "You've been gone a week and a half. Do you know how hard it was to keep Mom and Dad from going to Milo's to find you?"

He stands there, silent.

"I lied for you," I say, getting louder. "I covered for you."

I have the urge to punch him.

"You have no idea," I say, "what things have been like since you left."

My eyes water, and I guess that finally breaks through his tough-guy act, because he shakes off my grip on his arm and pulls me into a hug.

"I'm sorry," he says.

"Don't be sorry," I say, stepping out of the comfort of his hug. "Tell me where you were. Tell me what happened."

His stormy gray eyes are full of shadows. "I had to confront something from my past. Something that wouldn't let go of me."

"What? That's not an answer," I demand. I reach up and touch his bruised eyebrow. "Who hurt you?"

"I can't," he says, shaking his head. "I'm not proud of my past."

"You're my brother. I love you. I don't care about your past, I only care about you."

"We all have secrets, Grace," he says, with a hint of

accusation—or maybe that's me projecting my guilt about the secret I'm hiding. His gaze drops to his hands. "I have to keep mine."

I want to push him for more, to find out where he went and what he did. To make him tell me who hurt him so I can hurt them right back. But if I've learned anything in the last month, it's that some secrets are worth keeping. How can I fault him for keeping his secrets when I'm steadfastly keeping mine?

Maybe that's something I can make him talk about in the future, but at this moment, I don't care. He's home, he's mostly unharmed. That's all that matters.

"I respect that," I tell him. I lean in for another hug. "I'm just glad you're home."

He whispers, "Me too."

"Are you hungry?" I ask. "I bet you're starved. Let me see what Mom left in the fridge."

Before he can answer, I dash into the kitchen. I've just found the bowl of leftover vegetarian chili from last night when the doorbell rings.

"Got it," Thane says.

And just like that, everything is back to ordinary. As I pop the bowl in the microwave, I grin. Mom and Dad are going to be so overjoyed that he's home—even if they didn't know he went anywhere other than Milo's house. Life is going to be back to normal before I know it. Now, if we can just get Gretchen home, then everything will be perfect.

# CHAPTER 23

## GREER

When I ring the doorbell at Grace's apartment, I don't imagine anyone but Grace will greet me. I know I should have considered a scenario in which one of the other members of her household opens the door, but when the handle turns and the door swings open, I'm speechless to see a boy standing there.

His eyes are startling. A dark, stormy gray that sweeps over me like a spring thunderstorm. The look on his face—a face full of sharp lines and chiseled planes—is equally turbulent. Angry even. With his thick brows drawn into a deep scowl, it doesn't take second sight to know he's not thrilled to see me.

Oh dear. This is Grace's brother. What was his name again?

If I could go back in time five minutes, I would pull out my phone and call Grace instead of following another resident into the building and taking the elevator to her floor. I would stay on the sidewalk around the corner.

That's not an option now, though.

As lame as I know it is, I say, "Hi. I'm Greer."

He looks me up and down, his scowl deepens, and he turns and walks away. I watch his broad shoulders retreat into the apartment. Since he didn't slam the door in my face, I'm going to assume I'm welcome to follow.

I follow him to the kitchen door, where I can see Grace punching buttons on the microwave. She turns when he calls her name.

I brace myself for her reaction.

Her face drops, and I can practically feel her panic. Not that I blame her. If she'd been spotted at my school the other day, I'd have felt the same way. She recovers quickly though and gives me a little wave. "Hi, Greer."

"Grace?" her brother repeats.

She squares her shoulders, and I admire her bravery as she says, "Thane, this is my long-lost sister Greer. Greer, this is Thane."

He looks over his shoulder, the twisting motion pressing the edge of his arm against mine. Everything about him—the grim set of his mouth, the furrowed brow, the stiff stance—clearly indicates he is not happy with my presence.

I feel awkwardly uncertain. I don't have siblings—well, I *didn't* have, not ones I grew up with. I have no frame of reference for what goes on between brother and sister. I don't understand the dynamics.

"Greer," she says, "can you give us a minute?"

I nod and retreat to the living room next to the front door. Even though I try hard not to hear, some of their muffled conversation is unavoidable. Words like *blood* and *family* and *can't tell* ring clear.

All the words are Grace's. If her brother is speaking, I can't hear him.

As I sit there, trying not to eavesdrop, I can't get the image of his eyes out of my mind. Dark, gray, hard. Lonely. Longing. The image blurs and shifts, zooms out. Becomes something else.

I see him standing in the kitchen with Grace. Either this just happened, or it's happening right now.

*"She's my blood, Thane," Grace says. "My biological family."*

*"That's pretty obvious," he says. "How long have you known?"*

*"Awhile."*

*He scowls.*

*"A few weeks," she says.*

*He shakes his head.*

*"Thane . . ."*

*"I get it. I'm glad you found each other."*

*Grace hugs him. "Please. You can't tell Mom and Dad."*

*Thane says, "I know."*

*An echo of his voice says, "I already knew."*

"Greer?" Grace shakes me, pulling me out of the vision. Her eyes are puffy and her cheeks damp. A door down the hall slams shut.

I try to focus my mind, back in reality. "Are you all right?"

"Yes," she says, wiping at the tears beneath her eyes. "He's happy for me. He's just . . . shocked, I guess."

She drops down next to me on the couch. For several long moments she's lost in her thoughts. I want to comfort her, but I don't think telling her about my vision will help.

"I—" She sniffs. "I knew I couldn't keep this a secret forever. But I wasn't ready. Not yet."

And this is all my fault. "I'm sorry."

"No," she blurts, turning to face me with her whole body. "No, it's fine. I *should* have told them sooner. As soon as I found out. I was too scared, I guess. It's better that they know. Well, Thane knows. He won't tell Mom or Dad unless I ask him to."

"Will you tell him everything? Will you tell your parents?"

"How can I?" She shakes her head. "I'll have to. Someday. I just—I don't want them to worry."

I nod, but I don't really understand. If I told my parents about my heritage, my destiny, they would rush me to the nearest therapist. I'd be committed to a psychiatric ward for

251

life. They would never understand. They would never *want* to understand.

"It's okay. It'll be fine," Grace says. "So, why did you come over?"

"Right," I say, relieved to be back on solid ground. "I think I know how to get to Gretchen."

"Really?" she squeals.

"Well, I know how to figure out how to open the portal anyway."

"Okay," she says, slightly less enthusiastic. "How?"

I take a breath. "I need to hold the pendant."

"Oh no." Grace jumps to her feet. "No way—you heard what Nick said."

I rise to face her. "I know. But I had a"—I search for the appropriate word—"I guess, a vision."

Grace gives me a skeptical look.

"I did," I say. "Besides, what do we really know about Nick? What do we know about his motives? His background?"

"Gretchen trusts him."

"Yes," I say, "but even if he's trustworthy, that doesn't mean he's right. That doesn't mean he knows everything. What other options do we have?"

"I found a lead," she says quietly. "To our birth mother. Her name is Cassandra Gregory and I found a phone number from four years ago."

"That's wonderful," I say, not fully understanding the change in subject.

"We can find her," she insists. "She can help us. You don't have to take this risk."

I smile at her concern. "We don't have time," I reply. "If the number you found is old, it could take ages to find her again. If we can find her at all. *Gregory* is not an uncommon surname."

"But it's another option. I don't want your"—she wipes at tears—"brain to explode or anything."

"Grace," I say, taking her hand and looking her straight in the eyes. I feel as if I have never been more certain in my life. "Trust me."

She takes a deep breath, considering. I can read her thoughts in her expression. She's scared—for me, but also for Gretchen. She wants to do the right thing. She's just not sure what that is. I know she'll make the right decision.

Finally she says, "Okay. It's in my room. I'll go get it."

"Good." I sigh a relieved smile. "Then I think we should go to my rec room, to have plenty of space for whatever happens."

She nods. "Let me tell Thane I'm going."

"I'll wait out in the hall," I say, wanting to give her and her brother as much privacy as possible. "And when we get Gretchen home, we can start looking for our biological mother."

She smiles and heads for her room.

While she's gone, I take a moment to savor her news. Our birth mother. Cassandra Gregory. I could have been Greer

253

Gregory. Doesn't have quite the ring of Morgenthal, but I could have made it work.

A minute later, Grace is walking through the door, pulling a small cross-body bag over her head.

"Let's go."

She starts walking and I follow quickly behind. If she doesn't want to talk about her brother, I'm not going to force the issue. What do I know about sibling relationships? But I can't help wondering what that weird final echo in my vision was all about. What does it mean? Did he really already know about me, or was that some trick of my mind? I don't know enough about my power to be sure.

That's something I'll tackle after we use the pendant, after we get Gretchen back. Thane can wait; we've got a sister to save.


Grace and I sit on the floor facing each other, kind of like in a sacred circle or something. She pulls the pendant out of her bag, holding it carefully between her palms.

"You're *sure* you want to do this?" she asks.

I want to make a sarcastic quip, but I don't think that will alleviate her concerns. "Yes," I say. "I'm sure."

Holding out her shaking hands, she lets the pendant dangle. The light from the overhead fixture hits the gem, spreading golden beams throughout the room. I feel the magic drawing me closer. I take a deep breath and brace myself for whatever is to come. I reach for the pendant.

When my fingers first brush the gold, I feel a tingle. Kind of like the shock of static electricity. Just a little spark.

Emboldened, I clamp my fist around the whole thing. Instantly it feels like I've stuck my finger in a light socket. Flash after flash of pure energy jolts through me, over me, around me.

My brain swirls with the same kind of hazy image I saw earlier in Contemporary Civilization, only there is no solid object at the center. As much as I try to focus my mind, to rein in all the racing thoughts, I feel that I'm in free fall. Bursts of momentary clarity.

Knife.

Blood.

Prayer.

Then things turn darker. Amid the shadows I see glinting steel and tearing claws. Flesh shredded, bodies piled, deafening roar. It's like a vortex of blackness, of evil. And high above, I see streaks of purple and gold.

I can't draw breath. I feel like I'm drowning in air. The images narrow, shrinking down to a—

"Greer!"

My eyes flash open. Grace is screaming, leaning over me with a desperate look in her eyes. Her hands grip my shoulders, shaking me as if she's trying to bring me back to consciousness. To life.

I struggle to breathe for a minute, my eyes never leaving hers. Silver to silver. She's like my anchor, keeping me conscious and rooted in this world. Saving me from drifting back into that dark place that almost claimed me.

Finally, when I feel that I have control of myself and my mind, I say, "What?"

"What?" she echoes. "What! Are you kidding me?"

She moves off me and pulls me to a sitting position.

"You were screaming in terror," she says. "Gasping like you couldn't breathe. Your eyes rolled back into your head and—"

I place a hand over hers. "I'm fine."

"Fine?" She shakes her head. "Thanks to me. I had to yank this out of your hand."

She holds up the pendant, letting it dangle from her fingertips like a poisonous snake.

"I know," I say, pushing shakily to my feet. "Thank you."

Things are falling into place, the unconnected puzzle pieces clicking together to form a comprehensible picture.

I don't have time to think about that dark, scary place. Of where I might have ended up if Grace hadn't pulled me back. Right now, we have to save our sister.

"I know how to get to the abyss," I say. "I need a knife."

I can almost feel Grace's eyes follow me as I disappear upstairs. Moments later I return from the kitchen with a small paring knife. If I'm interpreting the visions clearly, this is what needs to be done.

"Why do you need a knife?" Grace asks.

"I'm going to open a portal."

"Then what?" she asks.

"Then . . ." I hadn't thought of that. "Then we go in after Gretchen."

"Just like that?" Her eyes widen. "We'll need supplies. Who knows what's waiting for us in there."

She's being practical. And she's right, we shouldn't go in without supplies.

I nod. We take a few minutes to gather some essentials. I retrieve a long-forgotten backpack from the depths of my closet, and we fill it with bottled water, granola bars, a pair of steak knives, and a handful of zip ties from the household toolbox. When we feel prepared, we return to the basement.

Grace pulls the backpack onto her shoulders and I grip the knife in my left hand.

Our eyes meet, we exchange a nod, and I draw the blade over my right palm. I clench my jaw to keep from wincing at the pain. I move the knife to my right hand and repeat the action, drawing a line of blood on my left palm. I toss the knife aside.

With a little prayer that this works, I clasp my two palms together.

At first, nothing happens. I stare at my steepled hands. Just the feel of blood against blood. Maybe I read the images wrong, or the images were about something else, or—

"Omigosh," Grace gasps.

I look up and see a black spot right in front of me. As we stand there, watching, the spot grows. It looks exactly like the portal Sthenno was dragged into, just like the one Gretchen dived into. It grows until it is nearly as tall as the ceiling and as wide as a set of double doors.

I take an instinctive step back.

Grace steps up to my side.

"Ready?" she asks.

Am I? I have to be. "Yes."

She takes my hand in hers and, together, we take a step toward the portal.

# CHAPTER 24

## GRETCHEN

We set out through the crack, a group of six, leaving the brightness of the cave for the darkness of the cavern. The golden maiden and I are accompanied by another pair of those obsidian-like guardians, Sillus, and a winged horse, a pegasus. The unicorn, whose name I've learned is Lex, stayed behind because the light from his horn might draw too much attention. Apparently, where we're going, staying under the radar is mission critical.

The pegasus is a majestic thing. Sleek and silver gray, his wings fold tight against his body as we walk. I remember enough of Ursula's mythology lessons to know that the pegasus is also a descendant of Medusa. This creature's ancient ancestor was born of the blood of my ancestor. I'm not sure I understand how it happened, but according to legend, when

Perseus chopped off Medusa's head, Pegasus flew out of the blood that dripped from her neck. It is amazing that something so beautiful can rise from such an evil act.

"You were traveling in the correct direction," the golden maiden says. "The Den is far downstream from here, at the place where the dark river falls to a great depth at the edge of Abyssos."

"The edge?" I ask. "There's an end to this thing?"

She pauses before answering. "Of a sort."

"What—"

"Quiet," one of the twin guards says.

We all freeze and drop low to the ground. The pegasus moves close to my side and lifts his wing, urging me into his protection. I'm not usually one to accept help, but when I hear the footsteps, even I know it's best to stay out of the way.

They are countless. Like the sound of an entire army marching by. The echoes draw closer and closer until it sounds like they are walking right over top of us. The protective wing tightens around me.

But I manage to push forward and peek out around the pegasus's chest. The mass of bodies, walking in tight formation, is huge. There must be hundreds, at least. I watch in silence as they march upstream, disappearing around a bend in the canyon. None of us says anything until the last of the echoes dies down.

"Clear," the guard says.

Everyone exhales and returns to standing positions. As we get moving, I ask, "What was that?"

"Nychtian Army," Sillus says.

"Army?" I echo.

"The Army of the Night," the golden maiden says. "The force that plans to take over Panogia."

"What do you mean?" I ask.

"The dark creatures of Abyssos wish to have free, unregulated access to the human realm," she explains. "The only way to do so is to attack the guardians once the seal is broken." She gives me a sad look. "They train now to overtake you and your sisters, to kill you so the door may remain open wide for eternity."

My stomach churns at the thought of that army taking on me and my sisters. Fighting monsters one or two or even five at a time is manageable. But an entire army?

"That seems like a pretty big army," I say, forcing the words out through a dry mouth. "Seems like overkill to send that to take out three little girls."

"You are no ordinary girls," the golden maiden says.

"More army still," Sillus says. "Humans fight too. Monsters hypnotize."

"Hush, Sillus," the pegasus says. "You will frighten her."

Too late. "Humans?" I ask. "They're hypnotizing humans to create a second army?"

The golden maiden nods, a sad smile on her face. Like she can already picture our defeat. She doesn't know me very well. Or my sisters. We won't go down easy.

"What's the point?" I ask. "Even if they succeed, couldn't the gods just reseal the door? Couldn't they wind up just as badly off as they are now?"

She shakes her head. "The original sealing ritual was very specific."

"Only three outcomes are possible when the Key Generation arrives," the pegasus says. "The triplets open the door and take up the guardianship."

"Keys open door," Sillus adds, "and leave unguarded."

"Or they seal the door," the golden maiden finishes. "For all eternity."

There is something about the way she says that, about the third option, that sends shivers down my spine. From my perspective, it doesn't seem like such a bad idea to seal the door. Makes my job, my life, a whole heck of a lot easier. Clearly it's not that simple.

"What happens if we seal the door?" I ask, almost fearing the answer.

Her golden eyes fill with dark tears. "Every creature in Abyssos dies."

The air in my lungs whooshes out and I feel hot and shaky all over. I look around at the creatures who are helping me, who are treating me like a friend and not a deadly enemy—even knowing I can kill them with a single bite. Even knowing I hold their collective fate in my hands. The reality that they would die, all of them, without consideration, is unthinkable.

If the run-in with the laestrygon taught me anything, it's that I'm a huntress, not a killer.

"I won't let that happen," I say. "I promise."

They look skeptical, but they don't know me. They don't know I don't make promises lightly. If I promise something, then I make sure it happens. My actions will show them the truth.

"I promise," I say again. "But right now, in order to get back with my sisters and do whatever we have to do to break the seal, I need to find my friend and get out of here."

"Of course," the golden maiden says.

As we resume the long trek to the Den, I make a mental vow to do whatever it takes to make sure the door doesn't get eternally sealed.


"What in Hades is that?" I whisper.

We've just crested a rocky hill, and on the slope below is a long line of monsters. Every creature known to man and mythology stands like it's waiting at the DMV or something.

"Line," Sillus says.

I throw him a look that says, *I can tell it's a line.*

Pegasus says, "That's the line to get out. For the next window into your realm."

I close my eyes and shake my head. There are so many. Countless. And they are all waiting to get out into my world, to attack humans, to hypnotize them, to hunt my sisters.

"How often does the portal—the window—open?" I ask.

"It used to happen quite rarely," the golden maiden says. "Perhaps once every two or three days in your realm. But recently—"

"It's been more frequent," I finish. "Yeah, I've been facing more and more beasties lately. And more than one at a time."

"That is because the time draws near," Pegasus says. "The Key Generation is reunited, which means the original ritual is weakening. The magic is falling off in preparation for the new era."

"In preparation for you," the golden maiden says.

"Soon," Sillus says, "monster after monster get out. Too many for huntress to fight alone."

"He's right," the golden maiden says. "Unless you and your sisters break the seal and initiate the next stage of the prophecy soon, the veil between our worlds will continue to dissolve away."

"Until the day the door is sealed forever," the pegasus says. "And any creature trapped within will die."

"Great," I mutter. "No pressure."

I stare out over the endless line of monsters, just waiting their turn to go cause mayhem in my world. They want to build up the greatest army possible, so that once my sisters and I break the seal they can kill us, leaving the door open and unguarded. When we do that, when we open the door, we'll be attacked from both sides. Overwhelmed by monsters streaming out of the abyss and those already positioned in the human realm, with their hypnotized human army at their side.

At the moment, I can't imagine how we might win. Even with help from the good monsters and the Gorgons, gods, and minor deities who want us to succeed, it seems impossible.

I wish my sisters were here with me. Or Ursula. Or even Nick. Someone, anyone who knows what's going on and who can guide me through this stuff I have to do.

I feel a cold palm on my shoulder. I twist my head and find the golden maiden looking down on me with wise, encouraging eyes. "We believe in you, Gretchen Sharpe," she says. "We have been awaiting your arrival for a long, long time. Whatever we must do to help you succeed we shall do."

I feel instantly better. She's right. I have to get out of my own head about this, I have to keep perspective on the situation. There are a lot of creatures—some good, some bad, some caught in the crossfire—relying on me and my sisters to get our acts together and figure things out. No point in standing around worrying about how I'm going to make that happen. First I have to get home.

"Right," I say. "Let's get moving."

"This is as far as we dare go," the golden maiden says. "To venture farther at your side will only increase the danger. Our numbers make you too conspicuous. And you may need to move faster and with more agility than we are capable of."

I glance around at the group, at the maiden's gleaming golden body, the giant feathered wings of the pegasus, and the massive bodies of the obsidian guards. They are kind of a presence. They don't look like they could move too quickly, or nimbly either.

"I go with," Sillus offers. "I blend."

I almost laugh. What is a little monkey monster going to do to help me? But when I see the proud, determined look on his furry face—and the way his arms are shaking at his sides—I can tell how seriously he takes this.

"Thank you, Sillus," I say. "I appreciate the help."

"The Den is beyond the line." The golden maiden points to a place where the rocky wall juts out into the cavern. "On the other side of that formation you will find a door. There is usually a single guard, a cacus."

A fire-breathing giant. I've taken down at least five in my hunting history. One more shouldn't be much trouble.

"Thank you." I offer my hand and am surprised when she pulls me into a hug.

"No," she says, squeezing me. "Thank *you*."

As I turn to walk away, she stops me.

"You will not fight alone," she says. "When the day of prophecy comes, you will have help. In this realm and in yours."

I nod, surprised by how relieved that makes me feel. My sisters and I won't be on our own. The knowledge gives me hope.

Sillus and I turn and head down the hill while the others stand on the crest and watch from above. We keep to the boulders and outcroppings as much as possible, but when we get to the bottom, there is nowhere left to hide.

I crouch down, hoping my dark clothes blend into the rock around me. The line extends in both directions: to the left for as far as I can see; to the right, it winds around to a small cave opening. That must be the door.

I can hear the roar of falling water, at the cliff where the river spills off into nothing.

"How am I going to get through that line?" I wonder out loud.

Who knows how long it could take to go around? The line could go on to infinity. Time is of the essence.

"No worry," Sillus says. "Sillus distract."

I look at the monkey skeptically. He is one tiny cercopes, and they're a whole bunch of big and nasty.

Before I can voice my concern, he's taking off toward the line. He whisper-shouts back over his shoulder, "You watch! Take opening!"

I growl to myself and get into a ready position. I have no idea what the little nut has planned, but if he succeeds, I need to be able to act fast.

He approaches the line, scrambling up to the biggest, nastiest thing there. A Hesperian dragon. The one time I had to take on one of those, it nearly beat me. They're crazy strong and just pure crazy, with a hundred heads. They fight like beasts with nothing to lose.

Sillus sneaks up behind it—drawing the attention of several other monsters that point and laugh—and then jumps on its back. He climbs up the big, nasty body, wraps his monkey legs around one of the necks, and covers the beast's eyes with his little hands.

Within seconds I see what Sillus has planned. The Hesperian dragon roars loud enough to shake the cavern and starts flailing around wildly. It knocks into monsters on all sides of it, beasts that don't appreciate being shoved around, even by something as terrifying as a Hesperian dragon. They're not terrified. They shove back, and shove into one another, and soon the entire line has erupted into chaos.

Sillus holds on for dear life, and the increasingly furious Hesperian dragon swings its other ninety-nine heads wide, sending creatures all around to the ground, creating a circle in the midst of all the fighting.

My opening.

I jump to my feet and take off at a dead sprint. I make a beeline for the circle, trying not to think about the sheer number of blood- and huntress-thirsty monsters around me. I make it to the line just as the gap is starting to contract. Then I'm through, racing on the other side and scanning the area for some cover. I spot a pile of rocks to my right, directly across from where the golden maiden said the Den should be.

Ducking behind the pile, I press my back up against the

rocks and suck in breath after breath. It's like breathing fire, in and out. My lungs are starting to calm down when Sillus appears in front of me.

"See," he says with a giant grin. "Sillus distract."

"That you did," I say, my voice breathy as I work on my recovery. "How'd you get out of there?"

He shrugs. Needing to witness this for myself, I peer around the rocks and see the Hesperian dragon on the ground, unmoving. Several other monsters are tying its necks together in bunches of three or four.

Looking across the space I just ran through and back up the hill, I see the faint glimmer of the golden maiden. They're still watching.

When I turn back, Sillus is gone and I'm staring at a pair of big, blackened feet that look as though they've been soaking in charcoal. Following the feet up the legs, waist, and torso to the hideous face on top, I realize I'm in big trouble. The cacus.

"Uh-oh."

It grins, showing rough, uneven teeth with dark growth along the gums. It bends down, grabs me around the arms, and hauls me over its shoulder.

Well, at least now I don't have to figure out how to get into the Den. The cacus is taking me there.

"Found this lurking outside, boss," the cacus says as he drags me into what looks like an office.

The walls are the same black, shiny rock as the rest of the abyss. But ceiling lights illuminate the space, so I have no problem making out the old metal desk and the telchis sitting in the burgundy leather desk chair, his slobbering pit bull head drooling all over his own chest while his seal flippers smack together enthusiastically.

Nor do I miss the boy sitting in one of two bright-orange fiberglass chairs facing the desk.

"Nick?"

All my worst imaginings flash through my mind. Nick being tortured for information. Nick being torn to pieces by a mob of angry monsters. Nick being cast into the fires of Hades.

But Nick sitting in the boss's office, casual as can be with a glass of what looks like iced tea in his hand? That never even crossed my mind as a possibility.

When he sees me, his demeanor changes. He looks scared. Not of the monsters in the room. He's scared of me. Why?

"What's going on here?" I ask.

"You two know each other?" the boss asks. "How wonderful. You've been doing your job well, Niko."

"Job?" I echo. "What job?"

"Gretchen, it's—" Nick doesn't finish, but he doesn't have to. The boss does.

"Niko here is one of our agents," he says, sounding like a proud father. "One of our best."

"Agents?"

Everything inside me goes still.

"Sent to find you, get close to you." He glances from me to Nick. "Seduce you if he had to."

I feel like retching. Right here, on the boss's desk. If I'd had anything to eat in the last few days, I just might have.

Betrayal like I've never felt before turns my body to ice. There's nothing to say. I clench my jaw and stare at the rough black wall behind the boss's head.

"What you want me to do, boss?" the cacus asks. "Toss her over the edge?"

"No, you idiot. We need her alive." The boss pushes himself to his feet, and I see that from the waist down, he isn't as human as his torso would suggest. On clacking goat hooves he rounds the desk and steps up close to me. So close, I can smell his putrid breath.

Disgusting. Dog head, human chest, flipper arms, and goat legs. That's one messed-up family tree. Or should I say family zoo?

"We need her and her lovely sisters to open the door," he says, taking a loose chunk of my hair between his fingertips. "Then we can kill them."

I let the saliva build in my mouth for a second before spitting in his face.

His fingers clamp down on my hair and yank. Hard.

"Ow!" I can't stifle my scream.

Nick lurches out of his chair. "Don't—"

The boss smacks a flipper against Nick's chest, keeping him at a distance.

"This is between me and the pretty huntress," the boss says. "You stay out of it."

"I don't need a rescuer," I say, forcing myself to show more boldness than I feel at the moment. "I can take care of myself."

I can't—won't—look at Nick, but I sense him backing off.

"I'm sure you—"

The boss doesn't finish his sentence before the door to the office flies open. Sillus appears in the doorway. With about half a dozen monsters at his back.

"There," he says, pointing at the boss. "Him."

I don't know what Sillus told the beasts, but they all lunge for the telchis. The guard releases me to protect his boss from the onslaught. Sillus jumps on the guard's head, just as he did with the Hesperian dragon in the line.

"Go!" he shouts, pointing at the door.

I nod.

I grab Nick, holding his upper arm in a death grip, and run. I'm not leaving the traitor to commiserate with his handlers, to tell them any more than he already has about me and my sisters.

I want the chance to interrogate him myself.

Sprinting from the office with no real idea of what I'm going to do once I get outside, I'm stunned to find the pegasus waiting for me.

"Get on, cousin," he says, looking nervously over his shoulder toward the line. "The portal is about to open."

The pegasus curls his front leg back, holding it like a step, and I shove Nick toward him.

"Get on," I say in a tone that is intended to let him know there is no other option.

It must, because he places his foot on the curled leg, swings onto the winged horse's back, and reaches an arm down to help me up. Ignoring his arm, I grab a handful of mane and yank myself up in front of him.

Sillus comes running out of the office looking very pleased with himself.

"Hurry!" I shout, holding out my hand to him.

He takes a leap and grabs my hand, and I settle him on the horse, right in front of me.

"Let's go!" I shout.

The pegasus spreads his wings out wide and, with one strong flap, draws us into the air. It is a strange sensation, to be flying through the air on the back of a horse. But as the monsters below notice us, I'm glad to have several feet of space between us and them.

Soaring over the monsters, toward the front of the line, the pegasus glides for the portal cave. As we get closer, I see the cave start to swirl and glow with a bright sky-blue spot in the center.

Just like the black portal in my world, this one grows and expands to a size large enough to accommodate the largest monster. Or, hopefully, a Pegasus with a full load.

The monsters below point and roar, and the one at the front of the line turns just as we fly by. He reaches for us but misses.

Then we enter the portal and the abyss disappears behind us.

CHAPTER 25

# GRACE

From a distance, the portals into the abyss always looked pretty dull. Big, boring black splotches in space. Like a piece of contemporary art or a flaw in an old photograph. But up close, staring at one right in front of me—and about to walk into it—they're a little terrifying. A great vacuum, an emptiness that makes me feel despair just looking into it.

I squeeze Greer's hand.

We step forward together, ready to face whatever shadows await in order to save Gretchen.

Before we get close enough to step inside, there's a low rumble—like the sound of waves crashing against rocks. Greer and I exchange a look, surprised by the sudden change. Then, before we can move or speak or do anything, a giant silvery horse flies out of the portal.

*"Whaaa!"* I scream, shoving Greer to the side as I jump in the opposite direction, out of the path of the flying beast.

"Whoa!" a girl's voice shouts.

I stare up at the horse, his giant wings thumping against the ceiling as he lands. Sitting on his back, looking a little gaunt but otherwise safe and whole, is my sister.

"Gretchen!" I shout.

Jumping to my feet, I feel a smile take over my entire face. She beams down at me.

"Grace?"

"Hello, Gretchen," Greer says from the other side of the horse.

Gretchen slides to the floor, pulling a body down with her. Nick. He looks unconscious, his arms bound by a pair of sturdy zip ties. There's a red mark, about the size of a fist, on his temple.

Gretchen tosses him aside like a bag of garbage. She looks up at the winged horse—a pegasus, I realize. "I wish I could let you stay."

The horse whinnies. "I understand. A horse wandering the streets of San Francisco wouldn't get far."

My jaw drops. Not at the talking horse—I've seen a lot of crazy stuff since Gretchen found me in that nightclub, so an animal capable of perfect English isn't too shocking—but at Gretchen being nice to a creature from the abyss.

The pegasus lowers his head, offering his neck to Gretchen. She hesitates and says something quietly into his ear before giving him a quick bite right below the mane. In a flash he's gone.

A little monkeylike creature that had been sitting on the horse's back crashes to the ground. He jumps up to his feet.

"Sillus stay," he says. "Sillus help."

Gretchen looks like she's considering, like she really doesn't want to send him back with the pegasus. The Gretchen I first met a few weeks ago wouldn't have hesitated. But in the end she shrugs. "Okay, but the first sign of mischief and you're back in Abyssos."

"Abyssos?" I ask.

"Abyssos is the true name of the abyss." Gretchen turns to me. "I missed you two."

Her silver eyes cloud over, as if a thick bank of fog has rolled in and shadowed her inner sunlight. I know how much it must have taken for her to admit that. I step forward and wrap her in a hug. She may not want one, but she clearly needs one.

Gretchen awkwardly pats me on the back. Then, in an uncharacteristic moment of emotion, she gives me a brief squeeze. She's stepping away before I can squeeze back.

"I take it you learned something about him," Greer says, indicating Nick's unconscious lump. "Or did someone else land the punch that knocked him out?"

Gretchen's scowl says everything.

"He's no protector," she says. "He was sent by the monster side to watch us, to help us until we open the door."

"And then?" I ask.

"Then, I assume, he'd help them kill us."

Greer frowns, twisting her head to the side. "Are you certain?"

Gretchen doesn't respond, but the set of her jaw indicates the end of discussion. "How long was I in?"

"An entire week," Greer answers.

"We were just about to come in after you," I say. At Gretchen's confused look, I explain, "Greer figured out how to open a portal." I'm proud of her even if the prospect of stepping into the abyss nearly scared me to death.

"Where are we?" Gretchen asks.

"In Greer's basement," I answer.

"No one comes down here," Greer adds. "Not anymore."

"Good," Gretchen says. "I need a chair. Something I can tie this traitor to while I interrogate him."

I'm a little shocked at the venom in Gretchen's tone. Then again, she doesn't trust easily, but she was starting to trust Nick. She thought he was someone she could rely on, and Gretchen doesn't rely on many people. I'm sure his betrayal cuts deep.

"How about a bar stool?" I suggest.

Gretchen shakes her head. "I want to be able to tower over him. I want the physical advantage."

Greer says, "I'll get one."

While Greer goes to get the chair, I ask, "Are you okay?"

"Fine," Gretchen says. Then, as if she remembers that

we're sisters, allies, she softens. "Hungry, actually. Haven't had a thing to eat in days."

"Of course." I can't begin to imagine what she's been through. Hopefully one day she'll tell us. Now isn't the time. "I'll get you something."

I turn to head upstairs to the kitchen.

"Grace," Gretchen calls as I reach the door. When I turn back, she says, "Thanks."

I rush back across the room and fling my arms around her again. "I'm so glad you're back," I say against her shoulder. "I'm so glad you're safe."

She pats me once on the back, and I know she feels the same way. Before I embarrass her by making her emotional, I head for the stairs. As I climb up to the kitchen, I hear her yell at Sillus, "Get off that, you little monkey freak!"

I smile. Now that Gretchen is back, I know everything is going to be fine. Whatever changed while she was inside, we'll get through it. We'll figure it out. Together.

## CHAPTER 26

# GREER

There is a stack of extra chairs in the storage room off the garage. Mother does not allow even our storage space to have an ounce of dust or clutter, and every inch is perfectly organized, labeled, and accessible. The chairs are in the back, and I weave my way between precisely stacked boxes of cocktail party supplies and winter clothing and Dad's grad school papers.

I'm almost near the chairs when a wave of dizziness hits me.

This isn't a gentle fuzziness, like if I've forgotten to eat or haven't had enough sleep. This is like a tsunami wave of numbness, and for a moment I think I'm going to faint.

I brace myself against a stack of boxes. When I close my eyes, I don't see the darkness of my lids, I see Grace's brother, Thane. He's standing in front of a mirror, shirtless. Three

jagged lines are carved into his chest, running from one shoulder to the opposite hip. After soaking a cotton ball in green liquid, he dabs it on the wounds. He winces and I reach out instinctively to ease the pain.

Then, just as quickly as it came, the dizziness is gone. The image of Thane is gone. I'm staring at my own eyelids, leaning against a box in our storage room.

It was such a strong, clear image. My stomach lurches back into place and my entire body is covered in goose bumps.

I take a deep breath and try to shake off the unsettling feeling. I struggle to bring myself back into the here and now. When I feel in full control of my brain and my body again, I continue to the chairs. Pulling one off the top of the stack, I carry it out of the storage room and back to the rec room.

Grace arrives moments later, a plate of leftovers in one hand and the bottle of mandarin orange soda in the other. I want to ask if her brother has those wounds on his chest, but . . . I can't. Besides, she might not even know.

Gretchen takes the food and tucks in, devouring it like a starving animal. I quietly carry the chair to the center of the room and set it down next to Nick.

I have no idea what happened to me in the storage room, but clearly it was a vision of some kind. Could my second sight be improving? I can't be certain what triggered it, but I've never had such a clear, realistic feeling before. Maybe it has something to do with the pendant. With its connection to Apollo. Touching it didn't send me into a coma. Maybe it amplified my powers or brought them closer to the surface. I'm relieved that Grace has it back safely in her possession. Until we can learn more about it, it's probably best if I don't come into contact with the powerful object again.

When Gretchen has cleaned the plate of food and chugged half the bottle of soda, she walks over to the chair. With her superhuman strength, she easily lifts Nick up to the seat.

"Help me resecure his wrists," she instructs.

Pulling a dagger from her boot, she slices through the zip ties. His arms fall limp at his sides. She grabs one and drags it around behind, pulling out a fresh zip tie and strapping his wrist to the back of the chair. She hands me another tie, and I do the same with his other arm.

Grace watches as we secure his ankles to the front chair legs and step back.

"How soundproof is this room?" Gretchen asks.

"Quite," I say. "Mother had the entire room re-insulated after my first slumber party. The noise was too—"

"Good," she says.

Taking a step forward, she swings her arm wide and slaps Nick square on the cheek. When that gets no response, she repeats the action. This time he groans but doesn't regain consciousness.

The dizziness hits me again. I grab the back of the chair to keep from crashing to the ground. This time, the image is of an analog clock face. The hands spin, zooming past hours in mere seconds. When the big hand has made several complete circuits of the clock, the image dissolves, replaced by one of Nick sitting in the chair. He shakes his head and his eyes blink open.

Then the image and the dizziness disappear.

"I—" I shake my head. "I don't think he's going to wake up for a few hours."

Gretchen nods. "Probably not. I hit him pretty hard."

Grace gives me a curious look, and I ignore it.

"Can I crash here?" Gretchen asks. "I'm exhausted, but I want to be around when he comes to."

"Of course," I say automatically, shifting into hostess mode. "Let me get you some bedding."

"Don't worry about it," she says. "I'll be fine with that blanket on the couch."

I want to argue—every etiquette-ingrained bone in my body screams, telling me to make her a comfortable bed—but frankly I don't have the energy. I feel drained. I don't know if it's that I'm still exhausted from holding the pendant or the act of opening the portal or the weird dizziness I've been having ever since, but I feel like I've been awake for a week.

"Actually," I say, "I think I could use a nap as well."

"Can I stick around? I don't feel like going home right now," Grace says.

She doesn't say as much, but I think she wants to give Thane some time to process her news.

"Of course," I say. "Make yourself at home."

"Can I use your computer?" she asks. "I have some research I want to do."

"Research?"

She gives me a meaningful look.

"Oh, research." As in tracking down our biological mother. "You can use the laptop in my room. I'll show you on my way to a long, steaming-hot bath."

"Great," Gretchen says as she drops onto the couch. Balling the blanket up like a pillow, she stretches out and closes her eyes. "Catch you later."

The little monkey creature curls up at her feet and follows her into slumber land. Long-lost triplet asleep on the couch, mythological monkey monster right there with her, and descendant of a goddess unconscious and tied to a chair. Clearly, the amount of normalcy in my life is severely limited at the moment.

I lead Grace up the basement stairs, through the house, and up the two flights to my room. She remains unusually quiet the entire way.

"There's my laptop," I say, pointing to the open computer sitting on my desk. "The password is greerthegreat, all one word, lowercase."

"Thanks," she replies quietly.

I can tell she has something on her mind, so I take my time gathering my clothes for after my bath. I'm just folding my cashmere lounge pants onto the pile with my silk

284

camisole when she says, "I'm so glad she's home."

"Me too."

"I'm glad we didn't have to go into that place," she continues. "Does that make me a coward?"

"No," I say, setting my clothes on the bed and crossing to her side. "That makes you brave. Because you were scared and willing to go in there anyway."

She smiles. "I guess so."

"And you're not alone." When she looks up I smile. "I was terrified too."

Her shoulders relax and I feel like I've done a good deed. I made her feel better, and that—I'm surprised to admit—makes me feel better. Maybe I'm getting the hang of this sister thing after all.

As Grace takes a seat at my desk, I grab my clothes and retreat to the bathroom. Steam billows through the room as hot water fills the pristine claw-foot tub. Moments later, I'm sinking into heaven, surrounded by the scent of jasmine bubble bath.

My eyes are already closed when the dizziness hits. I smile when an image of the Immaculate Heart gym, transformed into a dreamy paradise for the alumnae tea, drifts through my mind. I'll take a vision like that any day. And tomorrow I will make it a reality.

## CHAPTER 27

## GRETCHEN

Moaning. I wake to the sound of moaning, and for a few groggy moments, I think I'm back in the abyss. That entire place moaned.

But the surface beneath me is soft, padded, not rock-hard stone. The air is cool but not cold. The smell is tolerable. Nothing like the abyss. And my stomach isn't trying to gnaw its way out of my body.

Dragging my eyes open, I see the smooth white expanse of a ceiling, not green glow against shiny black rock.

Definitely not the abyss.

I roll upright and remember where I am—Greer's basement—and why.

Halfway through the portal, Nick started trying to explain what happened. Spewing garbage. How I was misinterpreting

the situation and he was really on my side and if I would just listen to him—

I turned around and punched him above the left ear. He slumped forward against me, and by the time we emerged in this realm, I had his hands zip tied.

In the chair at the center of the room, Nick's head is lolling back and forth, like he's struggling to regain consciousness. I need to establish my advantage quickly. Scanning the room to memorize the objects and their locations, I reach up and flick off the table lamp next to the couch. The room plunges into blackness. Darker, even, than the abyss, because my eyes are light blind.

"What happen?" Sillus asks.

"Ssssh." I forgot about the silly monkey. How had I missed him in the scan? He must be curled up in hiding somewhere. "Stay where you are. And stay quiet." He doesn't respond, so I assume he's taking my order seriously.

The couch squeaks as I push to my feet. Nick's moaning stops. I stealth-walk across the carpet, careful not to let my heels thud against the floor.

"Gretchen?" Nick's voice sounds rough and raspy.

I should have gagged him.

By now I'm standing over him, looming above him from behind. My eyes are adjusting to the faint glow of light seeping in beneath the door and I can see him try to twist in his chair.

The zip ties keep him in place.

"Gretchen, come on," he says, yanking at his binds. "I know you're here."

He struggles a little more and then must realize the futility of his attempts. He stills and, I think, sniffs the air. He turns his head to the side and I can almost feel his dark eyes rake over me.

"I can smell you," he says.

I lift my foot and kick the back of his chair, sending him thudding face-first into the floor. Unfortunately Greer's parents splurged on extraplush carpet. That probably hardly hurt him at all. The weight of the chair holds him down, but I rest my foot against the seat anyway.

"Let me explain," he says, his voice muffled against the carpet.

"Explain what? How you tricked me?" I shove my weight into the chair. "How you lied to me? Made me trust you? When, all the while, you were getting ready to betray me? To kill me and my sisters?" I shove the chair again, harder, and am satisfied when he grunts in pain. "Yes, please, explain that to me."

As if he could say anything—*anything*—to justify what he did.

"I'm a mole."

I jerk back. My foot falls to the floor.

"What?"

"A mole," he says. "Gretchen, I'm a double agent."

I reach down, wrap a hand over the back of the chair, and

pull it—and Nick—upright. The chair is still rocking to a standstill when I walk over to the door and throw the light switch, flooding the room with bright light.

When I turn back around, Nick is watching me. There's a red spot on his forehead that I'm sure is going to turn into a nasty bruise. Good. It'll go with the one darkening on his temple.

"Tell me," I say, crossing my arms and leaning back against the door. "Tell me everything."

He nods, his dark-blue eyes serious.

"You remember I told you about the factions," he begins, "about the two groups waging a war for control of the door? For control of the Key Generation?" I just stare at him. Of course I remember. "Well, there is a third faction. A group that wants neither of those things."

"Sthenno told us about them," I say. "Before your friends kidnapped her."

"They aren't my friends," he says, snarling. "That third side, the one that wants a return to balance. That's the side I'm on. We want the door opened and the guardians in place." He takes a deep breath and sighs. "We want the world back as it was meant to be."

"Who?" I demand. "Besides you and the Gorgons, who's on that side?"

He shakes his head. "I can't identify everyone involved. I honestly don't know. I've been undercover for a long time."

"Wrong answer." I start for him.

"But," he says, giving me a pointed look, "I can tell you what I know."

I return his pointed look.

"Euryale and Sthenno are the leaders."

"Welcome to yesterday's news," I say. "Tell me something I don't know."

"There are at least three Olympians, maybe four, on your side." He shakes his head. "On *our* side."

"Name them."

"I—" He starts to refuse but then changes tacks. "Hermes is the only one I know for certain. I think Demeter is another one. Maybe Aphrodite, but the gods are so good at falsities and double-crosses, I can't be sure."

"Sounds like someone I know," I mutter.

He ignores that. "Only the Gorgons know for certain."

"Well we can't ask them now, can we?"

It makes sense, though. With opposing sides wanting me and my sisters dead—either before or after we break the seal—Ursula and Sthenno knew we would need real power at our backs. That's reassuring, at least. Especially after what I saw in the abyss, the numbers on the monster side.

"So they sent you?" I ask. "The Gorgons asked you to go undercover in the monster world?"

"Not directly, no," he says. His eyes shutter. "I received my orders from Hermes, and I am acting on their behalf."

"What was your mission, exactly?"

"To infiltrate the monster faction. To become a trusted

member of their organization, to learn sensitive information about the Nychtian Army I could then relay to my contact."

"And how does befriending me get you that information?"

"It doesn't." His head droops a little. "I was too good at my job. The monster faction asked me to go undercover as well. After Euryale was taken, they sent me up here to keep tabs on you."

"You knew?" I push away from the door, intent on shoving his face back into the floor. "All this time you knew they had Ursula, and you didn't tell me?"

My hands are on his shoulder, ready to drag him to the ground, but the pained look in his eyes stops me.

"It's . . . complicated. There is so much riding on my success. How could I tell you without blowing my cover?" He shakes his head. "I wanted to tell you, to reassure you or help you or even fight by your side. I believe in your destiny," he says, "more than anything else. As much pressure as you feel to live up to your legacy, I feel just as much to make sure you can. I couldn't risk losing what advantage I'd gained."

I don't want to believe him, but I can't ignore the sincerity in his voice. "What's changed?" He shakes his head. "Why are you telling me now?" I ask. "Aren't you still afraid?"

"It's too late."

"What do you mean?"

"They discovered my true allegiance," he says. "My cover is blown. If you had burst into the Den a few seconds later than you did, I'd be dead."

I run through the scene in my mind. It all happened so quickly. I slow it down and try to play through the moments.

I see Nick, sitting on the chair facing the desk, drinking iced tea. The boss leaning back in his chair. He's holding something in his lap. I didn't pay attention at the time—I was a little too busy trying to figure a way out of the situation—but now I see it clearly.

He had his flipper curled around a nasty-looking dagger.

He could have been about to slice Nick's throat. Or he could just as easily have been showing off his favorite blade.

"How can I believe you?" I ask. "You've been lying to me from the start. How can I trust you?"

Again.

That bothers me more than anything else. I let my guard down, let him in, let him closer to me and my sisters. How can I trust my own judgment again?

And, maybe the most important question, why do I want to?

"I'll earn it back, Gretchen," he says. "I'll earn your trust back."

"How?"

"In whatever way I can."

I study his handsome face. His short, wavy blond hair. The steady set of his jaw. The unwavering look in his midnight-blue eyes.

I want to believe him.

But I've been burned before. And not just by Nick. I

always wanted to believe Phil when he swore he'd never drink again. Every time. Year after year. Twelve of them. Twelve long years of taking his anger out on me and Barb. Twelve years of convincing myself it would get better. It never did.

How can I trust this boy who has, admittedly, lied to me from start to finish? Even if he has a good reason for the deception, it's still a betrayal. It was still lies.

"I—"

"I get it," he says, stopping me before I voice my doubts. "I'll work for it. I'll do whatever it takes."

I nod. I'm still angry and confused, but I appreciate that he's giving me time.

"And the first thing I can do," he says, "is help you get the Gorgons back."

## CHAPTER 28

# GRACE

"Hi girls, I— What happened?"

When I return to Greer's basement, Nick is conscious but still tied to the chair, and Gretchen and Greer are facing off. They both have their arms crossed over their chests and are standing about ten feet apart with matching angry looks on their identical faces.

"I have been planning this for *months*," Greer says.

"Who cares?" Gretchen retorts. "It's a stupid tea."

"It is *not* stupid. It's a tradition."

"And this is your destiny."

"Destiny has waited this long," Greer sneers. "It can wait one more day."

Gretchen growls and lunges for her. I dash forward, putting myself between my sisters. Putting myself in harm's way,

if the stormy look on Gretchen's face is any clue, but better I get a little hurt than Greer ends up strangled on the floor.

I've spent the last four hours straight staring at Greer's laptop—getting nowhere on a current address for our biological mother—so my vision is swimming a little. And my patience is a little thin.

"What's going on?" I shout.

Gretchen looks at me like she's just noticing that I'm here.

"What's going on?" she echoes. "I'll tell you what's going on. The Ice Queen is freezing full force."

I roll my eyes—mentally, so I don't set Gretchen off on me. She and Greer have had personality conflicts from day one, so this isn't really surprising.

"Yeah, well, I'd rather be an Ice Queen than a thug any day," Greer snaps back.

"What's. Going. On?" I say, louder and more specifically.

With my sisters fuming at each other over my shoulder, I look at Nick.

He shrugs. "Gretchen wants to go after the Gorgons. Greer wants to go to tea."

"Go after the Gorgons?" I ask. "Really? We know where they are? We know how to rescue them?"

"Yes," Gretchen snarls. "But apparently we have to wait until after *tea*."

"I told you I have responsibilities," Greer says, her voice cracking, full of uncharacteristic emotion. "I cannot just abandon them."

No wonder Gretchen is frustrated. If she's learned how to get Euryale back, she's eager to do that as soon as possible. I'm eager too. I don't have the close relationship with Sthenno that Gretchen has with Euryale, but I want to rescue her.

"Greer," I say, "I think this is a little more important than—"

The look in Greer's silver eyes stops me cold. I've never seen this look on her face. I never thought I would. She looks . . . desperate.

It's like the image she works so hard to present to the world is shattered.

"Please," she says. "I need this."

"No," Gretchen barks. "It's ridiculous."

"Gretchen," I say, feeling torn between my sisters.

Before I can say more, Greer interrupts.

"I promise," she says. "Give me this one day, this one event—" She squeezes her eyes shut like she's trying to hold back tears. "Then I will commit myself without reservation. I just—" She pauses again and opens her eyes. "I need this one last piece of my normal life. Please."

Behind me, I sense Gretchen softening.

As much as we want to go after the Gorgons right now, when Greer agreed to join us, to embrace her destiny and ours, we promised to try to work around her regular life when we could. She's only asking for a day. Hopefully that won't make a huge difference to the rescue, and it will keep

Greer in the right mind-set. Going in with her angry and resentful can't be a good thing.

"We can wait a day," I say to Gretchen. "Can't we?"

Behind me, Gretchen grumbles. She may not like the situation, but she understands.

"Fine," she snaps, covering her sympathy with attitude. "But as soon as your tea party is over, we go in. Agreed?"

Greer nods. "Agreed."

She reaches out her hand to Gretchen, who reluctantly takes it. I sigh with relief. I'm not a big fan of conflict in the first place, but between my sisters . . . Well, we've already got enough conflict in our lives—we don't need any extra between us.

"Wonderful," Greer says, with a bit of her false cheerfulness returned. "You are welcome to stay here tonight. I'll be gone quite early to go set up. The tea should be over by four. I'll be back by five at the latest."

Gretchen grumbles again, but nods.

"Great," I say. "I need to get home soon. Curfew. But I'll be back here tomorrow afternoon."

Greer says good night and leaves us in an awkward silence.

"So," I say, trying to break the ice, "we're going to rescue Sthenno and Euryale tomorrow? That's great."

"Yeah, it's peachy keen," Gretchen snaps. "I need some fresh air. Can you stay with him?"

She jerks her head at Nick.

"Sure, but—"

"I'll be back in twenty minutes," she says. "I need to clear my head."

"Oh. Okay."

If she's fast I won't miss curfew.

Then, just as quickly as Greer before her, Gretchen storms out. I wonder if they realize how much they have in common. Strength. Confidence. Stubbornness. The ability to make a dramatic exit.

"Wait, huntress miss, wait." The little monkey creature pops up from behind the couch and rushes out after her. "Wait!"

I shake my head. When we met, Gretchen wouldn't have let even the most innocuous monster stay in this world any longer than it took to connect fangs with flesh. Of course, when we met, she wouldn't have jumped into the abyss after a boy either. A lot has changed in a very short time.

I expected to find Nick bloodied and battered when I came back down, but other than a darkening spot above his eye, he looks pretty much whole. Which is another mystery.

"You're a great mediator," he says. "That could have turned into a nasty fight."

I shrug. "We have bigger things to fight than each other."

"You can't always make everyone happy, you know?" He sounds way too insightful. "That's not always possible."

"You sound like you know something about that."

Now it's his turn to shrug. "When you have mixed loyalties," he begins, and then seems to realize how bad that sounds. "When you care about the cause *and* the person, then things get . . . complicated."

"I can imagine."

*Ring-ring-ring!* My phone sings out from my bag.

"That'll be my mom," I say with a small smile, grabbing my bag from the floor next to the couch. "Can you be quiet for a minute?"

He looks around, like *What have I got to talk about?*

I pull out my phone and punch the answer button. "Hi, Mom."

"I thought you were coming home early tonight," she says in a slightly irritated tone.

"No, I told you I was going to study at a friend's house." At least, I *think* I told her that. "I swear I did."

"You didn't," she says.

I'm still walking a fine line of being in trouble for disappearing last week. Mom especially has been extraconcerned over my whereabouts. I wish I could go back to the freedom I had before, but I'm stuck with the consequences of my actions. The consequences of my secrets.

Living a shadow life comes with a cost.

"We're going out for a family dinner," she says. "To celebrate Thane being back home."

"Mom, I—" I glance at Nick. I told Gretchen I'd watch him. She might not have beaten him to a pulp, but she still doesn't trust him enough to set him free or leave him alone. "I can't right now."

299

There is a heavy pause. "Why not?"

I hold the phone against my chest. This is the part I hate the most, the lying. The secrecy. I wish there were another way.

"We're right in the middle of a project." Kind of true, right? "I can't leave."

Also true. That doesn't make me feel any better, though. And when Mom sighs at the other end of the call, I feel like the worst daughter in history.

"I feel like you're drifting away, Grace," she says, her voice sad and soft. "You're barely home anymore. I can't remember the last time all four of us had dinner as a family."

I can picture her perfectly, staring out the tiny kitchen window, tears glistening in her eyes. Tears I put there.

I *really* wish there were another way.

"You know we can talk about anything," she says. It sounds like one last, desperate attempt to hold on to a daughter who's floating out of reach.

I can't tell her I'm not floating away by choice.

"I know, Mom," I whisper. We can talk about anything but this. I stiffen my spine. "It's just schoolwork. Everything at Alpha is much more challenging than back in Orangevale."

Another half-truth. More challenging, yes. But I'm still keeping up with my work without much effort. And it's not the schoolwork that's keeping me away.

"Okay." She sounds resigned. "When will you be home?"

"I don't know," I answer honestly. "I'll call when I'm on my way."

"Don't forget your curfew."

"I won't."

We say our good-byes and then I collapse on the couch. I don't mean to cry, but before I know it tears are running down my cheeks and I'm sobbing into my hands.

"Family is hard, isn't it?" Nick asks.

I sniff and wipe at my silly tears. "It is."

"It will get better," he insists. "Once the seal is broken, and the battle is over. Things will get—"

"Easier?" I scoff. "I doubt that."

"No," he agrees. "Not easier. But . . . steadier. Once balance is restored, you will find a rhythm. A pattern."

"But what about the rest of our lives?" I ask, because he seems willing to talk. And there's no one else around to ask. "Will we ever be able to have anything like a normal life?"

"I can't answer that," he says. "Only time will tell. But I can tell you the Gorgon sisters guarded the door in harmony for millennia. With lives and loves outside the destiny. Otherwise you and your sisters wouldn't even be here. They managed the balance until someone got it in their head to stir the pot."

Thanks a lot, pot stirrer.

Actually, that's something I've been wondering about. The truth about how all the lies began. I've found few clues about what really happened, other than that the story we learn in mythology is a lie. The book I saved from Gretchen's library makes only vague references to Athena and another power. It seems Athena is the face of the lies, but another deity is pulling the strings.

"You don't know who?"

"No one knows." He shrugs. "Most suspect Athena, because she sent Perseus to kill Medusa, but that seems the obvious choice. She is too blatant in her efforts."

"Who else could it be?" I ask. "Who else would have a vested interest in letting monsters loose in the human world?"

"Many. Hades, Hephaestus, Hera, Chaos, Nyx, Eris, Adikia, Epaphus. The list is long." He sighs. "Those of the third faction—our faction—have been trying to unmask the instigator since Medusa's death. Whoever is responsible is also clever."

We fall into a silence. My mind spins at thoughts of my family, my adopted family, the original Gorgons, the mother I can't find, the others I don't know about yet. Athena, the conspiracy, the seal. Destiny. Fate. I suppose those are two different things, destiny and fate. Destiny is a gift, something to rise to. Fate is something to make for yourself.

"Will it really get easier?" I ask.

Nick smiles. "It can hardly get worse."

I can see why Gretchen likes him. They have almost the same sense of humor.

I flop back against the couch. Maybe that shouldn't make me feel better—maybe I should be waiting for fate to say, *Ha, that's what you think!*—but it does. And besides, we're going to make our own fates. I close my eyes, just for a second, and next thing I know Gretchen is shaking me awake and telling me to go home.

Home. Not quite the refuge it used to be, but always the place I belong.

## CHAPTER 29

## GREER

The gym is transformed. As I stand in the doorway, I can no longer picture the space as it was only yesterday. A commercial cleaning crew sterilized it from top to bottom, erasing the horrid gymnasium smell. The committee and I arrived at dawn to work our magic, turning an athletic space into a corner of heaven.

Staying busy keeps my mind off the rescue I delayed. Off the promise I made. My mind can't deal with those things right now.

I'm proud of our work. Round tables covered with white linens are set up in the center, evenly spaced to make the arrangement pleasing to the eye. Along one wall of bleachers, now disguised by drapes in a soft golden yellow covering from the floor to the clerestory windows at the top, is a buffet

table with crystal punch bowls, real champagne flutes, and cocktail napkins in school colors.

Along the opposite, similarly disguised wall is a raised dais and the table where the principal, the heads of the alumnae association, and the tea committee will sit and speak during the tea.

Every place at every table is set to perfection. Beautiful gold-and-violet china, gilded flatware, crystal goblets.

It's all beautiful, but the ceiling . . . The ceiling is my triumph.

To hide the ugly light fixtures and the drab gray tiles, long swathes of dark-lavender silk hang in swooping swags. Behind the swags, bright white fairy lights twinkle through, giving the impression of the sky at dusk. The glow of sun streaming in the windows only enhances the effect. With the scent of peonies in the air, from the white-and-pink center-pieces on each table and the flickering candles adding to the aroma, I can almost imagine I'm standing outside. The fad-ing sun casting a violet hue on the world, the persistent stars twinkling through the haze.

The only thing that ruins the image is the clanking sounds of the caterers setting up in the hallway off the other end of the gym.

"Oh well," I say out loud to the empty space. "Perfection never lasts forever."

I set my bag down at my seat, on the end of the dais. I could claim the center as my due, at the left hand of the principal. But knowing that an emergency is inevitable at any event, I want to be in a position to act quickly.

I go about my duties, surveying each place setting, confirming the number of flutes on the buffet, checking on the caterers. Everything is in place by the time the rest of the committee returns, changed into their tea attire. I brought mine in a garment bag. Mostly—I'm not proud to admit—to avoid having to go home and face Gretchen.

We go over the schedule one more time, confirming who's speaking when. Who's responsible for seating which prestigious alumnae. When we instruct the string quartet to start playing.

We are minutes from the first guests arriving when the dizziness hits me. Harder than before—my knees literally buckle beneath me. Luckily, I'm next to the dais. If I'd come down on the buffet as hard as I just landed against the platform, there would be fruit punch and shattered glass everywhere.

"Greer," Annalise asks, "are you okay?"

"Yeah," I say. "I'm—"

The vision slams into me, hard and fast. My brain explodes with the image, with a high-definition movie playing in my head.

The gym, decorated as it is now, and full of women of various ages wearing mostly pastels and pretty hats. A dark cloud forms on the other side of the windows, blocking out the unusually sunny day. Then, with an explosion of glass and sound, the windows blow in and shards rain down over the crowd.

The movie goes into fast forward, so I only catch glimpses. Just beyond my reach. But I see enough. I know what's coming.

As the vision fades, leaving a pounding headache and weak muscles, I lurch for my purse. I pull out my phone, call up the messaging app, and send a desperate text to my sisters:

9-1-1

# CHAPTER 30

# GRETCHEN

In my standard black tank, cargos, and combat boots, I have never felt as out of place as I do walking into Greer's pastel nightmare. I want to turn and run. But I've been trying to call her since her cryptic message came through. The calls keep going to voicemail.

She needs me, and I'm here. Even if I'm not sure she'd do the same for me.

"What is this place?" Nick asks.

Deciding he might be useful, I sliced through his zip ties and brought him along. This might be a good chance for him to prove which side he's really on. If this actually is an emergency situation—I swear, if she asks me to wait tables or make an ice run, I'll deck her—we might need his help.

I scan the room, full of girly decorations and extremely

fragile-looking dishes, intent on finding Greer. I see her and Grace standing by the door at the other end of the room. Winding my way through the space, trying not to damage anything in the process, I make it to their location with a runny nose.

"Bless you," Grace says as I sneeze. "Hi, Nick."

"For the love of Medusa," I mutter. "I've never smelled so much perfume in one place."

That's when I first notice the signs on Greer's face. Her smooth brow is slightly wrinkled. Her jaw is set and she is biting her lip with her teeth. Her hands are fidgeting with the edge of her pale-purple dress.

Any of those things would have made me worry about Greer—she doesn't fidget—but it's the eyes that say it all. They're wide with fear.

"What?" I ask. "What's wrong?"

At first she doesn't speak. Then Grace gently nudges her and she says, "I had a vision."

"A vision?" I repeat.

"Yes. I've been having them since—" She and Grace share a look. "For a while now."

"And?" I prod. "What was this vision about?"

She looks up at the ceiling. "Monsters," she says. "Here. Lots of them. I sent everyone else away. Hypnotized them."

If nothing else clued me in, the fact that Greer is disrupting her precious tea means her fear is real. But I can't see anything to justify it.

I shake my head. "Maybe you're just worried?" I suggest. "The past couple of weeks have been tough. Maybe it's—"

In the space of a breath, the sunlight streaming in from the row of windows high above us disappears. It's like a cloud suddenly surrounds the gym. The lights inside flicker and then go out.

There is a terrible sound, a pressure, and then the windows above are shattering. Wind whips inside, pulling down the fabric covering the ceiling and blowing out the dozens of candles glowing on every surface.

"Move," I shout above the wind, pointing at the empty space in the middle of the gym, away from the raining glass. "Get to the center of the floor."

I don't know what's going on, but I have a feeling it's bad. Really bad.

"Keep our backs together," I say. "No one gets surprised."

Grace screams. Into the end of the room, through the doors I just used, marches a line of men. They are dressed in gleaming white-and-gold armor, carrying long spears and heavy swords. If the Nychtian Army from the abyss was terrifying in the dark evil radiating off it, this group is just as dreadful. They look trained and well armed, and if the hard looks on their faces are any indication, they aren't here to defend us.

"What the hell?" I ask.

"The Arms of Olympus," Nick whispers in my ear. "They are notorious for pursuing an order until it is fulfilled." His voice drops even lower. "They march for the side that wants you dead before you unseal the door."

"Great."

The line shifts, moving as one as they widen their stances and wield their weapons.

Together, we four back away, toward the other door.

Greer gasps. I look up. Streaming in through the now nonexistent windows is a flock of flying beasts. Black as night and with the scent of evil on their wings. The scent of blood.

The Nychtian Army.

I feel Grace and Greer squeeze tighter against my back.

Nick says, "Don't move."

I cut him a look. Right. I'm trapped between the army of darkness on one side and the Olympian soldiers with orders to kill us, and I'm going to . . . what? Try a karate chop?

"If we can get to the door," Greer whispers, her voice quaking, "the hall leads to a side exit."

A flying creature sweeps down, squawking at the line of golden soldiers that is starting to advance on us.

"We'll never make it," I say. "There are too many obstacles."

"The good news," Nick says, "is they'll be just as busy fighting each other as they are worrying about us."

"Well that's something," I reply. "Maybe we can—"

The door Greer wanted us to head for smashes open. A woman, dressed in a black flowing gown that waves in an unnatural wind, stands there with a dozen blank-eyed humans flanking her.

She walks forward, her eyes fixed on me. I gasp as I recognize her.

"Mrs. Knightly?"

The grin that spreads across her mouth gives me the chills.

"Are you ready for the war, Misss Sharpe?" she hisses.

Every hair on the back of my neck stands up. The screeching of the flying creatures and the clanking of the golden army's weapons fade away as I realize my biology teacher is somehow involved in this other world. How did I not see this coming?

"Gretchen?"

Greer's voice cracks as she says my name. I turn away from Mrs. Knightly, who is advancing across the gym toward us with her human drones, to see the Arms of Olympus approaching from the other side. We're caught in the middle, with the flying beasts swarming above.

Trapped.

"I think I can get us out of here," Grace whispers. "I think, if I focus, I can autoport all of us."

"We can't leave these creatures here," I argue. "Once we're gone, they're not going to be content to fight each other. The whole city will be at risk."

"I—I know what to do," Greer says. "Give me your knife."

"What are you—"

"Just give me the blasted knife, Gretchen!"

Shocked by Greer's outburst, I lean down and retrieve one of my daggers.

"Now," she says as she very calmly draws the blade over her palm, over another cut mark I hadn't noticed before. A thin line of blood appears, bright red with a shimmer of silver, like drops of mercury. Then she takes each of our hands, mine and Grace's, and slices matching marks in our palms. "When we close the circle"—she hands my blade back—"we will have to get out of here quickly."

Grace nods. "I'm ready."

As Greer presses her palm against Grace's, Grace places her other hand in mine. I glance at Nick and nod. He understands and wraps his arms around my waist.

I hold out my left hand. Greer looks me in the eye a split second before she places her right palm in my offered hand. I feel the zing of magic as our blood meets, the deadly fluid of my left vein, the healing of her right.

A black hole the size of a normal portal appears above our heads. Above our circle. As I watch, the portal grows. And grows. And grows until it practically fills the entire space above us.

"Now, Grace!" Greer shouts.

Grace squeezes her eyes shut, concentrating.

"Nothing is happening," Greer says.

Grace starts shaking. "Give me a minute."

The portal is still growing, taking over more and more of the gym, moving lower and lower. Some of the flying creatures scream as they are sucked back into the abyss. If Grace doesn't get us out of here, we'll be next.

"Now, Grace, we need to go—"

The world around me disappears, I'm blinded by bright white light for a moment, and then I'm in a living room. Nick is still at my back—I can feel him. Greer's hand is still tight in my left one, Grace's still in my right. We're together, whole, and out of that gym.

"Grace, you did it!" I shout.

I yank her close into a hug. Greer too.

"Ah-hem."

Grace stiffens. "Oh no."

Nick unwraps his arms and I release my sisters. Turning, I know I shouldn't be surprised to see a pair of adults and a boy our age standing there. It doesn't take Greer's second sight to know what has happened.

When Grace was trying to desperately get us out of that battle, she zapped us to the one place she always feels safe. Home.

"Mom. Dad." Her voice is breaking. "Um, I can explain."

## CHAPTER 31

## GRACE

Greer and Gretchen offer to go wait somewhere else—my room, the hall, maybe the moon even—but I think they should be here for this. I look around the dining table, my sisters on either side of me, Mom and Dad at either end, and Thane and Nick across the shiny surface. Nick seems unfazed by the situation, but Thane is unusually tense.

Everyone is looking at me.

I take a deep breath. Time to stop keeping secrets.

"It all started a few weeks ago," I explain, "when Milo took me and Thane to a nightclub."

Dad clears his throat.

"An all-ages club," I hurry to explain, as if that will be the most problematic part of the conversation. "That's where I, um, *met* Gretchen."

Gretchen shifts uncomfortably in her chair. For a girl who's used to being on her own, with only an open-minded guardian for company, sitting at a full family table is probably really awkward. Especially when she's a central part of the story.

"By then I'd already started seeing monsters," I confess. "It started almost as soon as we moved to San Francisco."

"At the dim sum place?" Thane asks. "That was the first one?"

I nod. "And then more at the nightclub. So when Gretchen explained what we are, it was kind of a relief."

"And just what *are* you?" Mom asks.

At least she's being open to the craziness I'm finally sharing.

Beneath the table, I take my sisters' hands in mine.

"We are descendants of the mortal Gorgon Medusa," I say. "Monster hunters."

"Huntresses, actually," Greer adds.

"I don't—" Mom shakes her head. "I don't understand."

I give my family a brief rundown of the story as I know it. About how Medusa was a guardian, about how her legacy has been skewed by history, about how we're the latest set of descendants, supposed to guard the door between our world and the abyss.

I leave out the part about us being the Key Generation because, really, that's not critical information right now. They're having to process enough already. I don't want them any more worried about me than they have to be, than I know they will be when I tell them the rest.

"So, what you're saying," Dad says, "is that when you've been telling your mother and me that you are studying at a friend's, you've actually been roaming the streets hunting monsters."

"No, not always," I say. "Most of the time I was at Gretchen's loft, studying. Training."

"Gretchen's loft?" Mom echoes. "That's where you were last night?"

My cheeks burn. "No, I was in Greer's basement."

"Gretchen's loft blew up," Greer offers.

I kick her under the table.

"What?" Mom gasps.

"It's nothing," I insist.

Thane glares at me across the table, and I swear his eyes burn like gray flames.

"I mean, we're fine."

Dad rubs his eyes. "Gracie, this is all very . . . inventive, but—"

"Don't be obtuse, Sam," Mom says. "We both saw her and her . . . friends appear in the living room."

"Did we?" He sounds tired. "Maybe we just—"

I knew he would take more convincing. He's an engineer, after all. You can't calculate for monsters and mythology with even the most complicated equations.

"Dad," I say. When he looks up, I open my mouth and let my fangs drop into place.

He blinks. Several times. "I don't . . ."

"It's real," Thane says.

I can't tell if he's just as much in a state of disbelief or if he's trying to convince Dad or if he actually knows more than he's letting on. He's taking this in pretty easily, without many questions. He and I can have a conversation later. Right now, I have more to tell Mom and Dad. I nod and smile, letting my fangs retract into my mouth.

"The thing is," I say, more nervous about this part than the rest, "everything is getting worse."

"What do you mean worse?" Mom asks.

"Because Gretchen and Greer and I have been reunited, things are starting to change." I take a deep breath. "And, um, a war is coming."

Mom gasps again.

"War?" Dad's eyes get wide. "What do you mean?"

"It's complicated, Dad, but basically some people—some gods—want us to guard the door. Others want us to seal it forever."

"Others want us—"

I kick Greer before she can tell my already freaked parents that there are gods and monsters out there trying to kill us.

She glares at me. "To open it and leave it unprotected."

"Yes," I say, relieved by her tact. I focus on my mom for this part of the reveal, because I think she'll be the most understanding. "In the meantime, while things get worked out, it's going to be kind of dangerous around here."

"Sounds like it already is."

I nod. "It's going to get worse."

As quickly as possible, I explain about the immortal Gorgons and the abyss and how we need to rescue them because they're the only ones with answers. Then I get to the hard part.

"Mom, Dad," I say, trying to sound as mature and responsible as possible. "Gretchen, Greer, and I need to go into the abyss. It's the only way to get to Olympus, to get Euryale and Sthenno back."

For five whole seconds, they stare at me, mouths agog. I know how this must sound to them—the fact that they're even taking me seriously is extraordinary—but I have to make them understand.

"Certainly not," Dad finally says. "If I believe anything you're saying, you are not going into that—"

"Please, Dad. Don't make this any harder. Things are just as dangerous at home." I turn back to Mom. "One monster already showed up here. In the alley. Monday last week."

I watch her eyes as realization dawns, as she puts the pieces together and figures out that, when I disappeared for hours the other night, I had a good reason. "Oh, Grace," she says. "I had no idea."

"I know, Mom." I smile, letting her know that I don't blame her for her reaction at all. She feels guilty, but I'm the one to blame. I'm the one who kept it a secret.

"I—" Her eyes fill with tears. "I don't like this."

"I don't have a choice," I say. "It's my destiny."

She nods and then looks at Dad.

"Please," I say to him. "Trust me."

His face softens. "Of course I trust you, Gracie."

"Then you have to let me do this." I glance at my sisters. "You have to let *us* do this."

He frowns, but I can tell the exact moment he relents. It's barely noticeable, a tiny shift in his eyes. I don't need their permission—this is something I have to do—but I'd rather have their support all the same.

I mouth, "Thank you."

"I'm going with you," Thane says.

I give him a pleading look. "Thane . . ."

"No," he says. "You're my sister too. I'm going with you."

Something passes between us, something he's trying to tell me. His stormy gray eyes are intent on mine, and I get the feeling this is about more than just being a protective big brother. Greer squeezes my hand, and when I look at her she nods. I don't know why that reassures me, makes me feel better. It just does.

I look back at Thane. "Okay."

Five of us will make this journey, then. Me, my sisters, Nick, and Thane. We'll have fractionally better odds, and that's something.

Twenty minutes later, Mom and Dad have packed our backpacks full of food and water. They've asked me if I'm sure about what we have to do about a million times. And I think they are finally accepting that this is something I can't—won't—walk away from.

They've also promised to be extracautious—to watch their backs when they leave or enter the apartment, to take off if things seem to be getting worse, to take care of themselves so I have two fewer things to worry about—until this is all over. Or, at least, settled.

At the door, Mom hugs me tighter than ever before. Dad pats Thane on the back.

"You take care of her, son," he says.

Thane nods. Considering the fights they usually get into, I don't think Dad has ever been prouder of him.

Mom turns and hugs Thane. "You take care of *you* too."

Then we're gone. They're staying home, staying safe. I'm the one walking into danger. But not alone. I turn to face Nick, my brother, and my sisters, struggling to keep the tears from my eyes. I was being so strong for Mom and Dad, and now I feel it crumbling away.

"Okay," I say, forcing positivity. "Now what?"

"Now," Gretchen says, "we gather the rest of the supplies. If we're going in, we're going in prepared."

She makes a list of what we need, assigns each of us a portion of it, and then we're on our own. I'm getting half a dozen flashlights and extra batteries. Thane is filling another two backpacks with food and water. Everyone else is on special errands and we're meeting in Greer's basement in two hours.

As we part ways to gather our supplies, I pull Thane aside.

"There's something you're not telling me," I say.

His face remains expressionless. "There usually is."

When he starts to turn away, I grab his elbow.

"Thane—"

"Now isn't the time. When this is all over, when we get back safely," he says, "then we can talk."

I want to push him for answers, but he's right. There's no time.

"I'm going to hold you to that promise," I tell him.

He grins. "I know you will, Grace-face."

I'm so stunned by his uncharacteristic smile that I stand silent as he turns and heads out on his errand. Then I shake myself back to reality. Time is ticking and I need to get moving too. Two hours until the scariest moment of my life. It may be selfish, but I'm glad Thane will be at my side. Who can a girl rely on if not her big brother?

# CHAPTER 32

## GREER

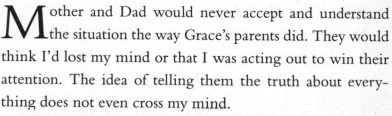

Mother and Dad would never accept and understand the situation the way Grace's parents did. They would think I'd lost my mind or that I was acting out to win their attention. The idea of telling them the truth about everything does not even cross my mind.

However, the danger to them is all too real. I can't keep them in the dark, going on with their everyday lives when the peril grows with every passing minute. When another monster might show up at our front door at any time.

Which is why, while the others disperse across the city to gather supplies for our trip into the abyss, I return home, calling my parents along the way.

Dad agrees easily, promising to swing by the house on the way to his afternoon meeting in the Haight. Mother is a more difficult sell.

"I'm sure this can wait, Greer," she says, sounding distracted. "We can discuss your *emergency* when I get home this evening."

I don't tell her that an emergency, by its very definition, cannot wait. I don't tell her, either, that she likely won't be home before I would normally be in bed asleep.

"Please, Mother." I hate to beg, even more than she hates seeing or hearing desperation, but I tell myself that in a short while she won't remember this conversation. "It truly cannot wait. Please come home."

I hear her sigh. Voice muffled, as if she's covering the mouthpiece of her phone, she tells her assistant, "Transfer the notes to my tablet. I'll read them on my way home."

"Thank you, Mo—"

The phone clicks dead in my ear. I stifle the brief surge of pain. No point wasting time and energy being hurt. She's coming home—they both are—and I will make them safe. That's all that matters.

Dad arrives first. He's on the phone, waving me off for a moment. "Absolutely not," he barks into the phone. "Those terms are unacceptable and they know it. Send them back to their garage to come up with something more reasonable."

He snaps his phone back onto his belt holster.

"What is the big emergency, Greer?" he asks, sounding more intrigued than concerned.

"I'd rather wait for Mother to arrive," I say. "So I can talk with you both at once."

"Your mother is coming home as well?" His brows lift in surprise. "Sounds serious."

Mother walks in, saving me from a temporary explanation.

"I'm here," she says. "Now please tell me what on earth is so very urgent."

As much as I would rather they sit, giving me the slight advantage of height over them, I don't have time. My sisters and the boys will be here any minute. I need to get my parents out of harm's way before that happens.

"You need to take a vacation," I say.

Mother snorts.

"You know that's not possible," Dad says. "But if you want to use the company jet—"

I step closer to Mother, focus my eyes on hers, and will the power to work. "You *need* to take a vacation."

She scowls, and then her face clears. In a hollow voice, she says, "I need to take a vacation."

"What?" Dad sounds stunned. As well he should. The last time I remember my parents taking a vacation was . . . well, never. I think they even passed on a honeymoon in favor of business school graduation.

"I need a vacation," Mother repeats.

Before Dad can figure out something weird is going on, I put myself in his line of sight, look him in the eye, and say, "Yes, you both need a vacation."

Immediately his face goes just as blank as Mother's. "We need a vacation."

"Somewhere warm," I say. "Without internet. Without cell phone service."

"No cell phone," Mother repeats.

For an instant, half a moment, I'm tempted to go one step further. To tell my mother I love her and hear her tell me back. But I know it won't be real. Mother doesn't express affection.

Instead, I continue my instructions. "You won't even pack a bag. You will get your passports. Take a car to the airport and make the travel arrangements when you get there. Buy everything you need when you get to your destination."

"Passports," Dad says.

Mother nods. "Destination.

"You will be gone at least two weeks," I add. "You will not check in with me because you know I'm fine."

"You're fine."

I glance at my watch, an antique handed down from my great-grandmother. I have only a few minutes.

"Go," I say. "Get back in one of the cars waiting outside and go. Now."

They turn to leave.

At the last moment, I can't stop myself. "Mother," I call out. When she turns, I say, "I love you."

"I love you," she echoes back.

If I close my eyes, I can almost believe she said it for real. Almost.

I rush forward, wrap my arms around her waist, and allow myself a moment of connection. Then I release her and they disappear into the shiny black car. I'm still watching the spot where the car vanished around the corner when everyone shows up.

"Are we ready?" I ask.

We all have fully loaded backpacks, with everything Gretchen thinks we'll need—or *might* need—in the abyss. Mine holds enough provisions for a week, at least, along with a fleece jacket and a pashmina that can function as a scarf, blanket, or pillow. Gretchen said it was freezing in there, and I have low tolerance for cold.

"Ready," Grace says, heaving her own bag of provisions onto her back.

The boys and Gretchen carry the heaviest loads, with not only their own provisions but also weapons and antivenoms Gretchen has retrieved from the safe house, extra provisions for everyone, and some other items that Gretchen and Nick were very secretive about.

The member of our party I understand the least is Thane. Grace's brother.

He doesn't have to be here, standing there like a statue with the heaviest bag of all on his back. He could have stayed home with their parents—*should* have stayed, maybe—and left the dangerous job to those of us with supernatural abilities.

When Grace was trying to convince him to stay home, I had a brief vision. We were somewhere dark and black—the abyss—and Grace and I were facing down a hideous monster.

The thing was about to slice through Grace with long, blade-like claws when Thane clobbered the thing from behind. He saved Grace's life. That's why I encouraged her to let him come.

Still, there is something . . . compelling about him. I can't stop sneaking glances at him. And I am *not* the sort of girl to sneak furtive glances.

Whenever I look at him, I get the feeling he's conflicted. I'm not sure if it's my keen Medusa sense or just intuition. Either way, he's an enigma. One that I can't help wanting to unravel.

"Let's do this," Gretchen says. She pulls out one of her daggers and swipes it quickly over her palms, drawing out twin lines of silvery blood. Then, dagger back in her boot, she asks, "Everyone ready?"

"Yes," I say.

Grace gives her a shaky smile. "Ready."

The boys nod, ready to follow in right behind us.

Gretchen smacks her palms together and the portal appears, at almost the exact spot in my basement where she came flying out on the pegasus just yesterday.

Grace takes one of my hands in hers, grabbing Gretchen's with the other.

We share a look, just between us three, and then Grace smiles. Gretchen nods. And I take a deep breath.

Hand in hand, we step forward into the abyss. Into danger and destiny.

# Dive into more magic from
# TERA LYNN CHILDS!

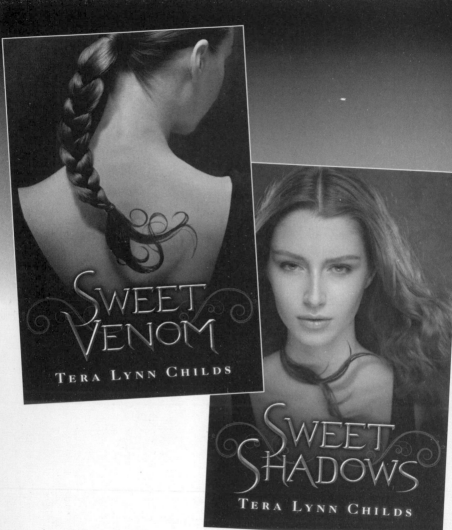